FIVE-STAR Reader ★★★★★ Reviews

"Brilliant! As a frequent visitor to Russia myself, I was captivated by [the author's] knowledge of the Russian culture and character . . . a can't-put-down read because of the intrigue. He beautifully combines his personal ordeal with his compassion for the Russian people and his knowledge of a changing society. This is a best-seller for sure!"

—Stanhope, New Jersey

"This story held me enthralled from cover to cover. Mike Ramsdell has captured perfectly the realities of life in Russia at the end of the cold war together with the spirit of the Russian people and wrapped this into a tale of suspense and intrigue. To this he added some deeply personal elements to reveal a sense of humanity to which we can all relate. A wonderful book with so many levels of enjoyment."

—Brisbane, Australia

"This book still amazes me. . . . It has everything from action to mystery with the best part being the love story. This book will change your life in the sense that it will make you want to be a better person. It also will help you believe in miracles and believe in the goodness of the human spirit."

—Snowflake, Arizona

"The author's writing style is captivating, you feel as if you are inside his thoughts. His descriptions are so clear you can picture the scenes in your mind as you are reading. . . . I really hope there are more books to follow, this one book is just too good to leave me being completely satisfied."

—Houston, Texas

"I was transported by the book to another place and time. The portraits of the characters, both major and minor, make them truly come alive. Its message of hope and faith in the face of seemingly impossible odds is beyond moving. It is a page turner that will leave you feeling wonderful."

—Hackettstown, New Jersey

". . . a very personal and human story. The first-person style of writing allows the reader to identify with the author. It has action and intrigue, but the valuable moral lessons throughout make 'A Train To Potevka' a must-read. Hopefully, my kids will read it next. I couldn't put it down."

—Brigham City, Utah

"Mike Ramsdell does a marvelous job in his book of bringing Russia to life. I found myself back in Russia with him. I decided that I'd better read it again, and found the second reading even more enjoyable than the first (and that's saying a lot since I was thrilled the first time)."

—Washington, D.C.

PRAISE FOR POTEVKA

"A beautifully written saga of faith and duty. Part spy thriller, part autobiography; it's from the heart and told with integrity. I couldn't put it down."

—Doug Summers

"Fascinating, intense, real . . . a wonderful book."

—Dean Hughes

"Terrific! One of the most incredible and fascinating books I have ever read."

—Kathie Barson

"A potential best seller; I hope there's a movie."

—Vadim Klishko

"This book will be read over and over for years."

—Val Karren

"First-time author Lt. Colonel Mike Ramsdell does a masterful job of weaving his heart-stopping personal accounts with the sights, sounds, and history of Russia." —Steve Crain

"Riveting. Rarely has a book so captivated my imagination." —Colonel Gary Wilkens

"This book is such a great story as well as a great history lesson." —Marillee Tueller

". . . heart pounding, thought provoking, inspirational; the perfect mix of action and emotion, intrigue and introspect, as it both entertains and educates. A must for every home library!"

—Lori Nawyn

"An amazing look into the world of covert OPS . . . one that makes you grateful there are people willing to risk their lives, with no thanks at all, to keep us safe and free!"

—Huntley Thatcher

". . . know that this is more fact than fiction. The details presented could only be recalled by one who had lived them personally."

—James R. Phillips

" 'A Train To Potevka' is the best spy novel I have read in years. Ramsdell is a master story teller which makes this book a true thriller. If you like spy novels, don't miss this one. 'A Train To Potevka' is about as good as it gets."

—Max B. Richardson

"Besides being a cliff-hanger spy novel, it gives powerful testimony to the basic goodness of man, and the power of faith and the human spirit."

—Steven S. Smith

A TRAIN TO POTEVKA

by

Mike Ramsdell

Всего Хорошего
(All the best)
Mike Ramsdell

A TRAIN TO POTEVKA

Library of Congress Catalog Card Number – Pending

Seventh Printing

ISBN 1-59872-030-9

Personalized books can be ordered at
www.michaelramsdell.com

Please send correspondence to:

Zhivago Press
P.O. BOX 1792
Layton, UT 84041-6792

or by email to:

michaelramsdell@aol.com

For speaking engagements, please call (801) 444-1776

Printed in USA FCPrinting Salt Lake City, Utah

To Bon, Chris, and Karen

Where there is great love there are always miracles.

Willa Cather

Table of Contents

Preface

Eighteen months prior to the publication of this book, I fractured my neck during a racquetball match. During the weeks that followed—as a diversionary tactic to get my mind off my injuries—I was encouraged by those close to me to use my recovery time to write about some of the experiences I'd had while living and working in Russia as an intelligence agent.

Throughout my school years and career, I had written papers, reports, and briefings, but never had I attempted to do any creative writing. Following several days of procrastination, one morning I set up my laptop at my bedside. After staring at the computer screen for two or three hours, finally the words started to come. By that evening I had a rough outline of several stories. But then the real work began—organizing it, evaluating it, and figuring out how to make it readable.

Initially, I decided to concentrate on a short, ten-page story as a gift for my sister. After it was finished, several people liked it enough to suggest that I give the story as a present to other family and friends. In the months that followed, those few copies turned into dozens of additional copies that were passed on from one family to another. I was grateful—mostly surprised—to know that what I had written seemed to be of interest to others.

As I continued to write, it was suggested that I create an anthology—a collection of short stories—

or consider the possibility of writing a book, although that was never my intention.

During the decision process, I contacted Dean Hughes, my good friend and famous Utah writer. I was hoping Dean could suggest a ghostwriter and I would simply provide the storyline. In his wisdom, however, Dean told me, "Mike, you've got to do it yourself. No one will care as much as you to get the stories right."

At the time, I had no idea what I was getting myself into and that writing a book would become such a monumental undertaking—one that, after I got started, I wasn't sure I could finish. As a first-time writer, so many times I thought about giving up, that no one would really care about what I had to say. Yet, whenever I was ready to quit, there was a quiet conviction that I *did* have a story to tell—a story to which others could perhaps relate and, hopefully, enjoy. Eighteen months and eighty thousand words later, *A Train to Potevka* was finally completed.

If the story provides a few hours of reading pleasure to some, I'll be very pleased. If not, at least my grandchildren will someday be able to read about *Papa* and some of his experiences in Russia at the time of the fall of the Soviet Empire.

I hope you enjoy the book.

Mike Ramsdell

Prologue

The setting for this book is based on events that took place in Russia and the former Soviet Union during and after the Cold War between 1988 and 2002. Within the context of the story, the book contains background information—albeit limited—regarding the *Bolshevik* Revolution, the establishment of the U.S. Diplomatic Mission in Russia, the Soviet KGB, the Russian mafia, and the Trans-Siberian Railway. Therefore, when you as the reader come upon such background information and it has no interest for you, please skip the material; my main objective is that you enjoy the story. I have also included a brief outline of Russian history and a glossary of possibly unfamiliar terms at the back of the book.

Although Russia was only one of the fifteen republics in the Soviet Union, it was by far the largest, both numerically and politically. As a result, in the book I use the terms Russia, USSR, and the Soviet Union interchangeably.

It is important to understand that, as a former intelligence officer, I had no other choice than to have this work categorized as fiction. The reason for this is three fold: First, I am subject to certain federal laws and regulations that govern what can and cannot be disclosed about my former work. Secondly, it would be foolish to put myself in possible harm's way by disclosing anything traceable regarding past encounters—both good and bad—with the KGB and Russian mafia. And, thirdly, it would have been impossible to write this book and not have the liberty to create dialog, description, and detail in order to make the story more readable and enjoyable. Thus, due to the foregoing reasons, several of the events, dates, places, and names in the book have been altered or fictionalized.

Finally, it was not my intention to write an academic narrative of historical fact. Therefore, if there are any mistakes or inaccuracies in this book they are entirely mine.

Mike Ramsdell

A TRAIN TO POTEVKA

By

Mike Ramsdell

It snowed and snowed, the whole world over,
Snow swept the world from end to end.
A candle burned on the table;
A candle burned.

Boris Pasternak
Doctor Zhivago

Chapter 1

THE BLIZZARD AND THE BUGS

When it was over, it was not really over, and that was the trouble.

Frank Yerby

Completely covered in ice from the sleet, snow, and pounding wind, the old train from Siberia, with its baggage of refugee passengers and frozen freight, looked like something alive as it struggled against the angry storm. It had the appearance of a huge white serpent, its large yellow eye peering out into the darkness, slowly twisting and weaving its way past the endless snow-covered towns and villages on its 6,000-mile journey across Great Mother Russia.

Fierce arctic winds blew heavy snow out of the North as the first major storm of winter caught up with us just outside the Russian city of Sverdlovsk. Severe conditions in the high mountain passes had forced the train crew to gear down the huge engines in order to push through the heavy snow, which already lay four and five feet deep in some places.

The storm was now a full-scale blizzard and showed no signs of letting up.

I was the only foreigner on board the train—an American intelligence agent—and desperate to get to an agency safe house several days away, somewhere in the middle of Russia.

In the last three days my world had been turned upside down: our agency's covert mission in Siberia had been compromised, my operational cover exposed, and my role as the person who had persuaded certain Soviets to work for us as informants had been revealed. At this very moment both the KGB and Russian mafia were trying to find me.

Safe—at least for the now—on board the cold, overcrowded train, trying to rest my aching, wounded body, I sat at my seat mesmerized, staring out through the ice-framed windows. As I watched the storm and the endless, frozen desolation of Siberia slowly pass by, I struggled to make sense of the improbable events of the last seventy-two hours—amazed at how fortunate I was to still be alive.

Only a few months earlier, I was back home in Utah, going through one of the most difficult periods I had ever experienced. It seemed that all at once I had lost so much that had been so meaningful in my life: my long, troubled marriage had finally ended; my mother had passed away after suffering from a prolonged illness; and the joy of my life, my son and only child, Chris, was about to leave for Australia to serve as a missionary for our Church. Considering all the major changes that were happening around me, I was, no doubt, at a definite crossroads in my life. Never, however, could I have imagined that only a short time later I would leave the Rocky Mountains for Russia and the vast wilderness of Siberia to participate in the most important, dangerous, yet, *life-changing* assignment of my career.

☆ ☆ ☆

It was the early nineties. The Soviet Union was in total chaos, with civil war a definite possibility. Mikhail Gorbachev's presidency was in serious jeopardy, the economy was in shambles, and the nation's *ruble* currency was becoming virtually worthless. Millions of people were near starvation. Worker strikes and protests were a daily occurrence throughout the country. In Russia's major cities, crime was running rampant.

Because of the anticipated implosion of the Soviet Union and the fall of its Communist government—leaving who knows what as the legal sovereign in Russia—the Department of State decided to make a bold, last-ditch attempt to locate four ex-Communist officials, take them into custody, and smuggle them out of Russia. These men would then be tried by our government before an international tribunal at The Hague in the Netherlands for the crimes of espionage and embezzlement, which they had committed against the United States.

These four corrupt officials, with the complicit knowledge of the Soviet government, had fraudulently siphoned tens of millions of dollars from the U.S. construction fund during the building of the new American Embassy in Moscow. Yet, more damaging than the pilfered millions, each of these political oligarchs, working in conjunction with Soviet intelligence, had played a major role in the KGB's successful efforts to compromise and render useless the hundred-million-dollar, top secret, crown jewel of the American Embassy complex—the newly-constructed U.S. Chancery Building.

I had been sent to Russia as part of a small agency task force that would conduct the covert operation under the direction of the Department of State. Our assignment was no small undertaking, and yet, because of the political uncertainty in the country, we were given only a ninety-day window to accomplish our mission. We had no illusions about what we could be facing. The close ties each of these now-criminal overlords had to the Russian mafia and KGB meant that our work would not only be difficult but also, possibly, very dangerous.

The KGB (Committee for State Security) began as a secret police organization that had its origins as the *Checka* during the *Bolshevik* Revolution. Its mission was to help the Communists seize, consolidate, and sustain power throughout the Soviet Union. Over the years, the KGB proved highly successful in its use of fear and terror to control the Soviet population. Under Lenin and Stalin, tens of millions of Soviet citizens simply disappeared—some to executions without trials, others to exile or imprisonment in a vast system of concentration/labor camps known as *gulags*. So powerful and far reaching was its influence, one of every seven Soviet citizens was said to be an informant for the KGB. This nation-wide system of informants—Big Brother is watching—was based on an insidious scheme of threats and intimidations by the KGB against both the informants and those being informed upon.

The KGB was responsible not only for all domestic and foreign intelligence but also, with the military, controlled the arsenal of nuclear weapons throughout the USSR. Roughly comparable to a combination of both the CIA and FBI, but much larger and less restricted in its mandate, at its peak the KGB had over 500,000 employees; more agents than all other Western intelligence agencies combined. It was common knowledge beyond the borders of the USSR that at least half of all Soviet Embassy personnel working abroad—including those in the United States—were in actuality KGB operatives.

After Stalin's death, the KGB significantly reduced its reliance on murder and kidnapping as its primary means of enforcement but still found ample opportunity for the application of intimidation and threats against their own countrymen. It is a widely accepted fact among Sovietologists and political historians that the Soviet Union and the Communist system could not have existed without the KGB's heavy hand of coercion and brutality.

☆ ☆ ☆

Moscow, Russia was considered the most important diplomatic post in the world; only the best and brightest U.S. Foreign Service personnel were assigned there. The new Chancery Building was designed as the center of operations—the heart and soul of the embassy. This, supposedly, state-of-the-art, impenetrable, top secret facility was to headquarter the offices of the ambassador, his deputies, senior diplomatic employees of State, along with representative of the Central Intelligence Agency (CIA), National Security Agency (NSA), Defense Intelligence Agency (DIA), U.S. Agency for International Development (USAID), and high-level representatives from each branch of the U.S. military.

The nerve center within the Chancery was the CPU (Communication Program Unit) where crypto machines transmitted messages—tens of thousands of characters per second—via satellite from Moscow back to Washington, D.C. and to CIA headquarters in Langley, Virginia. These encoded communications contained detailed information regarding CIA operations targeted against Russia, results of NSA eavesdropping on Kremlin communications, and directions from the State

Department as to how the U.S. Ambassador and our Moscow Diplomatic Mission were to deal with the Soviet government.

After years of construction and only months before its completion, it became evident that Soviet intelligence had penetrated the new Chancery Building along with several other strategic, classified facilities on the embassy compound. Much to the contrived surprise and, of course, the total denial of the Soviets, American technical experts electronically sweeping the secure areas of the embassy discovered that the entire Chancery Building had been bugged. Literally thousands of minute listening devices had been painstakingly imbedded by Russian intelligence into the modular concrete walls, floors, and ceilings during their pre-casting phase. Incredibly foolish but true, State Department construction management had then allowed Soviet workers to assemble these modular components at the work site on the embassy compound.

This penetration of our new embassy facilities by the Russians during the Cold War would come to be regarded as one of the greatest clandestine/covert achievements ever by the KGB and, in turn, one of the greatest blunders in the history of U.S. counterintelligence.

Had the KGB not been caught and their intelligence collection devices not detected, the Soviets would have been privy to *every* classified, top secret conversation that would have taken place within the walls of the Chancery.

The sabotage of our new Chancery Building by the Soviets was so thorough and pervasive that the entire high-rise structure was made useless to our diplomatic corps. So smug and arrogant was the KGB with their perceived success of pulling off such a remarkable intelligence coup, that when Soviet bricklayers finished the exterior façade on the front of the embassy Chancery, they were directed by the KGB to install a subtle brickwork design above the building's main entrance. At various times during the day, especially at sunup and at sundown, when rays of sunlight would shine at a certain angle across the face of the Chancery, the letters "*CCCP*" could be seen. These four Cyrillic letters represent, in English, the abbreviation *USSR*—The Union of Soviet Socialist Republics.

An amazing sight! Here was the newest and the most important American Embassy in the world and the USSR was flaunting—with brick and mortar graffiti—not only its most successful physical security breach ever, but also its clever prowess and perceived superiority over the United States of America.

After years of futile diplomatic negotiations with the Russian government in an effort to right this wrong, a top secret mission was put in place by U.S. intelligence for a covert task force to be sent into Russia to find the four responsible former Soviet officials and bring them out to stand trial before an international tribunal.

If the prosecution against these mobsters proved successful, then the United States, in turn, would be able to show the complicity of the Russian government and KGB in the crimes that had been committed.

☆ ☆ ☆

Helsinki, Finland is the nearest Western capital to Russia, and, as such, was selected as our base of operations. The actual preparation and training for our mission took place at a small port city on the Baltic Sea.

The task force members chosen for this mission came from various intelligence commands depending on each person's field experience, language capability, and physical qualifications. A few days after our arrival, we were divided into four teams of three men each. Our weeks of training were extremely busy and long—sixteen hour days—yet professional and well organized.

It was not long after our training had started, however, that I discovered the unfortunate bias that prevailed between some of the senior agents and those of us they felt to be inferior because we were not part of the so-called "Washington Intelligence Establishment."

Like one or two other members of the task force, I had not taken the normal career path of most intelligence officers. I had come from the military side where most of my training and field experience had been done outside of Washington. Those of us not known within the inner circles of the D.C. beltway had a definite strike against us when dealing with some of these "East Coast Blue Bloods."

At our first task force meeting, eyes rolled and snickers could be heard when a senior controller from headquarters introduced me as the "military agent from the boonies"—from Bear River, Utah, somewhere from the backwaters of the Rockies.

This particular agent seemed to have it in for me from the moment I arrived at our operations center in Helsinki.

"I see from your paperwork that you're from Utah," he said during my in-processing. "You're not one of those weird Mormons . . . are you?"

Shocked, I couldn't believe that a supervisor would behave in such an unprofessional manner. We had never even met, but already he had a strong prejudice against me. His negative attitude was certainly perplexing, not to mention discouraging.

I had been specifically selected to be part of this mission because of my experience in Germany and Russia and my ability to speak both languages. Yet it was evident that a few of those assigned to the task force thought me under qualified—a possible risk. This senior agent had already made up his mind about me. He, along with one of his good buddies, went out of his way to remind me—and on several occasions—that I was going to be a liability to the success of the mission.

I was determined to prove them wrong.

Chapter 2

CATCHING THE CAT

Some days the dragon wins.

Anonymous

My team's specific mission was to apprehend Vladimir Koshka, a powerful, wealthy Russian known to friend and foe as *The Cat*—which is the translated meaning of his last name. Vladimir Koshka was known for his ambition and ruthlessness but *especially* for his violent temper. Through his influence and power within the Communist Party, including his close ties with the KGB and Russian mafia, it was estimated that Koshka had personally stolen more than six million dollars from the U.S. Embassy construction project.

Since leaving government service, where he had served as a member of the Supreme Soviet (parliament), Koshka operated several mafia-connected businesses. One such business was a company in Siberia that sold drilling equipment to multi-national firms—German, French, and British—under contract with Russia to help develop her oil and gas fields in the Soviet Far East.

Posing as expatriates working in the international oil business in Siberia, each member of our team had specific mission responsibilities. Having lived in Germany for several years, first as a missionary for my Church and then later as a young officer in the U.S. military, my operational cover was that of Dieter Schultz, a field manager for a German oil company. Because I spoke both German and Russian, I was assigned as our team's point-of-contact with the Soviets we would need to recruit as informants in order for our mission to succeed. It would be my task to gain the trust and confidence of three or four of Koshka's subordinates and persuade them to work with us and provide us the critical information we needed concerning Koshka and his mafia operations. Most importantly, it would be my responsibility to get these informants to agree to testify against Koshka in an international court of law. This is where money would be such a determining factor in the success or failure of our mission. During these desperate times in the Soviet Union, as the economy and the government were falling apart, large amounts of money could buy almost anything.

Prior to our task force joining the mission, HQ had already established that during the last week of each month, Koshka usually made a visit to his mafia-connected business in Tayginsk, a small but growing city surrounded by dozens of settlements and labor camps in a remote area of Siberia. Koshka used this business in Tayginsk ostensibly as a front for his criminal activities in the Soviet Far East. Following three months of investigation and surveillance, our team was able to confirm Koshka's monthly travel routine to Siberia.

After an immense amount of work and the outlay of significant sums of money, we were able to convince three of Koshka's people to cooperate with our investigation. Yet, it remained a difficult and delicate situation—not knowing where our informants' true loyalties really lay. Regrettably, we were about to find out.

Three days before our clandestine operation was to conclude and we were to take Koshka into custody, our worst fears became reality. .

✯ ✯ ✯

In the early morning, just as the fog and haze were lifting and the city of Tayginsk was coming to life, I stood at the window in the musty, two-room flat I had rented, watching the pedestrians and traffic below. From my vantage point three stories up in the apartment complex, I looked towards the building across the street, something I purposely did several times each day. But on this particular morning my heart stopped cold. The worn street sign attached to the side of the old building across the street had been straightened to its upright position—a pre-arranged signal from our most trusted Russian informant that something with the mission had gone seriously wrong.

Our primary asset, Viktor Kozlov, a forty-year old Russian, lived with his wife, two children, and his elderly parents in a small, three-room apartment near the center of the city. Viktor had come to Siberia as an engineer from St. Petersburg with the promises of career advancement and triple the salary he was previously earning. After the Soviet government shut down the petroleum company that had brought Viktor to Tayginsk, he'd struggled finding work of any kind in order to keep his family fed. On the recommendation of a friend, Viktor had joined Koshka's company as a consultant. In a matter of months, he was put in charge of the company's inventories and warehouse.

Six months passed before Viktor realized that the company was also a front for Koshka's criminal activities in Siberia. When he attempted to leave the company, Viktor was threatened by Koshka personally. When he still refused to cooperate, Koshka threatened Viktor's family and children. Thus, under such great duress, Viktor agreed to stay on and handle his responsibilities as warehouse manager but refused to be involved in any criminal dealings.

In our efforts to find potential informants, I had approached Viktor when we learned of his loathing for Koshka. Following only two or three assessment meetings, he agreed to participate with our investigation and work for us as a mole inside Koshka's operation.

Viktor and I had agreed that in case of an emergency, straightening the sign on the building across from my apartment to an upright position would be a signal for the two of us to meet near the base of the bridge that spanned the Tayginka River in the city center. We were to go there at noon, six p.m. or at midnight and wait for at least fifteen minutes for contact to be made.

After seeing the sign moved to its upright position, I hurriedly notified my two other team members. Like me, they were unaware that anything had gone wrong. As far as they were concerned, everything was on schedule for the final three days of our operation. We agreed that they would provide surveillance and be in position as backups when I met with Viktor at the bridge.

Shortly before the noon hour, I watched from a distance as Viktor approached the outdoor market near the bridge. He stood there for several minutes while the three of us looked for any suspicious activity. Once the all-clear was given, I walked through the crowd to where Viktor was standing. When Viktor saw me he appeared very upset.

"Herr Schultz," he said, "Vladimir Koshka knows about you and your plan to smuggle him out of the country."

I stood in shock. "This can't be!"

"One of your other informants, a Chechen who works for Koshka, told him everything. He claims you were the person that convinced him to become an informant and that you paid him thousands of dollars to do so. And . . . I'm sorry to tell you this, Herr Schultz, but Koshka will have you killed if he can find you."

"Does Koshka know about you or the third informant?" I asked him.

"I think not. They said Koshka went into a wild rage, even destroying several pieces of office furniture, when he was told about your plan to kidnap him and take him out of Russia. After venting his fury, I was told that Koshka brought together a group of his hit men and set a plan in motion to specifically find you for some payback—*Russian mafia style*."

I didn't want to think about what Koshka and his henchmen would do to Viktor and our other informant if he found out about them and their involvement.

"When I left Koshka's business to come here," Viktor said anxiously, "there were several men in dark clothing—mafia men—standing around in the foyer. Herr Schultz, they will be out looking for you soon—if not already."

"Thank you for this information, Viktor." I said. I handed him an envelope of *ruble* bills. "You'd better leave before someone sees us together. I'll be in touch, and please be careful."

"You be careful, too, Herr Schultz."

Using hand signals to communicate with my two other team members, thirty minutes later we met back at my apartment. The realization that our mission had been compromised left us in shock and dismay. *After being so careful with every detail of our operation, how could such a thing have happened?*

I could almost hear the complaints of the doubters and senior agents back at headquarters—"See . . . I told you about that agent from the Utah backwoods!"

Intensely aware of the imminent death threat against me, and knowing of the reputation of the Russian mafia for violence—especially when getting revenge—we sent an encoded message to European headquarters through our embassy in Moscow explaining what had happened and stopping all plans for getting Koshka out of the country. We also asked for our team's immediate removal from Tayginsk. A half hour passed before HQ's reply came back, telling us there was not enough time for an extraction team to be sent into our location in Siberia and get us out.

Because I was the only member of our team that had actually met with each of the informants—they did not know of one another's cooperation—headquarters directed that the two senior agents working with me catch a flight out of Tayginsk as soon as possible. Since it was likely that Koshka's men, with of the help of the Chechen informant, would be looking for me at the airfield, I was not to risk going near there. In due time, I would be given instructions as to how I was to leave the city. HQ also warned me to stay indoors during daylight hours and to go out, if absolutely necessary, only after dark.

The only flights out of Tayginsk left three times a week—all in the late afternoon. Within an hour headquarters informed us there were seats available on today's flight. I was instructed to help in any way I could to make certain that my two colleagues were on that aircraft. The two agents returned immediately to their living quarters to pack their bags for their connecting flight to Moscow. As directed by headquarters, it would be my responsibility to stay behind and sanitize our three apartments and destroy all operational documents and materials.

With my cover now blown, I found it peculiar that HQ would assign *me* to remain in Tayginsk to close down our covert operation when *I* was the one being targeted by the mafia. Besides, such an important responsibility was always left to one of the more experienced senior agents.

Early in the evening, after the fog and winter darkness had covered the city, I went to inspect the apartments of the other two agents. I already missed their companionship, especially the security of having them with me in case something were to go wrong. I have to admit, during our earlier conversations with HQ, I was disappointed that my two cohorts had not shown a willingness to stay behind with me in Tayginsk so that we—as a team—could make it out of Siberia together. Yet I was glad for them just the same; they were now safely on their way out of Siberia on board a small *Aeroflot* jet.

Because of the urgency for them to get to the airfield to catch their flight, they'd had little time to pack their personal belongings, thereby leaving their flats in total disarray. It took me over two hours to sanitize, clean, and organize each apartment; this included the removal of all paper trails and other possibly incriminating evidence. After I returned to my own flat and put everything in order there, I made contact with headquarters to confirm that all three apartments had now been cleared. In the process of exchanging last-minute information, HQ explained that the plans for my own departure from Tayginsk had now been set.

Telling me they were concerned for my safety, after reviewing the documented brutality of Koshka and his mafia group, headquarters insisted that I get out of Tayginsk as soon as possible. They did not want to risk the chance that I might be found by the mafia or KGB. I was instructed—actually ordered—to leave on the next possible train, which would leave in a matter of hours from Zanushka, a small village less than an hour away. The disconcerting news for me was that this was not a normal long-distance train, but a common peasant train—the lowest type of passenger class. It was traveling all the way across Russia, from Vladivostok in the Soviet Far East to its destinations of Moscow and St. Petersburg in the West.

I was directed to travel only as far as Potevka, a small village four or five days away, where one of our agency's transit safe houses was located. According to HQ, the cabin was to be used only in case of an extreme emergency and for not more than forty-eight hours. My situation, however, would require an exception to the rules. According to HQ, I would be able to "lay low" at the cabin safe house for four days before continuing on to Moscow and the safety of the American Embassy.

Despite their claims of concern for my safety, it was not difficult to read between the lines. It was obvious that headquarters and the State Department didn't want me back in Moscow just yet. They needed time to prepare a response if confronted by the Soviet government about the real reason for my being in Russia—that I was not a German oil company manager working in Siberia but an undercover agent working for U.S. intelligence. Keeping me out of sight for a ten-day period—in transit on the train and a few days at the safe house—would give HQ the necessary time to prepare their contingency plans. This would also allow them to work out the details of a possible follow-on assignment for me now that our covert mission in Siberia had been terminated, unless, of course, a couple of our elitist senior agents got their wish and I would be sent back to the States early.

I was instructed to purchase my ticket at the train station in the village of Zanushka from where I would be leaving, forty miles down-line from Tayginsk at four o'clock in the morning. I had strong reservations about traveling on a long-distance train, but I had no other choice. I desperately needed to get out of the city and away from Koshka and his mafia men. It was the only transportation available—a slow, archaic train traveling westward across Russia along the historic route of the legendary Trans-Siberian Railway.

✯ ✯ ✯

Just after eleven p.m., I finished packing my clothes and gear. I gathered together a few items of food—five or six apples, a hunk of cheese, some jerky, and a loaf of bread—and put them in a knapsack. Food was something I'd had very little stomach for in the last several days. While worrying about the final, crucial events of our covert mission leading up to our confrontation with Koshka, not only had I been unable to sleep, but with no appetite whatsoever, I had eaten very little.

With great reluctance, but as ordered by headquarters, I disabled my communication transceiver and walked to a remote area of the Tayginka river, which ran through the city. I threw the radio device, my handgun, and ammo into the deepest part of the swift-running current. HQ insisted there was no way—as a foreigner—I could risk being caught with any of those items in my possession as I traveled across Russia. It was well known within the agency how random inspections were carried out on foreigners by the Ministry of Railways' Security Police—a shadow entity of the KGB—especially for those traveling on second or third class trains. I had carried the 9mm Beretta for the entire three-month operation, but never once did I have reason to think of using it to protect myself—not until now.

Chapter 3

MEETING THE MAFIA

Nothing in life is so exhilarating as to be shot at without result.

Winston Churchill

Around midnight I walked in a cold, light rain several blocks to a fourth flat, one which only I had used for my meetings with the informants. Headquarters had instructed me to double-check the apartment to make certain I had completely sanitized and sterilized the place, not leaving a trace of anything behind.

After I finished inspecting the apartment and was ready to leave, I went to the kitchen window and looked out on the courtyard six stories below.

I became concerned when, at such a late hour and in such miserable weather, I saw two men standing near the large double doors that served as both the entrance and exit for the building. They were standing in the night drizzle, smoking cigarettes, and looking around nervously as if they knew something was about to happen.

One of the men was wearing a dark hat, which obscured his features. But when the other moved closer to the light which hung over the entrance door, I immediately recognized him as someone we had observed during our months of surveillance of Koshka's operations. We had previously identified this man as an inept, discredited KGB agent who had been sent—probably exiled—by Moscow to this dead-end outpost in Siberia to act as the go-between for Koshka's mafia group and Soviet intelligence.

A sickening feeling immediately came over me, and in that moment I knew I was in serious trouble.

How did these men know I would be in the building and at this very hour?

For three months our team had been very careful to make certain that we were not under any type of surveillance ourselves, which might disclose what we were really doing in Tayginsk or where we were staying. Yet it had been necessary for me to meet with the informants, and, therefore, I had brought them to this flat several times for confidential meetings regarding Koshka's mafia operations. Our Chechen informant had, no doubt, tipped off the two men waiting for me below at the building exit.

As my adrenalin started to flow, I frantically began considering my options of escape.

The drab, gray apartment building was only a few years old. Because of its typical, poor Soviet workmanship, the building looked like it had already existed for ten or fifteen years. Our team had surveyed the structure the week of our arrival in Tayginsk. Like other Russian prefabricated buildings, it was several stories high with eight different stairwells, each having its own separate entrance. There were no elevators. On the top level was an attic, and below the ground level was a basement, which was used for storage. Due to the frequency of crime in such high-rise buildings, each individual apartment's entrance, like this one, was protected by an extra security door.

Leaving the kitchen, I quickly switched off the light in the small living room and went across the hallway to the bedroom, which looked down on the other side of the building to the inner courtyard. Desperate to discover another way down, I opened the window and looked out. There was no fire escape—nothing. I was trapped! Somehow getting past Koshka's two heavies waiting for me at the building exit below was going to be my only way out.

I reminded myself to remain calm, but my heart was beating so loudly I could hear it pounding in my ears.

Then I remembered something from our agency training: if trapped in a high-rise and nothing else is available, tie several lengths of bed sheets or drapery together as a makeshift rope. If I could make it down to at least the second story level, I could drop from there to the ground below.

Quickly I pulled the sheets off the bed. While searching the bedroom closet with my penlight for additional sheets, several loud knocks suddenly slammed against the outer security door. I froze.

This can't be happening!

Only a few hours earlier I'd had the help and security of my two colleagues, both well-trained, knowledgeable agents but now safely on a jet heading back to Moscow. I was left here alone in Koshka's backyard, my communication radio and handgun at the bottom of the Tayginka River.

Why hadn't headquarters anticipated that such a confrontation could occur?

Hurriedly, I resumed my search, frantically throwing blankets, pillows, and other linen around the bedroom. I knew I had very little time before Koshka's men might force their way into the flat. Finding only one other set of sheets in the closet, I began ripping them in half, then in half again, tying each length end to end.

The pounding at the door became louder and more frequent, then abruptly ceased. Moments later, I heard wood splinter and crack as if a crowbar was being used to break the frame and locks of the outer security door. Then silence. My muscles tightened like a knot. Not breathing, I stopped and listened for voices or movement. Still, I heard nothing. Without making a sound, I continued working as fast as I could, hoping and praying that my unwanted visitors had left the building.

Could it be they had decided I wasn't inside? Perhaps they didn't actually see me enter the building after all?

When I had enough sheet lengths tied together to make it, perhaps, a third of the way down the outside of the building, I heard glass from the small windowpane of the inner door shatter and fall to the floor. Fear bolted through my body.

"Don't panic," I told myself, *"Do not panic!"*

Again, I stepped to the open bedroom window and looked down on the inner courtyard. Even using the few sheets I had tied together, I knew there was no way I could fall from four stories up and not suffer severe injury. I threw the sheets onto the floor and moved quickly from the bedroom into the dark hallway next to the badly damaged inner door. Standing among the pieces of shard glass, I waited. My heart pounded in my chest and my mind raced wildly, trying to anticipate what was about to happen.

On the other side of the inner security door, through the small, broken window, I could see the movements of a large man. There was no doubt he knew I was inside the apartment. He was cursing loudly, but I couldn't understand his garbled Russian words. Then, through the hole in the broken window pane, a large, bloodied fist and arm appeared as the man reached inside and began to undo the door bolt.

Why in the world had HQ instructed me to throw my weapon in the river? And why had I been so foolish to follow their orders?

Knowing I had only seconds to react, I stepped to the side of the door, hurriedly zipped up my jacket, and pulled my gloves tightly on each fist. I took several deep breaths and readied myself.

At the moment the man pushed open the door, I lunged out and hit him as hard as I could with my right forearm to his head. Together we fell out into the stairwell with me landing on top of him. Frantic, violent blows were exchanged as we rolled and grappled on the landing. It was like fighting a wild, raging beast. After several minutes of frenzied struggle, I took a severe blow to the back of my head when the brute picked me up and slammed me against the metal railing of the stairs.

Momentarily dazed, I ended up on the cement floor with the huge man straddling me, pummeling me with his fists. Desperately, I tried to deflect his blows by covering my face with my hands and arms. While attempting to maneuver myself free, he grabbed me around the waist in an excruciating bear hug.

With the full weight of the heavy beast now on top of me, the stench of rancid body odor and noxious vodka acted like smelling salts to my senses. With panic and pain rushing through my body, I thrust two fingers of my right hand into his nostrils with such force that I heard the cartilage in his nose snap.

The big bear grabbed at his snout as a burst of blood splattered across my face.

Finally free from his grip, I struggled to my feet but found myself standing above him on the stairs, his wide body blocking my exit below.

Like a madman, he stood screaming incoherently at me as blood gushed from his nose down over his mouth and chin, spattering onto the front of his coat.

He came at me again.

Following another onslaught of wild blows, the man stepped back from me. Momentarily exhausted, he stood with his arms hanging down at his sides, looking at me with such poisonous hatred in his eyes as blood continued streaming from his nose.

Why didn't this man have a weapon . . . or was he under orders from Koshka just to give me a severe beating and break a few bones?

By now the lights in the stairwell were on. Several people had come out of their flats to see the cause of all the noise and commotion.

Standing for a brief moment face-to-face, I realized my assailant was not the KGB agent I had recognized earlier when looking down from the kitchen window. I had never seen my attacker before, even during all our weeks of surveillance.

The large man had thick, leathery skin; a pockmarked face; several gold teeth; narrow eyes; and dark, bushy eyebrows. He appeared to be around fifty years old. Because of his strange Russian accent when he spoke, I assumed him to be Chechen or from one of the southern Soviet Republics. Dressed in his distinctive, black clothing—slacks, turtleneck, leather coat—and with his shaved head, there was no doubt he was a member of the Russian mafia.

Despite his large, burly frame, his movements were slow and deliberate, which gave me hope in my ability to out maneuver him.

Six stories below us, the KGB agent guarding the front door of the building, kept yelling up to his comrade, "What's happening? Is he up there? Did you get him?"

For those suspended seconds, the thug and I stood looking at each other, our chests heaving as we gasped for air, both of us unable to speak. He ignored the repeated calls from his accomplice below. That's when, for the first time, I noticed the bloody brass knuckles gripped in his left fist. I then realized that the damaging blow to my head had not come from the stair handrail after all.

I reached up to check the back of my head. Blood was flowing from a sizeable puncture wound in my skull through my hair and down the back of my neck. The dark, red blood that now covered the stairwell floor was not just from the man's spewing nose but also from my head wound.

From the dim glow of a light bulb hanging at the end of a long electrical cord directly above us, besides the brass knuckles, something shiny appeared in his other hand—a stiletto knife.

Trying not to show any sign of fear, I stared directly at him and slowly slipped off my jacket.

Continually cursing while licking and spitting blood that oozed from his nose over his thick lips, he raised the knife chest high and gestured with it several times towards my stomach, as if to indicate where the first thrusts of his stiletto would land.

Then saying the first Russian words I could understand, "*Koshka skazal, Vraemya plateet.* (Koshka said, it's now payback time)," he took a step up the stairs towards me.

With my jacket off and my eyes focused on his every move, I slowly took a step backwards up the stairs. It was important that I maintain a two or three foot distance between us. I wrapped my jacket around my left arm in order to deflect the anticipated blows from his knife; I needed to keep my right arm free and unencumbered.

With each step he took up the stairs, I mirrored his exact movement.

Sporadically wiping the dripping blood from his nose with the sleeve of his coat, he continued swearing and mumbling about the message from Koshka and "payback time." Perhaps Koshka had ordered the two thugs to only break some bones or cut me up really bad, but from the look of rage in the man's bulging eyes—there was no doubt he wanted me dead.

Maintaining the space between us, step by step we moved in perfect unison like two out-of-breath boxers to the top of the seventh floor landing to where the attic was located.

I had already been inside the attic when our team surveyed the building; I knew its layout and remembered that there were no lights above the sixth floor level.

I wanted my attacker to follow me into the darkness of the attic where I hoped to elude him long enough to make my escape down the stairs. I would deal with his KGB cohort waiting at the building's front entrance when the time came.

With my eyes fixed on his stiletto, I continued to back away up the stairs from my attacker. The critical moment came as I slowly moved away from the top stair railing towards the attic door, five or six feet behind me. Pinching his nose with his thumb and index finger to stop the bleeding, the lug clumsily moved towards me. When my back finally came in contact with the attic door, I carefully reached behind me and turned the handle. My heart sank. The door was locked!

From his cynical, bloody grin of stained yellow teeth, I could tell that he, too, knew the door was locked.

I stood momentarily frozen, watching the twelve-inch stiletto get ever closer.

Thinking for certain that he now had me, the brute arrogantly hopped from one foot to the other like a huge, Russian, dancing bear.

Just as he was about to make his final move towards me, the building drunk standing on the stairs below us, whom I had seen asleep on a stair landing at the time I entered the building, reached up and grabbed the man's pant cuff. Momentarily startled, my attacker looked down to see who was there.

In that saving moment of distraction, I flung my jacket in his face and leaped around him. Unfortunately, he was still able to land a brutal kick with his heavy boot to my right side as I fled past him down the stairway.

As I dashed down the stairs, the mafia brute bellowed to his partner below, "He comes! He comes!"

With no time to think or plan what I was going to do next, I bounded down the stairs, hitting every fifth or sixth step as I ran. As I burst through the front door, from the corner of my eye, I caught a glimpse of a tall, dark figure standing just a few feet away. Suddenly, there was a flash—*Bam!*—then another—*Bam!*—as the deafening sound of two gunshots exploded in my left ear. The KGB agent guarding the building exit had fired two rounds from his handgun *point blank* at my head! A high-pitched ringing immediately began resonating through my brain.

At the sound of the gunshots, I instinctively dove headlong to the muddy ground and rolled wildly in different directions. I struggled to get to my feet while holding the left side of my head. I ran frantically out into the darkness, zigzagging across the soggy outer courtyard in an attempt to avoid another volley of gunshots. With my hand pressed tightly against my left ear, I ran flat out for two or three blocks along a slippery asphalt road heading towards the Tayginsk Railway Station. There, I hoped to lose my attackers among the hundreds of rail cars and locomotives.

In the frantic moments after the two initial gunshots, I didn't remember hearing any other rounds being fired. At point blank range, surely the gunman thought both shots had struck me in the head and that it was only a matter of time before I would die from the bullet wounds or from the loss of blood.

After sprinting for several minutes through the fog and drizzle as fast as my unsteady legs would take me, I couldn't go on. I came to a stop at the corner of a run-down, vacant building. Gasping for air, my lungs were ready to burst. The pain in my head and in my side was unbearable.

Hidden behind a stone wall, I looked back to see if the two men were following me. I couldn't see either of them—or anyone else for that matter. At this late hour, and in such miserable weather, it appeared I was the only person on the eerily deserted street.

Watching the road while holding my side and trying to catch my breath, I reached up and checked the back of my head. Because of the fight and my frantic escape running through the rain, I was soaking wet from head to toe. Steam from my body dissipated into the cold night air. Even my undergarments were soaked. *Or was it blood from a gunshot wound?*

It seemed there was blood everywhere. I was not certain if I had been hit or grazed by one of the bullets. As my shaky fingers nervously explored my head, I could actually feel the blood pulsing from a hole in my skull. Upon further examination, I determined that it was not a bullet wound, but rather a puncture wound made by the blow from the brass knuckles. I had a split bottom lip, a swollen left cheek, and severe pain on my right side from the kick I'd received. Other than the severe battering my forearms received while defending myself from the brass knuckles, at the moment it seemed I had no other wounds but these.

By the grace of God and the shooter's poor aim, both of his bullets had completely missed me!

In the dim light cast by a nearby street lamp, I could see that my shirt had turned dark red and realized that it and my undergarment were both soaked with blood. It had spread all the way down to the back of my trousers. I desperately needed to get the bleeding stopped. Without anything available to cover or plug the hole in my head, I discovered that the end of my little finger was an exact fit and would have to suffice until I could make it back to my apartment.

After resting against the stone wall for a considerable time, I was finally able to breathe somewhat normally.

As I started to collect myself, the irony of what had taken place during the last half hour flashed through my mind. I couldn't help but think how strange it all was, only a few hours earlier I'd been so upset that our covert operation in Tayginsk had been terminated. Yet tonight's events put everything into an entirely new perspective. After all my years of intelligence work and several undercover missions—for the first time in my career—I had come face to face with someone who *absolutely* wanted to kill me.

I had to pull my thoughts together. I needed to somehow contact headquarters, get medical attention for my head wound, and get out of these cold and sticky, crimson clothes. Also, I desperately needed to get something to drink; my mouth had been like cotton ever since the moment I first saw my two assailants waiting for me at the building entrance an hour earlier.

I stayed hidden behind the rock wall for another ten minutes until the pain in my side began to subside, and I had the bleeding from my head wound somewhat under control. Most important, I wanted to make sure that I was not being followed.

The cold night air and my wet clothes started to cool my body down, which caused me to begin shivering uncontrollably. The trembling, however, could also have been from the significant amount of blood I had lost.

As the night and everything around me seemed to slow down and return to its normal pace, I noticed, for the first time, that the cold drizzle had changed to a light snow—the first snow of the coming Russian winter.

Staying in the shadows, with the end of my little finger stuck in the hole in my head, I cautiously walked to my flat several blocks away. Before entering my apartment building, I stayed across the street out of view and surveyed the area to make certain I had arrived alone and that no one was waiting for me there in the darkness.

Once inside my apartment building, I climbed the stairs to the third level. Upon entering my flat, I bolted and locked the door behind me.

After washing the blood and mud from my hands, I gulped down several glasses of water. I pulled a change of clean clothes out of my packed duffel bag. The communal showers down the hallway by the WCs, shared by eight other families, were not an option for me now. There was no way I could take the chance of being seen in this condition and possibly be reported to the police. I took off my bloody clothes and stuffed them in a plastic bag, which I would discard later.

When I walked over to the sink, I was stunned by what I saw in the mirror—a pale, ashen face, framed by blood-soaked hair and beard. Carefully, I stuck my head into the sink under a trickle of cold water and slowly washed the clotted blood from my hair. Standing naked in front of the sink, with soap, water, and a washcloth, I proceeded to clean away the blood, sweat, and mud that covered most of my body. Already a huge purple bruise was beginning to form where my attacker had kicked me in the ribs on my escape down the stairs. I stepped back from the sink and rolled up the now-red, wet rug and placed it in the plastic bag with the bloody clothes.

I pulled a small first-aid kit from my duffel bag. I carefully applied a gob of disinfectant to my throbbing head wound and covered it with three small sterile pads and several lengths of gauze across and around the top of my head, using strips of adhesive tape to hold it all in place. I gently maintained pressure on the bandaged area with the heel of my hand.

I struggled putting on my clean clothes because of my weak, sore arms. When I was finally dressed, I sat at the edge of the bed and forced myself to take several slow, deep breaths.

The pain in my side was intense. The brute's kick had probably cracked, if not broken, several ribs. Also, the pounding in my head and the ringing in my ear were unrelenting.

Coming down from such an adrenalin high and losing so much blood was starting to make me feel unsteady and light-headed. I could also tell I was slowly losing my strength.

And with all I had ahead of me, what would happen if I were to pass out somewhere . . . ?

In spite of my aches and pains, knowing that I had somehow been able to survive and elude my attackers was a powerful high. This, in itself, started to make me feel somewhat better.

Clearly, I was now faced with a difficult decision, one that needed to be made almost immediately: Should I still try to leave on the Soviet workers' train, which would be departing in just over two hours, or should I stay another day in *Tayginsk* to regroup and try to see a doctor? However, I knew that visiting a Soviet medical clinic would certainly entail filling out paper work and possibly filing a police report—something I definitely could not risk.

What to do?

I had just gone through a living hell. Yet the good news was that I was still alive and in one piece. Less than an hour away was a small train station where I could purchase a ticket, which would get me away from Tayginsk, away from Koshka and his mafia thugs, away from the danger and threat I was facing. The decision was obvious—I needed to do everything in my power to be on that train and on my way out of Siberia.

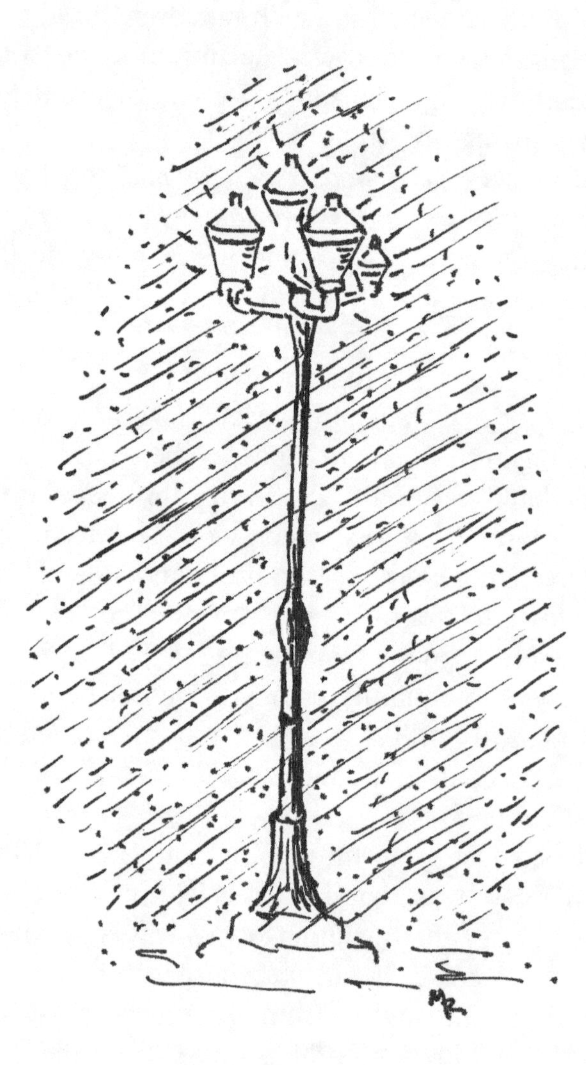

Chapter 4

IN THE BELLY OF THE BEAST

There is something about poverty that smells like death. Dead dreams dropping off the heart like leaves in a dry season and rotting around the feet.

Zora Neale Hurston
Dust Tracks

At two o'clock in the morning, I hitched a ride with a truck driver to Zanushka, the village where I would catch the train.

I was concerned while buying my ticket that I would have to show some type of identification. However, once I pulled a roll of *rubles* out of my pocket and passed the customary bribe to the cashier, not a word was mentioned about an ID. With my ticket in hand, I nervously waited outside in the shadows under the overhang of the train station.

A small group of peasant workers waited there also; talking, smoking cigarettes, and already drinking their first beers of the day.

The weather had turned much colder as the light snow continued to fall.

At four-thirty in the morning the old, long, green train rattled and screeched to a stop at the small station. This third-class, commoner train, which had departed days earlier from Vladivostok, would take twice as long as its famous, first-class tourist counterpart—The Grand Trans-Siberian Express—to reach western Russia. It would make well over a hundred stops in cities, towns, and villages as it traversed across the eleven time zones of the USSR.

Due to the on-going collapse of the Soviet Union, similar trains had been added to the trans-continental schedule in the past several months in order to move the multitudes of refugees leaving the despair of eastern Russia for the hopes and dreams of the West.

☆ ☆ ☆

The Trans-Siberian Railway is the longest continuous railway in the world. Covering almost one third of the distance around the earth, it took decades to build at a cost of billions of *rubles* and hundreds of thousands of human lives.

Before the railway's existence, the arduous journey across Russia took several months. People traveling this route were forced to use a combination of limited rail lines; motorized vehicles; horse-drawn sledges; and, at times, even steamships to navigate certain large rivers and to cross Lake Baikal, the four-hundred-mile long lake, so deep and vast that it holds one-fifth of the world's fresh water.

The Trans-Siberian Railway is considered one of the great engineering marvels of the last 150 years. In the spring of 1891, construction on this epic undertaking began at opposite ends of Russia—in the West at Chelyabinsk and near Vladivostok, almost five thousand miles away to the East. After constructing various subsections of the rail line along the planned route, masses of men and machines connected the two lines in Siberia twenty-five years later. The Trans-Siberian Railway was heralded complete. Government-sponsored celebrations of this unparalleled accomplishment went on for more than four years throughout Russia.

The manpower necessary to accomplish this undertaking was monumental. By the time the rail line was completed, millions of laborers had worked on the quarter-century project.

In actuality, the railway was built largely by social outcasts—criminals, military deserters, religious and political dissidents—who had been exiled by the government to a life of hard labor in Siberia. This banishment was even given to mental patients and people convicted of petty crimes—a punishment, which, cruelly, even included many of their family members.

It was a matter of simple economics; the Russian government desperately needed cheap labor to build the railroad. Rather than leave these men and women in the large cities to waste away in prisons, hospitals, or welfare wards, they were forced into exile to help build the rail line across the vastness of Russia.

The workers and their families suffered unthinkable hardships, but none more dreadful than trying to survive the horrible Siberian weather from late September to early April, when, in the dead of winter, it is not uncommon for temperatures in this brutal region to reach 70 degrees below zero. With limited resources in the Siberian wilderness and forced to live under such terrible conditions, hundreds of thousands of workers and their family members died from injury, disease, or the cold.

☆ ☆ ☆

Sitting on board the train, watching the refugee passengers, I was reminded that after seventy-five oppressive, corrupt years in power, the Soviet Communists were now losing control of the country and the people as their empire imploded around them. Tens of thousands of these desperate families, most of whose parents or grandparents had been exiled to Siberia by Lenin or Stalin, were leaving their meager homes and possessions behind in the East, hoping for a new life in the large industrial cities of western Russia.

The twenty-four rail cars were crammed with sixteen hundred refugee passengers—poor peasant families making the grueling, two-week trip across Russia. In addition to the horde of passengers, a crew of more than one hundred Soviet railway personnel was on board, responsible for keeping the long train moving toward its destination. Besides two or three cars of freight, there was a dreadful smelling food car, a postal car carrying hundreds of pouches of mail, and a communication rail car equipped with several large metal cabinets of telegraph and radio equipment in case of an emergency along the way.

There were no separate or assigned seats, only hardwood benches on each side of the aisle. The few sleeper compartments on each car were reserved for the conductors, car attendants, and other railway personnel working on board the train.

Each long-distance passenger was given a small, stained pillow and an even dirtier, gray, wool blanket for the entire trip. This was a poor-man's train and the lack of accommodations reflected the same. Passengers would have to endure the two agonizing weeks trying to rest or catch what sleep they could while sitting on a crowded wooden bench, or, as some of the men did, wrapped in a blanket, curled up on the cold, wet floor.

Each family had staked out its own space in the congested train, surrounded by their life's possessions stuffed inside bulging cardboard boxes, cheap plastic suitcases, and large nylon and burlap bags, all tied together with rope and twine to discourage the thieves that roamed through the rail cars at night.

Luggage, boxes, and bags filled the overhead racks and every available space under the seats. Excess baggage pieces were stacked in the aisle way, which was constantly covered in slush and mud from the boots and shoes of those getting on and off the train.

Throughout the rail car, stout, unshaven Slavic men with protruding bellies, wearing shabby coats over threadbare, nylon jogging suits, smoked foul cigarettes, drank too much vodka, and argued and fought with one another over the card games they played to kill the endless hours.

Plump, worn women in gaudy, flowered dresses covered with tattered coats and sweaters, wearing their ever-present headscarves, looked after the children and guarded over their possessions of boxes and bags like mother hens.

Rather than an outward display of hope or optimism, the mood among the passengers was one of quiet desperation. Like prisoners entombed inside the belly of this slow moving beast, many of the adults—especially the older women—behaved as if they were drugged, sitting listlessly hour after hour staring out through ice-framed windows with a lifetime of worry and fear etched upon their faces.

Mostly, I felt sorry for the children, strictly confined to the hard wooden benches next to irritable parents for the entire two-week trip, their muffled cries heard throughout the rail car both day and night. But then, perhaps, the children were the lucky ones, for they were able to sleep in spite of the constant jarring, rumbling, and stench of the old train.

At the time I boarded the congested train, I was relieved to find a small space in a corner of the very last passenger car next to a window. Like a stowaway, I sought to make myself as inconspicuous as possible and blend into the masses. I pushed my duffel bag under my bench and tied a piece of heavy twine from the bag to my boot. I placed my worn attaché and food sack next to me on the seat and propped my backpack at my other side.

As I looked out the window, I noticed that the light snowfall had picked up in intensity and was becoming a real winter storm.

A broken boiler had left the inside of the rail car freezing cold; the temperature couldn't have been more than five or ten degrees above freezing. The only heat seemed to be that generated by the mass of bodies inside the car.

I tried to stay warm, huddled in my corner seat, wearing a long Russian winter coat, a pair of thick work pants, two wool shirts, with my thermals underneath. In spite of my layers of German clothing, the only place on my body not numb from the cold was my aching head. Thankfully, the *schapka*—my large Russian fur hat—I had purchased three months earlier when I'd first arrived in Moscow, not only kept my head warm but also conveniently concealed my bandages.

Once settled on the train, I was overcome with exhaustion from my recent ordeal. I was hungry, but, for the time being, I chose not to eat anything from my knapsack. Not knowing about the availability of food, I wanted to conserve what few rations I had for the four or five-day trip. Besides, whenever I thought about eating, my appetite was quickly suppressed by the constant, nauseating stench inside the rail car: foul body odor, cheap eau de cologne, stale tobacco, strong vodka, and the pungent smell of sausage, onions, and sour cabbage.

Still, even more than the hunger and fatigue, I knew the worst part of the agonizing hours on board the train would be the constant *watching* and *waiting*.

No one was to know I was an American. In fact, no one should even suspect me to be a foreigner unless they saw my travel papers. I spoke both Russian and German and held a documented cover as a German oil executive working in Siberia. In my work clothes, field boots, and scruffy beard, I should be able to travel completely incognito.

Yet I was aware that there were certain KGB operatives who knew who I *really* was, what I was *really* doing in Russia, and they—along with members of the Russian mafia—were *really* trying to find me.

Each rail car had two attendants, called *provodniks.* The two assigned to our rail car, one male and one female, were trouble from the moment I met them. As Russians would say—they were both "stinking drunk" with their own importance, a strange phenomenon common throughout Communist Russia. No matter how little power or authority an individual had, that person could—and usually would—use his or her position to make others' lives more miserable.

I never understood why they did this. Perhaps such behavior had something to do with their meaningless job and having to endure the never-ending despair of a life without choices living under the Communist system.

The male *provodnik* was a short, bald, chubby man with a round face, probably in his mid-sixties. Spectacles hung from the end of his thick nose as he went back and forth through the rail car continually blowing on his fingers, which protruded from the ends of his worn out gloves. In constant motion, he always pretended to be overburdened by his responsibilities and paperwork.

When he first checked my documents, declaring me to be of German nationality, he let me know that he, too, spoke the language, having studied it several years at the university in Leningrad. Actually, he did know some German, but not enough to carry on a real conversation. Yet at least once each day, usually while checking my documents, he would passionately engage me: "*Jetzt sprechen wir Deutsch*" (Now we speak German.). But he would only do it for the sole purpose of trying to impress the passengers around him.

The female attendant, a tall, surly woman dressed in an official uniform at least two sizes too small, incessantly fussed with her hair, which was twisted and piled on top her head, making her look even taller than her actual six foot two or three. Her mouth of gold teeth was seldom seen due to the fact that she always seemed to be scowling, which made her look like a character right out of a James Bond movie.

I determined, if at all possible, that before I left the train I would somehow get a photograph of her, even though—especially as a foreigner—taking photographs of government property (the train) and government workers (the *provodnika*) was absolutely forbidden.

From my first hours on the train I sensed that both *provodniks* were suspicious of me, especially of my documentation. On more than one occasion they noted my pallid color and asked if I was feeling well. I assured them I was fine, that I was just getting over a recent bout with the flu.

They seemed to accept this explanation, but I'm certain they wondered why they never saw me with my head uncovered, and why, as a manager with a German oil company, I would be traveling on a slow, third-class worker's train.

Each day, as if it were pleasure rather than work, the *provodniks* would randomly go through the packed rail car checking tickets, passports, and other travel documents. They were actually looking to catch stowaways—exiles, criminals, dissidents, and military deserters—who were trying to escape their banishment to a life in cruel Siberia.

When I questioned him, the male *provodnik* told me for each deserter he found he was paid a bonus—an amount almost twice that of his monthly salary.

One would expect that after checking all my documents once, twice, or three times, this would surely be enough—but not for them. Every day, as the *provodniks* made their inspections through the train car, they required me to pull out *all* my credentials and travel papers. They were indeed drunk with the power of their positions, acting as if it were at their sole discretion that I, or anyone else for that matter, remained on the train.

Obviously, I didn't want trouble or to be reported to the authorities for some indiscretion, so I stayed in the shadows at my seat and cooperated fully whenever confronted by them. Yet each time they reviewed my documents and continued to ask the same probing questions over and over, I became increasingly skeptical of their true intentions. Were they just being the usual obnoxious *provodniks* or were they trying to catch me in a lie?

Because of my mistrust towards the *provodniks,* early on I became preoccupied with my rail map, trying to determine the train's progress and anxiously counting the remaining days and hours until I would be able to get off the wretched, lumbering train in the village of Potevka.

For some unexplained reason, there were times when the train seemed to crawl, moving only fifteen to twenty miles per hour. I couldn't imagine staying on the train all the way to

Moscow. Although I had been on board only a short time, I already needed a break from this slow-moving circus. I needed to rest my tired and bruised body on something other than a hard, wooden bench. I needed a *real* bed and some *real* food. Yet, according to my map and rough calculations, Potevka and the safe house were still several days away.

Chapter 5

FOOLS, FEAST, AND FAMINE

A crust of bread and a corner to sleep in,
A minute to smile and an hour to weep in,
A pint of joy to a peck of trouble,
And never a laugh but the moans come double;
And that is life!

Paul Laurence Dunbar
Life

While riding this insufferable train taking me to Potevka, I had another potentially serious problem. In addition to my painful head, ribs, and arms, my hearing loss, and constant fatigue, I had brought only the small knapsack of food for my journey, and I was still days away from provisions stored at the safe house.

Located in the middle of the long line of rail cars was the wretched smelling food car. Yet, I had *NO* intention of going there—no matter how hungry I got!

Headquarters constantly admonished agents to carry their own food when traveling on Soviet trains. This was because of the poor sanitation, which resulted in a high incidence of food poisoning from meals prepared on the second and third class non-tourist trains.

WARNING: DO NOT EAT THE TRAIN FOOD!

Yet, for whatever reason, it seemed that each agent assigned to Russia needed to learn the value of this lesson the hard way.

A few years earlier, during my very first assignment to the Soviet Union, at my orientation briefing, I received the standard warning about avoiding food prepared on the Russian trains. Unfortunately, I, too, failed to take the advice seriously.

Following a week of meetings and briefings at our embassy in Moscow, I took the over-night train, the *Krasnaya Strela* (Red Arrow), to Leningrad—now St. Petersburg. It left early in the evening around dinner time. I was traveling alone, excited at my chance to mingle with the bourgeois passengers and practice my Russian. It seemed I had spent years preparing for this moment. I was finally on my own, on assignment in the USSR, and eager for the chance to experience it all.

I put my things away in my assigned sleeper cabin and made my way to the dining car. With no thought to the warnings of my superiors, I ordered a variety of dishes from the menu. Besides, I had grown up a country boy in rural Utah and believed I had a cast-iron stomach. Surely, strange food could not affect me!

After a plate of *zakuski* (hors d'oeuvres), the main course, which after all these years I still distinctly remember, was a greasy yellow stew with lumps of *something* that the waiter assured me was chicken.

Wanting to spend as much time as possible in the dining car speaking Russian, I chose to extend my informal language lessons by ordering additional food items at various intervals throughout the evening: a plate of pickled sardines, a mushroom omelet, a traditional Slavic cucumber-cabbage salad, a bowl of the famous *borscht* (beet soup) accompanied by a half-loaf of Russian rye bread. Much of the food I willingly shared with the Soviet travelers seated at my table.

Following two hours of exhilarating conversation in the swaying dining car, I started feeling somewhat queasy. I excused myself from the table and hurried back through several passenger cars to my sleeping compartment.

While struggling with the rocking and bouncing of the train, my stomach began a rocking and bouncing of its own. When I finally reached my cabin—and not a minute too soon—I threw myself into a fetal position on the bed, holding my raging stomach. Within a half hour, I was sicker than I had ever been in my entire life. It was as if an alien creature was growing inside my stomach.

How could this have happened so suddenly? Had someone tried to poison me? And why hadn't I paid attention to those warnings about avoiding Russian train food?

Lying there for hours, I wondered if the excruciating pain would ever stop and if I'd be alive in the morning. And there I was traveling alone on a Russian train, in the middle of the night, speeding from Moscow a half thousand miles towards Leningrad.

As my angry stomach started going into convulsions, I knew I was going to die. And before the night was over, I was begging, even pleading with the Lord, *"Please, Lord, please. Let me die!"*

The following morning while departing the train, I regrettably passed by our rail car *provodnik.* He commented that I didn't look well, that I was the color of the yellow stew that was served in the dinning car the previous evening.

Desperately trying to forget anything about last night's stew, I asked him sarcastically: "Does Russia have anything like a department of health that inspects food and facilities in places like restaurants, cafes, and passenger train dining cars?"

He said he'd never heard of such a thing and thought it quite unnecessary. "Why would anyone prepare food for the public that was not fit for consumption?" he asked incredulously.

I bid him *da svidaniya* (goodbye), and staggered off as quickly as I could towards my hotel.

I never reported this experience to my superiors, but I'm certain some of them must have questioned my work ethic as a newly-arrived agent. I had been in the country less than two weeks when my supervisor at our embassy in Moscow received a call from me requesting two days of vacation time so I could stay in Leningrad and view the art treasures of the world-famous *Hermitage.* In reality, I never left my deathbed at the hotel for three entire days.

It would be another two years before I was actually able to view the masterpieces of Russia's greatest art museum.

☆ ☆ ☆

Despite this horrible experience with food poisoning during my first rail trip in Russia, my problems with food and Soviet trains were only to get worse.

It was now, while on this slow, unbearable, workers train from Siberia to Potevka, that I would experience another major food crisis. This incident—mercifully—would not make me physically sick but would leave me angry and disgusted, not only with myself, but especially with the deceitful behavior of the passengers in my rail car.

Early in the morning, during my first day on board the train, I made the inexcusable mistake of leaving my food knapsack—the one I'd brought with me from Tayginsk—at my seat when I left the passenger compartment to use the WC.

After I returned from the washroom, I immediately sensed that something was wrong; the noise in the rail car was subdued—almost silent. Adrenalin rushed throughout my body. Pretending as if nothing was wrong, I casually scanned the hushed car, expecting to spot the new face or faces that didn't belong there. *Had the KGB or mafia found me? Had the provodniks reported me to the Railway Security Police?*

When I got to my seat, I looked down—my food sack was gone. I stood in the aisle looking around, attempting to appear calm while collecting my thoughts, trying to decide what I should do.

Compared, however, to what I'd imagined—the presence of the KGB or Russian mafia—the missing food sack was almost a welcome relief. But I was still so upset with myself. Trying to conserve what little food I had thrown together for the four or five-day trip, I had not eaten a thing from my knapsack. And to make matters worse, during the frantic last few days of our covert operation, I had been too anxious and nervous to think about eating. I was now without any food and had several days yet to travel. *I should have known this could happen! Why on earth hadn't I been more careful?*

Defiantly, I stood at my seat looking around at the other passengers. My stolen food had forced me out of my dark corner. Surely, I would draw more attention to myself if I didn't confront the situation and react as a normal person would.

I looked at the passengers seated at my end of the rail car. In my best Russian, I asked, "Please, did anyone see what happened to my food sack?"

No one uttered a word. They kept their heads down or looked away to avoid my eyes. The only exception was a small, disheveled, dark haired boy sitting between two elderly people a few rows away. The boy seemed concerned, watching me intently with his bright blue eyes.

After a few, tense, awkward minutes, sporadic laughter suddenly broke out from the other end of the rail car where a small group of Soviet soldiers were sitting. Without thinking, I turned around, squared my shoulders, and defiantly walked the length of the car and stood before them.

"Excuse me for interrupting, but you seem to think it's funny that someone has taken my food sack. I have several days to travel and nothing to eat. I would appreciate it if one of you *honorable* soldiers of the *Motherland* would tell me what happened to my food."

The soldiers' laughter fell dead quiet. Throughout the rail car there was silence, only the rumble of the train's wheels beneath us. I addressed the soldiers again. Not one would look at me or respond to my question.

I was upset and angry but, especially, with myself. *Surely someone saw who took my food. Was it the soldiers? What kind of people were these? With food being so scarce for everyone, how could they be so callous and brazenly dishonest as to do such a thing and in front of the other passengers?*

I had now personally experienced first hand the dark corruption that permeated this Communist system from the highest levels of government politicians all the way down to the common peasants.

But now I possibly had an additional problem. *Had I drawn more attention to myself because of my reaction to the incident and standing up to the soldiers?*

As mad and disgusted as I was, it was still difficult for me to be truly angry in light of what was happening in their country. The lack of food throughout the USSR was becoming a crisis. The famous hammer and sickle emblazoned on the red Soviet flag represented the Marxist ideology of *Industry and Agriculture.* Yet for the suffering masses, agriculture always took a back seat to the government's obsession with building a great Soviet industrial/military power. For decades one of the many Communist government's propaganda mantras had been "Guns before Butter."

Russia has more arable farmland than any other country in the world; however, historically and still today, they have never been able to adequately feed their people. In 1914, Russia entered World War I woefully ill prepared. Hundreds of thousands of farmers were taken off the land to fight in the war, causing a great void in food production. As a result millions of men, women, and children starved to death.

Since the end of the First World War and the *Bolshevik* Revolution, the low food production has been a result of the corruption, mismanagement, and ineptness of the Communist system. The scarcity of reliable farm equipment was a major issue, but the most significant factor was the defiant attitude of many of the *kolkhoz* (collective farm) workers who would have their crops unilaterally taken from them by the government year after year, leaving them with little or nothing for all their toil and suffering.

Now, as the USSR was coming apart, there were major food shortages in the large cities and towns—even in the villages of the farm country. People were beginning to panic.

The only comfort I got from the loss of my knapsack was the realization that the person or persons who took it probably needed the food a lot more than I did.

I was now faced with the decision of whether or not to report the incident to the *provodniks. Would they help me or would I just be setting myself up for more trouble?* It was likely that I had actually drawn more attention to myself by confronting the soldiers. Telling the *provodniks* about the incident would probably cause even more attention than I could afford.

As I sat back down at my seat, I determined that no matter what, or how hungry I got, I still would not revert to eating anything that came out of the rank-smelling food car. Like a cat that had already used up a couple of his nine lives, I had gone through a great deal in the last seventy-two hours, and I wanted to live another day! Still etched in my mind and stomach was the harsh lesson I had learned years earlier with the chicken stew during my first experience on a Russian train.

The young boy seated a few rows away, who had obviously witnessed what happened to my food, seemed genuinely concerned. He kept staring at me as if he wanted to tell me something. *Just what had he seen?* The boy asked something of the old man sitting next to him—most likely his grandfather—who repeatedly shook his head, whispering emphatically to the boy. "*Nyet, Nyet, Nyet!*"

☆ ☆ ☆

It was during this same time period that those in our diplomatic corps stationed in the Soviet Union thought themselves immune from the growing food crisis until it showed its ugly head, even in the capital city of Moscow itself.

The very week I had arrived at the American Embassy in Moscow in preparation for this mission to Siberia, three Russian men broke into the apartment of an American diplomat in the middle of the night. The young attaché officer was living with his wife and young baby a short distance from the American Embassy compound in one of the old high-rise, Stalinesque apartment buildings.

The diplomat had obviously been seen taking groceries into his apartment each week, which he would purchase at the small commissary at the embassy. With the Soviet food crisis growing worse day by day, the U.S. State Department had established an emergency program of flying in foodstuffs from abroad for the embassy personnel posted in Moscow.

As the thieves entered the attaché's apartment brandishing handguns, they took the baby hostage from the hysterical mother. Never asking for money, they said they would return the infant unharmed once she and her husband emptied their flat of all food.

After two anxious hours of carrying boxes of food stuffs from their apartment to the thieves' car near the building exit, the thugs gave the baby back to the frantic parents and then drove off in a Russian *Zhiguli* loaded with the couple's entire supply of food.

The incident stunned the foreign service community to its core. It put everyone on notice that they, too, were vulnerable to the effects of the food crisis that had gripped the entire Soviet nation.

☆ ☆ ☆

Following this episode with the loss of my food, I retreated to my corner seat on the train car and left only out of necessity; i.e. visits to the gruesome WC at one end of the rail car or, at the opposite end, to fetch the only liquid sustenance available—Russian black tea.

The WC was unbearable, shared by over sixty people. There was no hot water. A broken window allowed snow to blow inside. The floor of the toilet room, just like the aisle way in the passenger car, was constantly covered with muck and mud.

Located at the other end of the rail car was a large *samovar*-looking teapot, which the *provodniks* kept full with a thick mixture of strong, Russian black tea. In order to make it drinkable, the heavy concentrate needed to be diluted with water from the nearby hot water tank.

Because it was the only sustenance on the train guaranteed not to contaminate, I forced myself to keep drinking it in order to replenish the fluids in my body due to the amount of blood I had lost.

For my remaining days on the train, I tried to suppress my hunger with cup after cup of the pungent, bitter stuff. Sugar cubes were available for only a few *kopeks* (pennies), until someone made off with our rail car's entire two-week trip allotment during my first night on board.

I would be on the train a total of five days before we reached Potevka; I couldn't imagine that the majority of the passengers would be on the train for two full weeks. As my hunger increased, my anxiety over the KGB and mafia began to diminish. There were times when I thought about visiting the food car to see what might be available, but the thought of food poisoning or becoming sick—knowing there was only one lavatory for the entire passenger car—was more than enough to keep the temptation at bay.

Furthermore, I overheard someone say that the only things left in the food car for sale were sickly cucumbers and ample bottles of vodka. Perhaps it was the availability of the latter that sustained the adult passengers, helping them dull their senses to the long, grueling journey.

Chapter 6

A POSTCARD FROM SIBERIA

Heavy the sorrow that bows the head
When love is alive and hope is dead.

W.S. Gilbert
H.M.S. Pinafore

After what felt like a thousand miles swallowed up by the *Taiga*, a forest of pine, birch, fir, and aspen so immense that it encompasses almost one-fifth of the forestland of the world, it seemed the old train would take forever to cross the endless miles of the barren Siberian *steppes*. Beyond the frozen windows, whenever the storm slowed enough, the snow looked like an ocean of silver sand stretching as far as the eye could see. The bleakness of the landscape—a world of numbing cold and desolation—rarely changed.

Every settlement we passed looked identical to the last: clusters of small log homes hidden behind broken picket fences; ramshackle barns with malnourished livestock—bony workhorses, cattle, and milk cows; woodsheds, outhouses, root cellars, and frozen garden plots; small, sad cemeteries, each mounded grave fenced by weathered-gray log poles and marked with a simple wooden cross. Chickens and geese, goats and pigs could be seen scavenging while wandering the rutted roads—most of which were unpaved and forever mired with mud or frozen solid when the harsh temperatures of the Siberian winter plunged brutally below zero and remained so until the thaw of late spring.

The monotony of the vast, empty landscape would sometimes be broken whenever we passed through one of the large industrial cities where a murky, brown haze hung over the entire province. Huge smokestacks belched chemicals and pollutants, contaminating the land, forests, lakes, rivers, and air for miles around—no doubt damaging the health of the local populace as well. A brown grit coated the buildings, houses, streets, and sidewalks. At times, even the snow on the ground had a rust-colored hue to it.

It is well documented that parts of Russia and the former Soviet Union continue to be ecological disasters of immense proportions; a problem not only for bordering countries, but for the whole world because of the amount of toxins and radioactive waste emitted by their nuclear, defense, and industrial plants. International experts agree that the Chernobyl disaster was not the first Soviet nuclear catastrophe—nor will it be the last.

Along the endless rail line, gaunt solitary soldiers in long, gray military coats could be seen standing watch with their German Shepherd dogs at every railroad crossing, every bridge, every tunnel, and every remote military outpost. They were part of the lies and propaganda created by paranoid Communist Party leaders at the Kremlin who were continually trying to convince the Soviet people that at any moment the United States and her allies would attempt to invade the USSR. As a result, it was the duty of every Soviet citizen to remain vigilant against these would-be aggressors. Thus, throughout the whole of the Soviet Union, countless soldiers stood guard to protect Mother Russia.

This fear of invasion was not without cause. During World War II, when Hitler's Nazi forces invaded Russia, they made it all the way to the outskirts of Moscow before they were finally repelled by the Soviet military and able-bodied Muscovites. Russia lost twenty-seven million people in what is still referred to as *The Great Patriotic War*. Even now, over fifty years later, a great deal of mistrust remains towards Germany. Many of the older Russians still advocate: "We will *never* forget!"

I found myself wondering, *Perhaps the operational cover that the agency gave me—a*

German oil company supervisor—was not the best of ideas after all.

Looking out at the passing landscape, once in awhile, one of the small, abandoned, wooden churches would appear. Whenever I saw these churches, knowing of the deliberate, malicious efforts by the *Bolshevik* Communists to destroy religion in Russia, it made me angry to think of how, for seventy-five years, most of these people had been deprived of a place to worship and how religion and hope had systematically been taken from their lives. So often when hope is taken away, as it had been for the majority of the Soviet people, life can be tragically difficult and heartbreaking.

I will always remember a scene, indelible in my mind to this day, of a moment late one frozen afternoon when I was standing in the rail car opposite my seat in the vestibule next to the exit door. The stench inside the passenger compartment had driven me to seek some fresh air that was blowing in from a small broken windowpane near the exit.

As I watched the passing, frozen landscape, the storm unexpectedly calmed. The snow and sleet stopped; the clouds partially opened. Suddenly rays of bright sunlight spilled across the valley onto a small village directly in front of me, illuminating the frozen ponds and marshes and windows of the dozen or so cabins off in the distance.

On that dingy, gray day, my eyes were immediately drawn to the first truly bright color I had seen in days. I saw a young girl, six or seven years old, about thirty yards from the tracks, walking down a muddy road in *bright red plastic boots*. She had on gray leggings and wore a heavy, dark coat several sizes too large for her tiny body. A large, brown scarf covered her head. In one hand she held a long stick; in the other she swung a small bucket. Immediately in front of her, a gaggle of geese scurried along the muddy road that headed back towards the village.

As our train passed by, she stopped, turned, and watched. She removed her scarf and slowly waved it back and forth above her head. Perhaps I only imagined it, but her comely, young face had a longing, wistful look, a look that seemed to ask . . . *What dreams could be mine if only someday I could be on such a train.*

In that suspended moment, for whatever reason, my own situation seemed to mirror that of the girl; she seemed so alone in such a dark, forsaken land. The young girl and the moment broke my heart.

Our train moved beyond the clearing and re-entered the storm. In an instant she was gone. I have often reflected on that occasion and the young girl in those bright red plastic boots. Who was she? What has her life been like? And where is she today?

☆ ☆ ☆

Inside the rail car, the only thing that ever changed was the empty faces of the Russian workers getting on and off at each stop. The length of each stop depended on the size of the city, town, or village. I watched closely as the new faces silently boarded our rail car. I carefully observed if there was anything unusual, perhaps something in the way a person looked or behaved, that would tell me this was not just a simple peasant worker but possibly trouble—the KGB or Russian mafia.

After each stop, when the train began to roll forward, I felt a temporary sense of relief from my fears. Unfortunately, my reprieve would only last until the next stop. The fatigue, worry, and constant vigilance were all taking their toll on me; plus my aching body was still mending from the beating I had suffered in Tayginsk.

The days and nights leading up to the final hours of our failed covert operation, including the life-threatening confrontation with Koshka's men, were more mentally and physically exhausting than anything I had ever experienced. Now on board a train, heading thousands of miles across Russia, I was so emotionally drained that things began to take on a surreal quality, like none of this was actually happening, that it was, indeed, all a distant dream.

☆ ☆ ☆

Whenever the train made a long stop during daylight hours, passengers would get off in order to breathe some fresh air, to stretch, walk around, try to buy something; but mostly they did it to break the monotony of being trapped inside their temporary tomb. The larger the town or city, the greater the number of passengers that would disembark. Many times I was tempted to get off myself, but never did; I was too concerned about what could possibly go wrong if I left the train, even if only for a few minutes. I needed to avoid any potential problems no matter what.

From my window seat, each large, dismal railway station appeared indistinguishable from the last. Like a huge, concrete stage—its walls covered with faded Communist propaganda posters—the same cast of characters played out their parts in this tragic, real-life drama: endless lines of bent *babushkas* (old women) standing shoulder to shoulder along the sidewalks pedaling tobacco, homemade beer, *piroshki* (cabbage rolls), and smoked salt-fish; drunkards struggling to remain vertical or, having already lost the struggle, lying on the muddy ground; brooding gypsy women surrounded by their dirty, malnourished children, begging for money from passersby; small groups of skinny uniformed soldiers talking to giggly teenaged girls; absurdly long queues in front of a Soviet state-run store having, *surprisingly*, something to sell to the local residents; wiry, rough boys burning old tires on side roads near the rail station; wrinkled old heroes of Word War II wearing worn suit coats covered with military medals, sitting on broken wooden benches near a statue of Lenin in a grassless park named after Karl Marx; and then there were *always* at each rail station the packs of starving dogs that hunted the cats that hunted the rats.

Another permanent fixture around the railway stations were the hefty female railway workers dressed in their orange canvas jackets, winter leggings, ever-present headscarves, and black storm-trooper-like boots. Normally sweeping up garbage or doing maintenance on the tracks, now in the winter, they could usually be seen chipping ice from the frozen rail switches.

Women, who make up the majority of the Russian work force, are usually relegated to the menial, hard-labor tasks. Unlike my feelings towards Russian men, I have a great admiration for Russian women. Historically, and still today, they remain the strength and character of Russia. The women are the powerful bond that holds the family, village, and nation together. Perhaps that is why these people refer to their homeland as *Great Mother Russia.*

Surprisingly absent from most small communities were automobiles. It was not uncommon to pass through a village or small town and not see a single vehicle other than, perhaps, an occasional farm truck or tractor. Even in the larger cities there were few cars compared to Western Europe. This stemmed from the fact that, under the Communist regime, only a small percentage of the population was able to afford an automobile. And for those who were able to purchase one, there was an inordinate waiting period—sometimes as long as five to seven years. Understandably, many of the vehicles were owned by the government and provided to high-ranking members of the Communist Party. Others were owned by certain citizens held in favor by the party: collaborating lawyers, scientists, professors, and doctors. The greater part of the populace was relegated to the poorly maintained and often unreliable public transportation of buses, trams, and trains. I wondered how we as Americans, with our obsession of the automobile, would have tolerated living under such conditions.

As the Russian landscape rolled endlessly by, I thought back to my student days at Utah State University. It was while enrolled in my political science classes—especially those taught by Professor Milton Merrill—that I became intrigued with the Soviet Union. His knowledge and insight into the world of international politics and U.S. Foreign Policy left a great impression on me. I was drawn in by the mystique of the world's other super-power—its people and culture, politics and military, and its tumultuous, thousand-year history. I was fascinated how this country, with its tyrannical leaders and arsenals of nuclear weapons, had become such a threat to the rest of the world.

During those early years of study, a dream of mine began to take shape—a dream that someday I would be able to experience this vast, intriguing country as a tourist on the famous Trans-Siberian Express. Never, however, could I have imagined that my dream to journey across Russia would end up being anything like this.

Chapter 7

THE MAN WHO CHANGED THE WORLD

Alone he rides, alone. The fair and fatal King
Lionel Johnson
The Statue of King Charles I at Charing Cross

Although he had been in power for only a few years, Mikhail Gorbachev, Secretary General of the Communist Party and leader of the Soviet Union, was boldly implementing major reforms across the USSR. Since the years of Stalin, Russia had never seen such a revolutionary leader. But unlike the cruel Stalin and the dogmatic dictators who followed him, Gorbachev genuinely cared for the

Soviet people and their welfare. He realized that the Communist system of government was in need of drastic change or it would eventually collapse. He instituted needed reforms within the *politburo* (Soviet party leadership) and allowed unprecedented freedoms to the Soviet populace. Idealized throughout the world for his visionary leadership, yet despised by the majority of Soviet people—they blamed Gorbachev for their personal poverty and the continuing downward spiral of the nation—Gorbachev's policies of *perestroika* (economic restructuring) and *glasnost* (openness) were changing the face of Soviet society.

Stirred by the winds of change from Gorbachev's reforms and seventy years of Communist oppression, the USSR was coming apart at the seams. The government was losing its strangle hold over the people, the economy was in shambles, and food was becoming scarce throughout the country. Out-of-control inflation had made the Russian *ruble* worthless. Overnight tens of millions of pensioners had lost their life's savings. Although illegal to have in one's possession, the currency of choice for the Russian people was the American dollar—surely Lenin and Stalin were kicking in their coffins!

Driven in recent years by a reawakening of nationalism within the Soviet Republics against the oppressive policies and iron-fisted control of Moscow, the walls of the infamous *Iron Curtain* were being torn down, along with the Communist régimes in Poland, Czechoslovakia, Bulgaria, Yugoslavia, Romania, Hungary, and East

Germany. The whole of Eastern Europe was in great turmoil.

Months earlier in Moscow, a group of hard-line Communist leaders attempted a political coup to overthrow President Gorbachev. As a result, the government's major political factions were positioning themselves one against the other, desperately trying to hang on to their power and authority.

Against the vehement protests of Communist Party hardliners, Gorbachev had finally opened the door to reveal the Soviet Union's dark past—permitting the ugly truths to be known. The result was the gradual demise of the world's other great superpower. A once mighty and proud nation, the USSR had sunk into a state of despair, paralyzed by the fear of what the future might bring—and their leader, Mikhail Gorbachev, was to blame.

I had arrived in Russia the week of the attempted coup against Gorbachev and watched from a Moscow hotel room window as tens of thousands of Soviet citizens converged on the Russian Parliament to protect it from the coup conspirators, a group of arrogant Communists who were determined to take control of the government and re-implement the hard-line rule of the old *Bolsheviks*. The Soviet Union was at another critical crossroads in its tumultuous history.

The people of the USSR, and those in the Soviet satellites, had lived under tyranny and terror for decades. Now, as the Communist barriers were coming down all around Eastern Europe, these people were willing to do anything to be free from their years of oppression. They knew very little about democracy, but many were willing to die for the chance to embrace it—and some did die.

For someone who had spent a significant part of his schooling in Russian studies and career work in Soviet intelligence, there could not have been a more uncertain and perilous, yet intriguing time for a foreigner to be there—especially an American—to be an actual witness to the fall of the great Soviet Empire.

Chapter 8

BAD KARMA IN BAVARIA

Communism is the corruption of a dream of justice.

Adlai Stevenson

While traveling on the train to Potevka, I spent hours trying to comprehend the chaotic, historic events that were now taking place throughout the USSR. *Would the Soviet Union really cease to exist? Would Communism be able to survive?* I wondered what these changes would mean for the future of this country and for the rest of the world. Pondering these questions, I couldn't help but think back to years ago and of my friend, Yuri Novotny, wondering, *What would Yuri think if he were here with me tonight, traveling across Russia and witnessing what was happening to this once mighty nation?*

Throughout history governments have sought secretive information in order to gain advantage over another country or to eliminate uncertainties when conducting foreign affairs. The espionage games between the United States and the Soviet Union were being played out even before the two countries established diplomatic relations in 1933. During the decades of the Cold War, spy tradecraft was developed into a fine art and became of utmost strategic importance—superpower against superpower, warhead against warhead, and spy against spy.

When I look back, it all seemed so simple. Russia was the great evil in the world, and it was America's duty to save the world from Russia.

Right out of resident intelligence school, I was young, inexperienced, and naive; unaware of the realities of the covert world of espionage and how quickly the game could turn so very deadly.

✯ ✯ ✯

The first time I saw him was when he walked into the classroom and sat in the seat next to me. He was strikingly handsome, over six feet tall, with olive complexion, blue eyes, and black hair. His summer uniform was starched and pressed, his shoes polished to a high-gloss shine. His handshake was strong and firm. He introduced himself as Jiří (Yuri) Novotny, a captain in the U.S.

Air Force, assigned to a Strategic Air Defense Unit in southern Italy. Along with sixty other students, he was beginning his first day of class in a month-long, security course at the U.S. Intelligence School in Oberammergau, Germany. As a young officer recently assigned to the school as an instructor, it would be a month of my life I would never forget.

Located in the German Alps, the village of Oberammergau is one of the most charming, picturesque places in all of Europe. Below the towering mountains, narrow cobblestone streets meander through the village of gingerbread houses and façade-painted shops. Austria, Switzerland, and Italy are less than an hour away by train or motorcar.

Oberammergau is renowned for two reasons. First, every ten years it hosts the world famous *Passion Play,* which depicts the last days of Christ here on earth. This tradition began in 1634, when the villagers made a pledge to honor the Lord with a grand, religious production of Christ's crucifixion and resurrection in exchange for His protection from the Black Plague, which was sweeping its way across Europe, leaving millions dead in its path. The village was spared, and, with the exception of World War I and II, the play has been performed throughout the summer every decade for the last 370 years. The second reason for its fame is that the village of Oberammergau is known world-wide as the European center of the centuries-old art of wood carving.

This area of Bavaria was like a second home to me. Having served for two years in southern Germany and northern Switzerland as a missionary for our Church (The Church of Jesus Christ of Latter-day Saints), I felt extremely fortunate to be assigned back there as part of the U.S. military. I was captivated by the beauty of the country, its people, the culture, and I especially loved the *wunderbar* German food.

Originally known as Hoetzendorf Kaserne under Hitler's Third Reich, the military compound at Oberammergau was occupied by American forces at the end of World War II. The small military complex was renamed Hawkins Barracks and eventually became the European Training Center for U.S. Armed Forces.

The school compound sat on a slope directly under the 5,000 foot peaks of the Bavarian Alps. The campus was made up of approximately thirty buildings, interspersed with huge pine trees and surrounded by a massive, twenty-five-foot high stone wall. The view from campus down towards the village, across the Ammer Valley, was spectacular.

The school, often referred to as O'gau, provided resident courses in several specialized military disciplines for select U.S. and NATO allied personnel from various commands throughout Europe. Only the most qualified and brightest students were accepted at the school. Due to the nature of the subject matter to which the students would be exposed, a top secret security clearance was mandatory for attendance.

The weather in Oberammergau on our first day of classes was exceptional. The sky above the mountain peaks was a bright, crystal blue; a soft, summer wind blew down across the beautiful Ammer Valley. I sat in the class room among the students dressed in a Soviet major's uniform.

Because I knew Russian and could speak English with a heavy Russian accent, I was chosen from among our teaching cadre to pose as a visiting Russian military officer from the Warsaw Pact. I had even grown a thick *Bolshevik* mustache to enhance my disguise.

After welcoming the students, Lt. Colonel Dunn, Department Director of the Intelligence School, would go over the administrative details and discuss the classified curriculum. He would then begin the first hour of instruction for the month-long course entitled *The Soviet Military Threat*.

As Lt. Colonel Dunn would proceed with his teaching, it would be my role, as the visiting Soviet officer, to take issue with most everything he said. The dialog between the two of us had, of course, been carefully choreographed beforehand. Following numerous interruptions from the Guest Russian Officer—me—Lt. Colonel Dunn would pretend to reach his boiling point. He would grab the lesson plan from off the podium and slam it to the floor, making sure pages flew in every direction. He would then challenge me, "Well if you're so d--- smart, then you get up here and teach the course!" He would then storm out of the classroom in a huff.

For the next two or three minutes you wouldn't hear a sound in the entire classroom. American and NATO military officers and senior NCOs (non-commissioned officers) would sit in their seats shocked and speechless.

I was then to act somewhat reluctant but to eventually get up from my seat and walk to the front of the class. I would pick up the pages scattered across the floor and place them back on the podium. Fifty-nine of our military's best would sit in stunned silence as this presumed Russian officer would begin to explain that the American colonel had been teaching them lies and propaganda about the failures and weaknesses of the great Soviet Union.

By the time I took over at the podium, there would usually be less than ten minutes before the students were allowed their first scheduled morning break, which they were required to take outside the building or in the student lounge.

During that first break, staff and faculty would stand with ears pressed against the wall opposite the student lounge and hear students' comments such as: "And they call this an intelligence school?" or "This faculty needs to be reported to European Command Headquarters in Heidelberg," or "How could they be so stupid as to invite a Russian officer here to the Intelligence School?"

As the intercom would sound and the students re-entered the classroom, most would notice my conspicuous absence and the empty seat. From the podium, Lt. Colonel Dunn would apologize to the students. “Inviting a liaison officer from Russia, obviously, was a bad idea,” he would tell them. “We thought it might add value to the class. We’re sorry it didn’t, but at least we tried.”

He would again review the course curriculum, but this time he would introduce each of the instructors who would then, one by one, join him at the podium. Now dressed in my real military uniform, I would be the last to be introduced. I would proceed to the podium from the back of the room, usually to fifty-nine surprised, smiling faces and always to a loud ovation.

We always had a good time with this Soviet officer skit; but more importantly, it set a positive tone for the students and for the seriousness we placed on the instruction and information they would receive during the next month at our school.

As the primary instructor of Soviet studies at O’gau, at the start of the second hour of class, I would begin a four-day block of instruction on the Soviet Union, specifically *The Soviet Military Capability* and *The Soviet Military Threat.*

During the morning’s first long break, Captain Yuri Novotny came to my office and re-introduced himself. “Do you really speak Russian?” he asked, smiling, still amused about the skit.

“Yes, I do, but not as well as I’d like,” I replied. “I just need more practice.” He then proceeded to speak Russian with me, something we tried to do every chance we got during the next month. Although Yuri was native Czech, his Russian was excellent, significantly better than mine. And I wasn't about to pass up this chance to improve my language skills.

Yuri's mother and father were both Czech citizens and had worked for the Soviet occupational forces in Czechoslovakia after World War II. He spoke highly of his parents, especially his father. Several times during the next month, Yuri related how much his father had sacrificed so Yuri could have the very best education and career opportunities possible, even immigrating with the entire family to the United States.

Yuri was born in Prague. As a boy, he lived with his parents in Russia and attended grammar school in Moscow, then moved with his parents to America when he was sixteen years old. He'd received his officer's commission through the Air Force ROTC program at Ohio University.

Both company-grade officers in the military, we were about the same age and seemed to have a great deal in common. We both loved sports, especially football, tennis, and skiing. We had both married our college sweethearts, and each of us had a one-year-old son. Yuri's wife, Jenni, and their little boy, Andrew, were the love of his life.

During the long class breaks, both in the morning and in the afternoon, Yuri would usually come to my office to chat and help me practice my Russian. He was an outstanding, patriotic officer and at the very top of the class academically. My respect for him grew with each passing day and we soon became good friends. I appreciated his willingness to help me with my Russian, but what I enjoyed most was listening to him relate his experiences of living in Russia and Czechoslovakia during the years of Soviet occupation.

Inasmuch as we were both without our families—his in Italy and mine on home-leave in the States—one or two nights during the week we would go down to the village to have dinner together at one of the German pubs or restaurants. On Saturday mornings we battled each other on the tennis courts down the mountain at the AFRC sports complex in Garmisch. Although I was able to hold my own against Yuri, I considered myself fortunate the times when I was able to win a set. Besides being outstanding at most everything else, Yuri was also an exceptional athlete.

One Saturday after tennis, I played tour guide for Yuri as we spent the rest of the day visiting Innsbruck, Berchtesgaden, and Salzburg, all within a two-hour drive. The next day, Sunday, we drove down the Brenner Pass through northern Italy to Venice. While we drove we shared stories of our families, how we grew up, where we went to school, our military experiences, and what we hoped for our future. The common thread throughout all his conversation was the love Yuri had for his wife and little boy, and the pride he felt being able to serve as an officer in the United States military. He spoke longingly about someday settling down, after retirement, with his family somewhere in small-town America.

✯ ✯ ✯

There were over three hundred personnel permanently assigned to the Oberammergau school, more than half of them support staff. Forty-two of us were officers. As with most military installations, each officer at O'gau was required to take his turn at an extra duty assignment, commonly known as the SDO (Staff Duty Officer). Newly-arrived junior officers, such as myself, were normally given four or five months to get acclimated to their new teaching assignments before their names were added to the SDO duty roster. The main responsibility of this position was to act on behalf of the school commander once he left the headquarters facility for the night.

Colonel Hart was the Commandant of the Intelligence School. Six months from retirement, he was a soft-spoken, rotund southern gentleman, and a grandfather figure to most everyone. During our SDO briefings, we were admonished by the school S-2 (staff intelligence officer), Major Green, that he did *not* want Colonel Hart disturbed once the colonel left campus for the evening—only unless World War III had begun.

Interestingly, over the three years Colonel Hart had spent as school commandant, he had been called from his home back to the command center only twice. Regrettably, on each of these occasions, I happened to be the SDO on duty.

The first incident happened on a summer evening during my very first SDO assignment. A serious fight—a free-for-all—broke out at a German pub down in the village between several American soldiers and a group of German gang members. Several of these German thugs took quite a beating—some even requiring medical attention. According to the witnesses we interviewed, the Germans had provoked the altercation and deserved what they got at the hands of the American soldiers.

As the SDO, I briefed Colonel Hart and his staff when they were called back to headquarters, then spent the rest of the night at the command center filling out pages of extra paperwork documenting the incident.

The next day I was summoned to Major Green's office. He was not happy, to say the least, and reprimanded me—as if to imply that *I* was the one who had somehow instigated the free-for-all. What a guy!

Just six weeks later, during my second SDO assignment, two young German boys, hiking in a restricted area on the mountain above campus, got trapped on a sheer cliff several hundred feet directly above the school. In an attempt to get down, one of the boys slipped and fell from the cliff, landing on a rock ledge approximately forty to fifty feet below.

That evening, with the assistance of the 3rd German Mountain Brigade, based out of Garmisch-Partenkirchen, eight of us scaled the mountain and brought the boys down. The boy who had fallen sustained serious internal injuries and remained unconscious for several months.

The hours spent bringing the injured boy down the mountain and watching him fight for his life greatly affected each of us that participated in his rescue.

Again, I spent part of the evening at headquarters briefing Colonel Hart and filling out extra reports and paperwork.

In the morning when I again briefed him and his full staff, I could tell the Colonel was somewhat troubled about his new lieutenant from Bear River—now an instructor at his school.

When we left the staff room, Major Green pulled me aside and told me to report to his office the following morning at six a.m.

Major Green had been the staff intelligence officer since his arrival at the school three years earlier. He was a short, stocky man with thinning hair and a Napoleon complex as big as his home state of Texas.

As I stood before him the next morning, he looked at me and explained: "Ramsdell, I truly think you're jinxed—I just don't want the risk of any further aggravation. I'm removing your name from the SDO roster until I feel differently about your ability to handle the job."

It was hard to understand his over-reaction to the situation. Being a young lieutenant, my attempts to reason with a senior major—as usual—fell on deaf ears. The events that happened on my SDO watch could have happened to anyone, but Green would not budge from his irrational position.

Needless to say, I was concerned about the label he was placing on me; not only that I was jinxed but that I was not pulling my share of the extra duties at the school and unable to handle the responsibilities expected of a junior officer.

Under normal circumstances, the SDO's responsibilities at O'gau were actually quite minimal. Besides answering telephone calls and taking messages, the SDO was required to be at the post theater just before the start of the nightly movie for the playing of the national anthem—a tradition at all U.S. military facilities. Between ten and eleven p.m., he was required to make a security drive through the housing area. His final responsibility for the evening was to make a physical security check of certain buildings on campus and verify that they were properly locked and secured for the night. This security check was done by inserting a special master key into a timer box, which would electronically record the SDO's visit.

Of the twelve buildings on campus to be physically inspected, ten of them were facilities in which money was transacted. The two other facilities to be checked, the Intelligence-Military Police building and the NATO building, were the two most security-sensitive facilities on campus due to the number of highly classified documents stored in each building's repository.

The NATO facility was the most important building on campus. It was under the operational control of Supreme Headquarters Allied Powers Europe (SHAPE). Representatives of the sixteen NATO nations made up the faculty and staff. Extremely sensitive, top secret classes were taught there; information the Soviets would desperately want to get their hands on. It was here that select U.S. military officers and senior allied commanders learned about NATO weapons systems and the deployment of nuclear armaments in Europe.

Because of its security classification, anyone that entered the building, including the SDO, needed not only a special clearance but also a particular access code. Upon entry, a person's clearance and access would be checked and verified by high-tech, state-of-the-art, electronic equipment.

It was the first week of July, almost one year to the day since I'd last served as SDO, when I was shocked to see, in the weekly campus newsletter, my name on the upcoming SDO schedule. My assigned duty would fall on Thursday night, the very night before our students' final exam.

For the rest of the week the few other junior officers assigned to O'gau would not leave it alone. "Ramsdell," they would jest, "we're all taking leave next Thursday and Friday. We don't want to be anywhere near this place with *you* at the helm!" I had great friends among the junior officers and these fellows weren't about to let me forget the great "love" that Major Green held for me.

At 3:00 p.m. on the appointed Thursday, I reported to the S-2 office at the command center in the headquarters building.

"Ramsdell," said Major Green, "I don't want any problems on your watch tonight, okay?

Still intimidated by what had happened a year earlier, I assured him, "Not to worry, sir. Everything will be under control."

"You know, Ramsdell" he continued, "I was thinking about you this morning and your problems with this SDO responsibility. I was wondering if putting you back on the roster was a good thing or not. Do you have any idea what the words *Bad Karma* mean?"

"I think so, sir," I replied, irritated that he would even suggest such a thing.

Major Green, again, reminded me of his displeasure that Colonel Hart had to be called back to the school during my two previous SDO assignments. After some further mean-spirited remarks, he had me sign for the building keys, the special access card, and the security code.

At six p.m. Colonel Hart was the last to leave the command center. He poked his head inside the S-2 office and gave me a smile. "Everything gonna be all right?" he asked in his warm, southern drawl.

"Yes, Sir," I assured him. "Everything will be just fine."

He gave me a thumbs-up and bid me good evening. To this day I still remember his parting words: "Lieutenant Ramsdell, now you're sure I'm not gonna see y'all until seven o'clock in the morning? Right . . . ?"

"No, Sir," I said. "I promise you won't hear a peep from me. Have a good evening Colonel, and please give my regards to Mrs. Hart."

At least one person affiliated with the school's command structure was sympathetic to my two previous SDO misadventures. Mrs. Hart had grown up in the Rockies—in nearby Wyoming—and was very proud of it. And, more important, she seemed to like me—or at least I thought so.

Following our unit's SOP (standard operating procedure), just before seven p.m., I walked up the hill to the theater. From my vantage point near the stage, everyone stood while the national anthem played over the loud-speaker system. I stayed for the first few minutes of Disney's *Lady and the Tramp*, and then went back to the headquarters building, where I busied myself updating my teaching lesson plans.

At ten p.m. I locked up the building and walked proudly to where my new, green Camaro was parked. Just out of college and now in the military, for the first time in my life I had a regular monthly paycheck—thus, my first new car. I slowly drove through the housing area, hoping those still out taking a late-evening stroll might notice me and my Camaro. Everything appeared normal in our quiet little neighborhood.

Before returning to the command center, I made a pass by the student dorms. Most of the lights in the rooms were still on—students, obviously cramming for tomorrow's big final exam.

When I returned to headquarters, I spent the next hour filling out the required SDO paperwork. The only area left blank on my report was the one involving the physical security checks of the twelve campus buildings, which I was to begin at midnight.

Later, while sitting at Major Green's desk, catching up on some reading, I heard the twelve strikes of midnight chime from the church tower down in the village. I grabbed the ring of keys, locked the building, and walked back up the hill to the top of campus.

My first security check was at the theater. I unlocked the heavy oak door, turned on the foyer light, and locked the door behind me. There was now an eerie feeling in the place with everything so still and quiet, when only hours earlier the theater had been packed with parents and noisy kids.

While making these security checks, I certainly would have been more comfortable carrying some sort of communication device in case something unexpected were to happen. But then again, nothing ever happened in sleepy O'gau.

Before leaving the theater, I placed the master key into the timer box hanging on the wall. It made a quiet hum followed by a click, indicating the box had electronically recorded my visit.

One down, eleven to go.

Next to the theater was the campus snack bar. Once inside I checked the cashier's cage and office door; everything appeared normal. From there I checked the Rod and Gun Club, the NCO Club, the mess hall, the mail room, the commissary, the gas station, and the Stars and Stripes Bookstore. I drove my Camaro to check our O'gau Officers Club, located a short distance from the school. Upon my return to campus, I made a security check of the post-exchange located on the first floor of the headquarters building.

At each facility I went through the same routine as the others. By one-thirty a.m., I had completed all my security checks, all but one, the NATO building.

Just before two a.m., I walked from HQ across the broad cobblestone street to the NATO school. Of all the buildings on campus, it was the newest, not more than ten years old. It was three stories high and built with the usual superb German craftsmanship.

With the appropriate key, I unlocked the outer door and locked it shut behind me. Ten feet inside the foyer, I took out the special NATO access card and placed it into a white metal box located next to the large electronic door. I punched in the security code.

A soft click sounded, and the door opened. I walked inside. Five seconds later the access door automatically closed behind me.

On the wall to the right of the electronic door was a timer box. Once the appropriate key was inserted, it made the normal hum and click, recording my visit.

I walked down the hallway to where a second timer box was located, a row of small overhead lights softly illuminated the long corridor. While inserting the key into the box, I thought I heard a sound from one of the floors above me. For a moment I contemplated going up to check, but dismissed the sound as my imagination or that of an echo. I turned around and walked back towards the exit.

My duties were now finished for the night. The last thing I would have to do at the command center would be to fill out the rest of my SDO report. It was past two in the morning. At this late hour, both the village and campus were sound asleep.

I felt relief that Lieutenant Ramsdell had *finally* come through for Major Green, and that Colonel Hart would be able to enjoy a full, undisturbed night's sleep.

When I was approximately halfway down the corridor, again I heard something from one of the upper floors. I stood motionless, listening. Nothing. *So, was it just my imagination?* As I was about to move on, I distinctly heard the noise of a file drawer being opened or closed. I froze. *How could this possibly be? There was definitely someone else in the building.* My adrenalin began to stir.

The first thing that crossed my mind was that one of the NATO school instructors was probably working late. But that seemed strange. I knew that after 1700 hours (five p.m.), Monday through Friday, and on weekends, the NATO facility was closed and off-limits to everyone.

Perhaps, however, an instructor did have reason to be in the building. Maybe he was working on a special project that Command forgot to mention to those of us assigned to SDO duty for the week. Yet Major Green had not said anything to me.

So, who was in the building, and what were they doing here?

Again I heard the sound of a file drawer. I stood in place, debating what I should do. I could quietly lock the doors of the facility and make my way back to the command center and call Major Green, who in turn—following standard operating procedures—would have to notify Colonel Hart. *No way was that going to happen!*

For a young officer, being selected as an instructor at the U.S. Intelligence School–Europe was a significant honor, one that could definitely jump-start one's military career. Four junior officers had been transferred from O'gau in the last year for incompetence; I certainly didn't want to become the fifth. I needed to handle this situation like an officer. I needed to take charge and show some leadership by resolving this problem myself rather than passing it on to someone else. There was no written SOP for what I was about to encounter, but I was determined to handle it on my own. And there was no way I was going to have Colonel Hart come back to the school—*no matter what!*

The sounds I heard above me were not people speaking; only the occasional file drawer being opened or closed. I quietly placed the ring of keys inside my garrison cap and laid it in the corner opposite the electronic door. After checking that my flashlight was still secured to my belt, I took a couple of deep breaths and started down the corridor.

The stairs to the upper levels were located in the middle of the first floor hallway. When I got to where the stairs began, I stopped. The sounds of a file drawer sliding on its tracks continued intermittently above me. Quietly, I made my way up the steps. Halfway to the second level, the stairs made a U-turn.

Upon reaching the second floor, I slowly moved my head into the corridor, which gave me a full view in both directions. To my right, near the end of the hallway, I saw an open door. The lights of the room were not on, but whoever was inside the room was using a flashlight. My heart began beating overtime.

As I silently moved further down the hallway, I saw above the open door a sign: CLASSIFIED DOCUMENTS ROOM.

Who could possibly be working here at two o'clock in the morning?

Again, I tried to convince myself that the person in the room was an instructor finishing up some special project. At this late hour, if I walked to the open door and announced myself, I would surely scare the person to death. My mind raced.

Standing ten to fifteen feet from the document room entrance, I took a deep breath and spoke. "Hello. Is someone there?"

Everything became deathly quiet. I waited.

Again I asked, but in a much louder voice, "Is someone there?" Still no reply. *Was the instructor so focused on what he was doing that he couldn't hear me?*

I moved to the center of the hallway and walked towards the open door. Five or six feet away, I stated in a loud, firm voice: "Hello! Is someone in there? I'm the staff duty officer, making a security check of the building." Still no answer—only complete silence.

The room was now totally dark; there was no longer any sign of the flashlight. When I moved to the open door, I heard movement and a rustling noise. I took a few steps forward, which put me directly in front of the entrance.

As I reached down to pull the flashlight from my belt, suddenly a large object came hurtling out of the room towards me. I had no chance to react. It hit me squarely in the chest with such force that it knocked me back into the hallway and then crashed to the floor. Papers and file folders scattered in every direction as a large metal file drawer came to rest a few feet from where I lay.

Grabbing at my neck and chest, I started to panic, unable to breathe. An edge of the file drawer had struck me directly in the throat, making it impossible for me to swallow. In the moment when I was knocked to the floor, I caught a glimpse of a dark figure running out of the document room and down the hallway towards the stairs.

The situation had now taken on an entirely new dimension. Someone had obviously entered this classified facility in an effort to obtain top secret NATO information. I didn't know if the intruder had run to the exit and tried to get out or if he was still somewhere in the building. But what I *did* know—there was no way I was going to pursue him by myself, especially without a weapon.

The military police platoon needed to be activated, and, regrettably, Major Green needed to be notified. I needed to get out of the building as quickly as possible and get help.

Fifty yards from the NATO facility, yet out of view, was the main entrance to the campus. There, the security gate was controlled twenty-four hours a day by at least two military policemen. I ran down the stairs and through the front door as quickly as I could and began shouting at the top of my voice in the direction of the guard gate.

Fortunately, one of the MPs had just left his post to go use the latrine. When he heard my yelling, he came running towards me. I told him that I had discovered an intruder in the NATO facility while making my security check and the person could possibly still be in the building or hiding somewhere on campus. Surely, the man would have a difficult time scaling the high, stone walls that surrounded the school compound.

I instructed the MP to run back to the main gate and order his coworker to activate the security platoon and then return to my location immediately.

After the young MP had done as I requested and rejoined me in front of the NATO building, he pulled out his sidearm and stood next to me, visibly shaken.

Within seconds the lights of the distant MP billets came on, and the place became a hive of activity. The head of the security police platoon, Sergeant Spencer, appeared on the steps of the billet in his skivvies. Perhaps sixty yards away, he looked towards me, yelling out orders to his men before running back inside.

Within five or six minutes, the first of the security platoon members reached our position. Others, still half dressed, followed close behind, lacing their boots, strapping on their field gear, and readying their M-16s.

As the first of the MPs arrived, I instructed them to charge their weapons and surround the building. Moments later, Sergeant Spencer stood next to me, anxious to know what had taken place. After giving him a quick overview, he ordered one of his men to switch on the floodlights that illuminated the immediate area between headquarters and the NATO facility.

Sergeant Spencer asked, "Lieutenant Ramsdell, have you called Major Green?"

I looked at him and shook my head in the negative. "There isn't time to wait for Green, Hart, or any of the command staff. We need to find the intruder before he gets away, and we need to do it now!"

Sergeant Spencer directed one of his NCOs to return to the MP billet where duplicate keys to all the buildings were kept in a vault. Leaving several of his men surrounding the NATO facility, Sergeant Spencer assembled the rest of his platoon in front of the building.

I stood at his side as he explained to them what had happened. We then assigned three-man teams to make physical security checks of each of the buildings on campus. Spencer, with the help of an assistant, passed out the building keys and instructed his men to re-assemble in front of the NATO building once they finished their inspections. We also instructed three of the teams to make a perimeter check on both the inside and outside of the high stone wall that encircled the campus. Each team was given a two-way radio, which they were to use to contact us if they came upon anything suspicious.

The MPs surrounding the NATO facility were ordered to remain in place with their weapons charged—but locked. The soldiers were instructed to apprehend anyone exiting the building, preferably without firing their weapons.

Sergeant Spencer chose two members of his platoon to accompany me and him into the NATO facility. Upon posting a platoon medic at the building entrance, he handed me his 45mm pistol with two magazines of ammo. I loaded one magazine into the 45 and stuffed the other in my belt. Spencer and the other two MPs charged their M-16's. Following a review of hand signals, the four of us walked to the NATO building entrance.

After unlocking the outer door, we stood in the foyer listening for any sound. We heard nothing. I placed the access card into the control box next to the electronic door and entered the security code.

As soon as it opened, the four of us hurried through. While walking down the first floor hallway, we tried to open each door. All of them were locked. Quietly we made our way up the stairs. When we reached the second floor, to the right we saw the scattered papers and files strewn across the corridor. The metal file drawer remained undisturbed from where it had landed after striking me in the chest.

With our weapons ready, we walked quietly to the entrance of the document room. We saw no one—we heard no one. Upon entering the room, I switched on the lights. We were stunned by what we saw.

Several of the classified cabinets were open, top secret files and documents were lying open on a large table located in the middle of the room. Following a cursory check of the rest of the room, we used hand signals to indicate that our next move would be up the stairs to the third level.

With my flashlight in my left hand and Sergeant Spencer's sidearm in my right, I took the lead with the others directly behind me. As we made our way up the stairs, we noticed large drops of blood on several of the steps. *How could this be—I hadn't fought or struggled with the intruder at all.* Perhaps the individual had cut himself on the file drawer when he threw it at me.

When we reached the third floor, the blood became more evident. It led us to the right towards the end of the hallway. All the ceiling lights on the third level were broken, and small pieces of glass covered the corridor. Pointing the flashlight farther down the hall, more blood was visible. It was obvious the person was seriously wounded.

Following the trail of blood, we made our way down the corridor, again, checking each of the room doors. After a several more steps, the beam from the flashlight reached the end of the hallway. There in the corner lay a body. As if on cue, the four of us disengaged the locks of our weapons.

As we slowly approached, I asked: "Who is there? I order you to stand and face us." The body did not move. The four of us inched closer.

"We are military police," I said. "We are ordering you to stand and face us."

Suddenly the body moved slightly and gave off a groaning sound.

The person lay face down in a large pool of blood, which spread from underneath the body to the end of the corridor nine or ten feet away. The man had obviously been shot to have lost so much blood. With our weapons at the ready, we surrounded him and waited for a response.

Observing only the movement of the man's labored breathing, I stuck the handgun into my belt, handed Sergeant Spencer the flashlight, and knelt down beside the body. I reached out and grabbed the man's shoulder and carefully rolled him over.

The first thing I saw was several deep cuts on his left wrist. It appeared that the tendons in the wrist were nearly severed. As I struggled to apply pressure to the man's arm in order to stop the bleeding, Spencer moved the flashlight up to the man's face.

My body reeled backwards—I couldn't believe my eyes! There in the pool of blood lay my friend Yuri Novotny.

Yuri was dressed in an Air Force summer uniform, which was now completely soaked in blood. On his feet he wore black tennis shoes. A gray back-pack lay at his side.

While one of the MPs knelt next to me, helping to apply pressure to Yuri's arm, with a handkerchief I tried to wipe the blood from Yuri's eyes. Underneath the blood and sweat, his face color was chalky white. He reached for my hand and weakly squeezed it.

"Mike, I'm . . . so sorry. I . . . I . . . didn't know you were going to be the SDO on duty tonight." he said, grimacing in pain. "Please help me, Mike." Tears flowed from his eyes and mixed with the dark red of his blood-covered face.

Still in shock, trying to comprehend what had just happened, "Yuri," I said, "you need to stay calm. We're going to get you help. But you need to tell me, have you been shot?"

He moved his head slowly from side to side. ". . . No." He started shivering uncontrollably. "Mike . . . I don't want to die. I can't believe . . . that I did this."

"Are you injured anywhere else besides the cuts on your wrist?" Again I felt his weakened hand try to tighten in mine.

"Mike," his words almost inaudible, "please don't let them tell my wife what I've done. She doesn't deserve . . ."

"Yuri, we're going to get you medical help as soon as we can. You need to tell me if you were alone in the building."

He slowly nodded his head. "Yes."

"Mike . . . Jenni and my mother . . . they know nothing about my double life."

As his other hand reached for me, I saw that it, too, had several deep wrist cuts. Sergeant Spencer took his first-aid kit from his web belt and knelt down beside me. While the MP and I held Yuri's arms up, Spencer tightened lengths of gauze wrap a few inches above the deep gashes on each wrist.

"Please God, . . . please . . . don't let me die. I just panicked, Mike, I panicked."

"Yuri, we've got to move you to the command center so you can get a doctor's help. Do you have a weapon on you?" I asked.

He shook his head and whispered, "No."

He then gestured with his eyes towards the corner of the corridor. There, several feet away on the floor, lay a multi-purpose Swiss Army knife, the main blade still open and covered in blood.

"Mike . . . I'm sorry I brought you into this . . . I didn't know . . ." he moaned. "I'm so . . . so cold, so thirsty."

Spencer took his canteen from his web belt and handed it to me. With my arm supporting Yuri's head, I held the canteen to his mouth as he drank down several swallows.

Sergeant Spencer instructed the two MPs to shoulder their weapons and carry Yuri to the command center. Yuri struggled to raise his hand to stop them and looked up at me.

"Will . . . will you please do it, Mike? Will you help me?" he asked.

"Of course I will, Yuri."

I gave the security access card to one of the MPs, along with the security code, and told him to bring the medic into the building immediately.

Spencer instructed the other MP to run to the main gate and place a telephone call to Dr.

Kunstman and tell him that an emergency had happened at the school and that a car and driver would be at his house in ten minutes to pick him up.

Sergeant Spencer and I slowly got Yuri to his feet. I placed his left arm around my shoulder and grabbed him around the waist with my other arm. Spencer steadied Yuri from the other side. We made it down the hallway as far as the stairs when Yuri suddenly collapsed. He had lost so much blood his strength was completely gone.

After an awkward few minutes trying to maneuver him down the stairs, I moved a couple steps below Yuri and pulled him towards me over my shoulder. With Spencer leading the way, we made it down the stairs and across the cobblestone street to the headquarters building.

When we finally reached the S-2 office, I laid Yuri down on Major Green's leather couch. The platoon medic immediately cut off the make-shift tourniquets from Yuri's wrists. Sergeant Spencer and his MP kept Yuri's arms elevated while applying pressure to prevent any further blood loss.

Yuri's skin was cold and clammy; his face ghostly pale. His breathing became labored as his body appeared to be shutting down. I assured Yuri that medical help was on the way and that everything would be all right. However, deep down, I was frantic—worried if Yuri would be able to hang on until Dr. Kunstman arrived.

While I again tried to clean the blood from Yuri's eyes, nose, and mouth, the composed voice of the young medic kneeling next to me kept repeating, "Keep him talking, Lieutenant. . . . Keep talking to him."

Yuri reached for my hand and pulled me down to his face and whispered, "Mike . . . I don't deserve to live. My family doesn't need . . . this shame," his words faltered, "especially . . . my little boy." His ashen face was streaked with tears. He asked for more water.

An MP walked into the room and informed us that Major Green was on his way.

I looked over at Sergeant Spencer and gave him a nod—an acknowledgement that within minutes we would have to face Colonel Hart and his staff.

It seemed that an eternity passed before we heard the car arrive outside. Concerned voices moved up the stairs.

Dr. Kunstman hurried into the room carrying a black medical bag. Sleep hung on his face, his white hair went in every direction, spectacles hung on the end of his long, pointed nose.

Seventy years old, Dr. Kunstman was retired from his medical practice down in the village. For the last five years, he had run the dispensary on campus. He understood more English than he could speak. His primary work was prescribing pills, giving shots, and comforting the sick. Anyone requiring medical attention, beyond basic prescriptions and injections, was sent to the U.S. Army Hospital in Augsburg, a two-hour drive away.

Dr. Kunstman checked Yuri's vital signs and immediately pulled a syringe from his bag. Within moments of the shot, Yuri's labored breathing slowed and he stopped shaking. After evaluating Yuri's injuries, the doctor cleaned the cuts, then applied antiseptic, bandages, and a clamp device over the lacerations on both of Yuri's wrists.

"Der man hast lost much blood und ist in shock. Vee need him to go *schnell* (quickly) to ein *krankenhaus* (hospital)," Dr. Kunstman said in an anxious tone. I clarified the doctor's German to those in the room.

Suddenly, I felt a strong, comforting hand on my shoulder.

"Mike, ask the doctor if the captain can survive the two-hour trip to Augsburg." It was Colonel Hart standing directly behind me.

Dr. Kunstman understood the question.

"I do not know, Colonel" he said. "Der man hast lost much blood. He needs ein *krankenhaus* very soon as possible."

"Mike," asked Colonel Hart in a calm, reassuring voice, "what do y'all want us to do?"

"Sir, we might be running out of time. I suggest we forgo the two hour drive to Augsburg and move Yuri down the mountain to the German hospital in Garmisch. It should take only thirty or forty minutes."

Colonel Hart turned to his staff. "Ok, men, let's make it happen. Lieutenant Ramsdell is in charge here. Do what y'all have to do."

"Colonel Hart," I said, "this officer is a friend of mine. I'd like your permission to ride with him in the vehicle with Dr. Kunstman and the MPs down the mountain."

"Of course, Mike." he replied. "That'll be fine."

Unexpectedly, Yuri suddenly reached for me. He struggled as if he wanted to sit up. I knelt down next to him and put my arms around his shoulders to help. As he opened his mouth to speak, his head and body slowly fell back to one side. While trying to steady him, air gurgled from his lungs in an ugly, mournful sound.

The final decision of how best to get medical help for my friend had been answered. At 3:45 a.m., U.S. Air Force Captain Yuri Novotny died in my arms.

The aftermath of Yuri's death was almost as bad as the circumstances of how he died. For those of us teaching and working at the school, our idyllic, sheltered life in beautiful Oberammergau had been tragically shaken. The day Yuri died, a dark shroud of sorrow seemed to come down from the mountain tops with the morning fog and cover the entire campus. It lingered there for months.

A CID (criminal investigation division) team from Munich arrived at eight a.m. and immediately cordoned off the NATO facility.

I spent the morning answering their questions and filling out paper-work. Those of us involved in this dreadful event were strictly ordered by CID not to discuss the incident with anyone.

At ten a.m. a medical van from the military hospital in Augsburg arrived to pick up Yuri's body.

Just before noon, Colonel Hart insisted that I be allowed to return to my quarters to clean up and get a few hours of rest before CID continued their interrogations.

I left HQ and walked to my apartment building not far from campus, thankful that my wife and little boy were back in Utah on home leave for two months.

I went to the bedroom and took off my blood-covered uniform. Next, I took a long, hot shower, hoping to somehow wash away the tragic events of the last twelve hours.

Dressed in my sweats, I walked into the kitchen where I poured milk onto a bowl of cereal. I stared at it for ten minutes before finally pouring it down the sink.

A huge knot was in the middle of my chest. I couldn't get out of my mind the image of Yuri's wife's reaction when she would learn of the tragic news.

Back in the bedroom, I pulled the window blinds closed and lay on the bed. For two hours I tried to sleep, but there was no way my mind would let it go, trying to figure the how and the why.

My soul ached. I sat at the edge of the bed with my head in my hands staring at the floor.

How could Yuri get involved in such a grave, criminal act, and why would he be so willing to take his own life?

I thought about my own life—my wife and my little boy. I thought of how fragile and irreplaceable life is. I thought of how insane this Cold War was and the games being played between the two world superpowers. And now a young wife was without her husband, a little boy without his dad, and parents without their son.

Death is just a bi-line in the newspaper until it visits you personally and suffocates your empty heart.

I was especially worried as to how I was going to handle a specific request from Colonel Hart regarding Yuri's wife.

Once we received word from Italy that Yuri's commander and unit Chaplin had met with Jenni, I was to call her and explain who I was, answer any questions she might have, and offer our help and support. Colonel Hart also wanted me to place a call to the United States and talk with Yuri's parents. The CID team would later insist that the conversation be taped by them, especially when I spoke with Yuri's father.

When I returned to the command center to meet with the CID team, I first placed the call to Yuri's wife in Italy, but was unable to speak with her. She had become so distraught over the news of Yuri's death that she had to be sedated. Three days would pass before I actually spoke with Jenni by telephone; she did have a request of me.

The following week, I was granted five days administrative leave. I packed a small suitcase and drove my Camaro through the Austrian Alps and down the boot of Italy to a small seaside community not far from Sorrento where Yuri had lived with his wife and son. Jenni was there with her parents who had flown in days earlier from Miami.

On the day of my arrival, she and I spent the entire afternoon walking along the beach. It was one of her and Yuri's favorite things to do with their little boy. She loved Yuri dearly and wanted to tell me every detail of their relationship since they had first met in college until his last phone call to her from Oberammergau the night before he died.

Jenni and I never discussed the dark side of Yuri's death. Following command orders from CID, I was not allowed to mention it. A full-blown investigation was already in the works, an investigation that would last for over a year. Even Yuri's body was not turned over to the family for burial until a certain portion of the inquiry was completed.

Back at our school, American and NATO criminal investigation teams arrived from various European commands and from the Pentagon, trying to determine the extent of Yuri's espionage activities, how long he had been working for the Russians, and who his accomplices might be. These visits went on for several months. I tried to be as helpful as I could, but to say I wasn't glad to see the last investigative team leave Oberammergau would be a lie.

Those of us involved with Yuri's death had answered every conceivable question probably twenty or thirty times. Yet, while trying to bring some closure to this tragedy, when we attempted to find out about the disposition of the investigation, especially concerning Yuri's father, our inquiries were always rebuffed with the proverbial excuse of: "Sorry, it's a matter of national security . . . the need-to-know rule applies in this case too."

It was finally time to close this chapter in our lives and in the life of our school, a U.S. military training center located in the beautiful Bavarian Alps, where teaching classes on *The Soviet Military Threat* would never be quite the same.

Over the years I've thought about Yuri many times and tried to make sense of what it was that motivated him to do what he did. Time and again during my career, I'd had the opportunity to see first hand the deceit, corruption, and evil perpetrated on the Soviet people by the Communist system that ruled over them.

Still to this day, I'm bewildered how Yuri, after having enjoyed all the opportunities and blessings of living in America for so many years, could make such a deliberate choice—not only to commit treason against the United States—but to even take his own life. However, not knowing or understanding the control and influence Yuri's father had over his son in order to corrupt him and get him to do what he did, I have compassion for Yuri, and I mourn his tragic death. I still miss my friend.

Chapter 9

A STARVING NATION

There is nothing so shameful as rags and
there is no greater crime than poverty.

George Farquhar
Beaux Stratagem

That first day on the train taking me across Russia towards Potevka, the day my food sack was stolen, I truly expected some kind, understanding person would come forward and offer me something to eat. I was certain that most of the passengers, particularly those sitting at my end of the rail car, knew exactly what had happened to my food and who had taken it. However, throughout the rest of that day and evening, no one offered their help.

Because of my injuries from the fight with Koshka's men in Tayginsk, I'd boarded the train in poor physical condition. It took all the energy and stamina I could muster to force myself to try and stay awake—*watching and waiting.* I was afraid that at any one of the seemingly endless stops, the KGB or railway police would come to my seat, escort me off the train, and then—*Who knows what?*

There were several times when I jolted awake, having dozed off into a deep sleep at my seat. Whenever this happened, I would immediately check for my briefcase, backpack, and duffel bag to make certain they were still with me. With the adrenalin of fear stirring again, I would survey the rail car, looking for anyone or anything that seemed to be out of place.

During the early morning darkness, my second night on the train, I awoke with a sudden jerk. Again, without intending to, I had fallen into a heavy sleep. It was almost impossible not to do, considering my condition and the continuous, hypnotic clickity-clack of metal wheels on metal rails, along with the rhythmic rocking of the train car. I sat up and looked around the darkened passenger car; everything appeared normal.

As I moved my hand down along the twine to make sure that my duffel bag was still attached to my boot, I felt something on the seat at my side, next to my briefcase. I reached down and picked it up. Wrapped in wrinkled butcher paper, I could feel a round, small object, something not much larger than a lemon. Without thinking what the item might be, I unwrapped it. There in my hand was a *kartoshka*—a small boiled potato. Its earthy smell immediately caused my heartbeat to jump and my mouth to salivate.

I clutched the small potato in my hand and scanned the dim rail car, expecting to see the Good Samaritan looking in my direction, watching for my reaction to this deed of kindness. Other than the sound of the wheels on the tracks, the train car was totally silent; all the passengers seemed to be bedded down for the night.

I took out my Swiss Army knife, put the potato on my knee, and carefully cut it into quarter pieces. Knowing this might be the only food I would have until I got to the provisions at the safe house, still days away, like a wily mouse, I forced myself to slowly nibble at the pieces. I was able to make my meager potato meal last for more than half an hour.

This incident of kindness raised my spirits so much that I found it quite easy to stay awake and alert for the rest of the night. With a blanket pulled over my coat and clothes, I sat in the darkness, rocking back and forth with the swaying of the rail car.

I spent the hours thinking of home and the recent loss of my mother. I thought about my son, Chris, now somewhere in Australia serving as a missionary. I thought about my dear friend, Bonnie, back in Salt Lake and wondered what she might be doing tonight. I thought about my family. I missed home, and I missed those that I loved.

Especially, I thought about the kindness of the individual who had left me the *kartoshka.* I wondered, *Would the person identify himself to me before I got off the train in Potevka?*

For the first time in a long time, Russia and its people—even this old, frozen, lumbering train—didn't seem so bad. Maybe there was reason to hope after all.

The next morning, as daylight penetrated the storm and made its way into the rail car, the passengers began to stir. The men stood and scratched and stretched; the women folded bedding while looking after the waking children. With blankets and pillows now packed away, the families brought out their food stuffs for their morning meal.

As was the case each morning, a long queue formed outside the WC. The line slowly made its way towards the end of the rail car, past the bench where I was sitting.

On this particular morning, out of the corner of my eye, I noticed someone standing next to me but not moving with the rest of the people in the line. As I cautiously shifted around in my seat, our eyes instantly met. His small hand held firmly onto the back of my bench seat, helping to steady himself from the swaying of the rail car.

There stood the young, unkempt boy who had appeared so concerned when my food sack was stolen the day before. His bright blue eyes sparkled underneath his shaggy, coal black hair. He gave me a warm smile.

Without saying a word, his gaze moved down to my seat where I had found the potato during the night and then back up at me. He gestured with his head and eyes, as if to ask, *Did you find what I left for you last night while you were sleeping?*

I smiled at him and nodded, "*Da* (Yes)."

"*Zdrasst'ye* (Hello)," I said.

"Dobraye utra (Good morning)," he replied in almost a whisper.

"Kak vas zavut (What is your name)?" I asked.

"*Minya zavut . . . Gennady* (My name is Gennady)."

Then a raspy voice yelled out from a few rows away, "Gennady!" It was his grandfather telling him to get back in the queue for the WC. The boy didn't move, maintaining his hold on the back of my seat.

Suddenly the grandfather stood and walked towards us. He grabbed Gennady's arm and jerked him back down the aisle to where they were sitting. The old man shoved the boy down into his seat. Hurt and embarrassed, Gennady doubled over in his seat and hid his head in the blankets and coats that were piled there.

What could I do?

If I were to intervene and tell the grandfather of the boy's kindness, in all likelihood Gennady would be reprimanded for giving away the potato from the old couple's food supply.

For the rest of my time on board the train, I never saw the boy without his grandfather at his side. There were moments, as the old man slept, when Gennady and I would exchange a glance or a smile—a secret communication between just the two of us. Not able to speak to one another, still, I'm certain he knew of my gratitude for giving me the potato and how proud I was of his courage and kindness.

The young Russian boy with the tousled black hair and brilliant blue eyes represented, for me, the hope and future of this once great nation.

✯ ✯ ✯

During my third day on board the train, I became extremely nauseated from hunger pains. I determined that if I were able to purchase just a single loaf of bread from one of the *babushkas* selling it at one of the large railway stops, it would be enough to get me through until I got to the Potevka safe house and the supply of field rations—MREs (Meals Ready-To-Eat). Yet I couldn't leave the train car for fear of someone taking my seat. And because most stops were very short, there was no practical way to get off the train with my bags and hurry back on again.

Late that morning, a peasant laborer boarded the train and stood in the aisle a few feet away from where I was sitting. He was one of a dozen or so workers traveling from the province where he lived to the place where he worked.

A large, muscular man, possibly thirty-five to forty years old, the man had hollow eyes and a chiseled chin. He wore frayed work clothes covered by an old, worn, military coat.

At first when he boarded the train, I became concerned as he seemed to continually stare in my direction. But after I saw his rugged, calloused hands, there was no doubt he worked at some sort of hard manual labor.

After watching him sway back and forth in the aisle for almost two hours, hanging onto an overhead luggage bar, I came up with a sure-fire plan as to how I could get the loaf of bread I so desperately needed. I reviewed in my mind the necessary Russian words of conversation, then stood up and motioned for the man to take my place.

"Sir," I said, "please, sit down here in my seat and rest your feet and legs for a while."

He nodded his head in a thankful gesture and sat down.

"Thank you, comrade. Thank you. I will sit for only a short while and then you can have your seat back."

Like so many Russian men, he reeked of alcohol.

"Where are you headed?" I asked.

"I've been home to see my wife and child over the weekend. I'm traveling back to Bazador, a few more hours away from here where I work at the steel mill."

"How long have you worked there?"

"For twelve long years," he replied.

"So, is your factory at full production?"

"Not at all. The party leaders who control production have laid off more than two-thirds of the workers—over five thousand people. And those of us who still work there have not been paid for over three months. Everything in this lousy country is falling apart," he said, in an angry tone of voice while looking around at those who might be listening.

"I'm sorry things are in such turmoil here in your country. Perhaps, we can help each other," I said quietly.

"What exactly do you mean . . . ?" he asked.

I moved closer to him and explained: "Unfortunately, I have no food, and I still have days to travel. Someone on the train stole my food sack my first day on board. I cannot leave the train because of the baggage I have with me and because of the risk that I'll lose my seat."

I patted my breast coat pocket where I kept my *rubles*. "I will give you a hundred *ruble* bill if you will purchase two loaves of bread for me at the next large station."

"Of course I'll do that for you. How much did you say you'd pay me?"

"I will give you one hundred *rubles*. Each loaf should cost no more than fifteen or twenty *kopecks*, and you can keep the rest."

"And . . . I keep all the rest?" he asked in disbelief.

"Yes, you keep the rest of the money," I assured him.

Our financial arrangement would probably leave the man more *rubles* for five-minutes of work than he would make at his factory in an entire month.

"I travel this route twice each month to go home and see my wife and little daughter. The next large station is Bazador. It's another two hours away, the very stop where I get off."

"Sir, you sit there and rest," I said. I reached in my coat pocket and discreetly pulled out a hundred-*ruble* bill and handed it to him. "Here's the money. Take it now and put it in your pocket so we won't have to make the exchange while people are getting on and off the train at Bazador."

"Thank you very much, comrade," he said. "This will be a great help to my wife and me."

Sitting in my seat, he leaned back and closed his eyes. In five minutes he was sound asleep—snoring.

Weak and sore as I was—especially my bruised ribs—the following two hours hanging on to the overhead luggage bar were pure agony. Finally, the train began to decelerate. I eagerly tapped the shoulder of the man sitting in my seat.

"Sir, the train is about to stop in Bazador," I told him.

He stood for a moment, looked around, and pulled on his backpack.

"My friend," he said, "I'll be right back with your two loaves of bread."

As he walked away, I was almost giddy with excitement, waiting to see him walking back to our rail car with the bread. I immediately began to calculate in my mind how many meals there would be before we reached Potevka and how thick I could possibly cut the slices. Russian black bread and Russian black tea, definitely an acceptable combination for someone as starved as I was!

When approximately ten minutes had passed, I started to become concerned. While keeping an eye on my bags, I stepped towards the door where, at any moment, I expected to see the man walking towards the rail car. Another five minutes passed, but still no sign of him or my two loaves of bread.

The train's whistle screeched as the huge engines started to slowly pull us away from the station. I stood next to my seat, hurt, humiliated, and mad.

Why hadn't I given him just enough rubles to purchase the bread, and then the rest of the money when he brought the loaves back to me?

He was probably by now at a local liquor store, waiting his turn in line; not to buy bread but to buy that which would help him escape from another day of his empty existence: another bottle of vodka.

It was the second time in only three days I'd been ripped-off since leaving Siberia! My only solace—at least I had my hard bench seat back to rest my weary, aching body.

☆ ☆ ☆

As the families brought out their food stuffs during mealtime, the pungent smells of sausage, smoked salt-fish, and sour cabbage permeated the entire rail car. I was so hungry.

I coped with the odors by thinking of *real food*—American food: a huge juicy cheeseburger, greasy French fries, and a tall caramel shake, served car-side at the Peach City Drive-Inn in Brigham City, Utah.

Continually consumed with thoughts of food, at the same time I kept myself full of tea whenever my aching stomach began to growl like a starved lion. Also, I kept reminding myself there were MRE rations at the safe house only a few more days away.

I resigned myself to stay at my seat and try to stay warm, pretending to read German and Soviet oil trade magazines, but all the while dreaming of something to eat—*worrying, watching,* and *waiting.*

Chapter 10

A BROKEN BABUSHKA

The wind blows out of the gates of the day,
The wind blows over the lonely of heart,
And the lonely of heart is withered away.

William Butler Yeats
The Land of Heart's Desire

After five seemingly endless days, my wretched journey out of Siberia was finally over. In the darkness of the winter night, the frozen train from the Soviet Far East moaned and groaned to a stop in the village of Potevka twelve hours late.

Weak and famished, I stepped from the passenger car into the storm with my duffel bag, backpack, and briefcase. I stopped for a moment by a platform wall outside the small station to see who else might get off the train or who might be there waiting for me. No one.

In the back of my mind, I was hoping that HQ might have an extraction team waiting here in Potevka to take me back to the safety of the American Embassy in Moscow or even out of the country. Unfortunately, there was no one from our side here to greet me. But then again, thankfully, there was no one from the Russian side either.

Relieved, I told myself the worst was finally now behind me, thousands of miles away back in Tayginsk—back in Siberia. Still, as I made my way across the tracks through the storm towards the small train station, I said a silent prayer that no one was here in the shadows of Potevka waiting to make my life more difficult.

☆ ☆ ☆

Like so many other small, neglected railway stations throughout the USSR, the Potevka station was in need of major repairs. A huge Soviet hammer and sickle iron crest, broken and rusted, hung over the entrance. As I walked inside, I couldn't help but notice the foul stench of urine and decay.

I stood looking around when an elderly, frail *babushka,* carrying what looked like an empty mailbag, walked toward me.

She wore a tattered blue railway overcoat with a new, official-looking, red armband pinned to one sleeve. The heavy coat enveloped her small frame, obviously several sizes too large. She wore dark leggings and large, black felt boots, which caused her to shuffle as she walked.

When she got closer, I could see her sallow skin and deep set eyes. She looked to be at least in her eighties or older.

What was a woman her age doing—still working and in such terrible conditions as these?

"*Vam nuzhna pomosch, tovarisch* (Do you need help, comrade)?" she asked, appearing surprised that someone had actually gotten off the train in her small village, especially in such a snow storm.

"*Nyet, spaseeba* (No, thank you)," I replied.

As I looked at the old woman, I couldn't help but stare. She reminded me so much of my mother—her size, her age, her appearance, even her mannerisms.

Two years earlier, my mother had suffered a debilitating stroke. Since that time, until her recent death, she was confined to a rest home in Box Elder County in northern Utah. Mom had passed away just a few months before I accepted this current assignment to Russia. I was grateful to have been back home in Utah when she died. Rarely did a day go by that I didn't think about her.

I smiled at the old *babushka*, thanked her again, and nodded my head in a respectful gesture of goodbye. After zipping up my coat and fastening the Velcro straps, I put on my backpack, lifted my duffel bag carefully over my shoulder, and slowly walked to the exit. When I reached the front door I paused, still thinking of my mother. It was as though she had just walked into my life again—however, this time she spoke Russian.

Sensing the *babushka's* genuine kindness and still amazed at how much she reminded me of Mom, I turned around and walked back to the old woman. I set my things down, took off my gloves, and unzipped the inside pocket of my coat where I kept my Russian *rubles*. I removed several large bills from my billfold, folded them and placed them in the *babushka's* gloved hands.

"Thank you for your offer to help me," I said. She looked down at the money and then back up at me.

"You're most welcome, kind sir," she replied softly, staring again at the rubles. "You're not Russian, are you?"

The old woman slowly removed her frayed gloves and gently grasped both my hands. I looked down as tears welled in her eyes. Her wrinkled face and withered hands depicted the years of want and suffering.

"You remind me very much of my mother," I said.

"The train was very late," she replied. "I've been waiting here for more than thirteen hours. The firewood I brought for the stove ran out several hours ago." She looked down at the floor, as if ashamed for her words. "I take the mailbag from the trains that stop here every four days and deliver it to the *kolkhoz* store where the villagers pick up their mail. The government pays me very few *rubles* for my work. It's the only income I have."

"I'm very sorry you had to wait so long," I said. "The storm was terrible coming out of the mountains. There was so much snow the train had a very difficult time."

Feeling the suffering of the old woman, I wanted to pull the rest of the *rubles* from my billfold and give them all to her.

Standing in front of me, still holding my hands, she looked towards the window at the storm.

"When I was a young girl, during a heavy snow just like this, I attended a winter parade in Moscow with my father. We went there in a *troika* (an ornate three-horse sleigh) pulled by three beautiful black horses. I sat between my mother and father in the sleigh, covered with a white bear skin to keep us warm. It is one of my favorite childhood memories of Papa, Mama, and me. He was such a wonderful man. My father, you know . . . he was a well-known lawyer in St. Petersburg before the revolution," she said, her voice full of pride.

"At the parade, we saw Czar Nicolas with his wife and children. Those were such happy times for us. Then . . ." her voice began to quiver, "only a few months later . . . the Czar and his family were captured by the *Bolsheviks* and taken away to Ekaterinburg where they were murdered . . . by a group of Communist cowards. Our country has known only despair and suffering ever since."

She let go of my hands, turning her head away as tears rolled down her beautiful, worn face.

"I'm very sorry," I said.

With one end of her scarf she wiped the tears from her eyes.

"Two years after the revolution . . . some men came to our flat in St. Petersburg during the night and took my father away." She struggled with the rest of the words. "Mother and I . . . we never saw Papa again."

"I'm so sorry," I said.

"Mother was never the same after that. She spent the rest of her life worrying and praying, waiting for Papa's return."

I could only imagine the misery this poor woman had gone through in her life, not only from the loss of her father and the suffering of her mother, but also being forced to live under the tyranny of Lenin, Stalin, and the other Communist despots who followed after.

With a huge, stained picture of a brooding Lenin looking down at us from an otherwise empty wall inside the station, we stood opposite one another, not saying a word. The only sounds were the howling wind and the deep rumble of the waiting train's idling engines. It was a surreal moment—one I will never forget—an old, Russian *babushka* and an American intelligence officer, sharing a moment of respect in the middle of a raging snowstorm, in the middle of the night, in the middle of nowhere.

Suddenly, the shrill sound of the train's whistle broke the night's silence. Covering her head with her worn shawl, the *babushka* turned from me, grabbed a signal light from off a shelf, and walked out into the storm onto the station platform next to the train. I watched as she struggled to swing the heavy light back and forth above her head. It was as if she were trying to show me—even at her age—her defiance against the Communist system by encouraging the blizzard and snow demons even more.

After only a short time at the station, the train from the Soviet Far East belched huge black clouds of smoke as it came to life and lumbered from Potevka into the white, frozen night.

From the exit door, I waved goodbye to the old woman. I put on my backpack, picked up my duffel bag and briefcase, and walked anxiously out into the storm for my long trek to the safe house, where food—*glorious food*—was waiting for me there.

The dim lights of the Potevka train station quickly disappeared in the storm behind me—but not the beautiful face of my mother.

Chapter 11

APPLES AND A SAFE HOUSE MOUSE

There's small choice in rotten apples.
Shakespeare
The Taming of the Shrew

The mile-long walk through the storm to the safe house cabin was a struggle. Although headquarters had given me verbal instructions regarding its location, the swirling, blowing snow made it extremely difficult to find my way. It took me twice as long to get there as I expected. After toiling against the storm for almost an hour, I felt a great sense of relief when I realized I was finally in the right place. While walking the last hundred yards towards the safe house, a large murder of crows, nesting in the nearby trees, squawked irritably at me before scattering into the snowy night.

By the time I reached the *izba* (a cabin or wooden home in rural Russia), I was numb with cold; I couldn't feel my fingers or toes.

I had a difficult time finding the key, which was wrapped in a piece of cloth, hidden under a huge rock next to the side of the *izba.*

Following several unsuccessful attempts because of my frozen fingers, I was finally able to unlock the door and push it open. The temperature inside the cabin couldn't have been much above zero, but at least I was finally out of the snow and bitter wind.

As directed by headquarters, before building a fire and locating the food rations, I was required to check through the cabin for any sign that the KGB had been there. After setting my duffel bag and briefcase in the middle of the room, I took my penlight out of my backpack and carefully searched for surveillance devices in all the likely places. Thankfully, I found none.

The few agency safe houses located in Russia were scattered strategically throughout the country, primarily in the larger cities so our field operatives could more easily blend into the masses.

Seven months earlier, with the help of one of our Russian assets, headquarters had designated the Potevka *izba* as a transit safe house. However, it was to be used only in the case of an extreme emergency. This particular *izba* was chosen because of its ideal location between two important Soviet military facilities, which were only a few hundred miles apart and both being monitored every few months by another entity of U.S. intelligence.

Tonight I was grateful for the suggestion of my superiors that I lay over for a few days in Potevka. Here I would be able to rest, recuperate, and regain my strength. Regardless of the events in Tayginsk, I wanted to be able to stay in Russia and show headquarters my willingness to complete the remainder of my six-month assignment. These last few months had been long and arduous—the most difficult of my career. Following the failed Siberian operation, several days at the *izba* safe house—away from the KGB and Russian mafia—were exactly what my weary body and mind needed.

In the major cities of the former USSR, most of the people live in mammoth, prefabricated, high-rise, tenement buildings. However, the majority of the nation's 300 million plus people live in wooden or log homes, which are the common dwelling structures throughout the infinite number of settlements, villages, and towns of the former Soviet Republics.

There were sixty to seventy cabins in Potevka in which people permanently lived. The other dozen or so were occupied on holidays or sometimes on weekends by people who had once lived in

Potevka, but had moved out to work in one of the large industrial cities a few hundred miles away.

The safe house was located on the outskirts of the settlement in a secluded area near the forest and several hundred yards from the nearest cabin. Like all the other structures in the village, it was made of logs cut from the nearby forest. So simple is the construction of such a typical peasant home, it can be built in a few month's time. After the log side walls are erected, a clay and straw mortar is used on the roof and between the logs to keep out the elements. Once sheets of tin or galvanized metal are fastened over the roof, the roof is then sealed with tar. The chimney is made from bricks or stone with mortar. The traditional decorative gables and eaves on the outside of the safe house were weatherworn; the original light-colored logs of the *izba* had turned a charcoal gray with age.

The inside of the cabin was one large room with a few pieces of crude, handmade Russian furniture. As I entered, I could smell mildew and rodents. It appeared that, with no other inhabitant claiming residence, Ma and Pa *meeshka* (mouse) had moved inside for the winter. *Well,* I thought, *at least I'll have some company during my four-day stay.* I removed the metal bar lock from the cabin's only window and cracked it open a few inches to let in some fresh air.

In one corner of the cabin stood a large, ornate, cast-iron stove used for heating and cooking. Above the stove, a wall cabinet, covered by a blue drop-cloth curtain, held the bare essentials of dishes, pots, and pans. A heavy oak table and two mismatched wooden chairs stood under the window. A small peasant bed with a canvas mattress stuffed with straw occupied the opposite corner.

As in most Russian *izbas*, there was no running water—thus no toilet or shower. Water needed to be carried from one of the two communal wells in the village. The outhouse was located among several large pine trees twenty-five yards from the cabin near the edge of the forest, not exactly a good location for something so important—especially during a storm like this.

Having checked the cabin for any KGB detection devices, my priority immediately turned to finding the MREs. I had to get something to eat—anything! My stomach was aching as much as my sore head and bruised ribs.

With my flashlight I anxiously looked through the cupboards, yet, every shelf appeared empty. I checked the back closet, but found nothing there either.

It was agency policy for a safe house to have at least one week's supply of food reserves. Surely that included transit or emergency safe houses too.

So, where were the rations that HQ had assured me were here?

In many instances provisions and critical operational items were hidden in some inconspicuous place inside a safe house. Without specific instructions of knowing where to look, finding the MRE pouches could sometimes be a definite challenge. Regrettably, it was not unusual for agents to occasionally make a game of how clever they could be in hiding the rations from the next occupant. Tonight, I was in no mood to play such a ridiculous game of hide-and-seek.

The only thing I managed to find during my search, on one of the shelves under the cupboard, was a bowl of apples. Unfortunately, they looked as if they had been at the *izba* for months. They were wrinkled, most of them rotten and not at all edible.

After making an unsuccessful search of the rest of the cabin and considering how tired and sore I was and how late it was getting, I decided to put eating off for a few more hours until morning. Besides, I'd be more likely to find the MREs with the light of day. At this late hour there was not a chance of getting food anywhere in the village, and the next cabin was possibly a quarter-mile away. Also, the village market would be open by mid-morning, where I would be able to buy additional foodstuffs to get me through my four-day stay in Potevka.

Mike, I told myself, *you've made it several days without solid food. You can make it through a few more hours until daylight.*

A fire would help warm the place, but the agent who last used the *izba* had failed to restock the woodbin next to the stove. Tired and weak, I decided the effort to brave the snow storm and chop wood at this late hour was more than I could manage. Tonight, I would sleep in my clothes with several blankets from the closet piled on top of me to keep warm.

After checking my head wound and putting on new disinfectant and the last of the gauze wrap, I secured the slide-bolt locks on the window and door. I placed my boots and backpack under the bed. I pushed the oak table across the wood floor and braced it against the door. This would give me more time to react if some unwanted guests decided to pay a visit during the night. Surely, not even the KGB or Russian mafia would be foolish enough to be out on a night in weather such as this.

Considering all I had gone through to get to Potevka, I had every reason to be upset—to finally get here and discover there was no food or supplies in the cabin as HQ had promised. Yet, in spite of not finding the rations, I was so thankful to finally be off that frozen, slow-moving train; to be at the safe house for a few days of rest. I was grateful I was alive and safe, away from the threat of Koshka, the Russian mafia, and the KGB. Desperately hungry and hurting, still, I felt that my stay in Potevka was going to be a positive one.

Now it was time to finally get some *real* sleep in a *real* bed!

I pulled three small, framed photographs from my backpack, set them on the small table next to the bed and bid them goodnight. Cold and exhausted, I knelt down and struggled through a quick prayer. I crawled onto the bed, reached down and pulled the pile of blankets over me. Totally spent, I was out before my head settled into the straw pillow.

Having grown up in the Rocky Mountains, I had occasionally experienced severe snowstorms and temperatures near zero for days at a time. This, however, was my first winter in the Soviet Union, and I was definitely *not* accustomed to temperatures of thirty and forty and fifty degrees below zero for weeks at a time. At these temperatures, exposed flesh could result in severe frostbite within minutes.

Welcome, Comrade Ramsdell, to real winter weather—Russian style!

Heavy snow fell on Potevka throughout the night.

Chapter 12

PRESIDENT CARTER'S FOLLY

Politicians are the same all over. They promise to build a bridge even where there is no river.

Nikita Khrushchev

The black, frozen night slowly gave way to the cold gray of morning.

A sudden, loud banging against the side of the cabin shattered my deep sleep. Immediately gripped with fear, I sat up in bed. *Where was I?*

My eyes darted about the strange room while my heart pounded heavily in my chest. After a few anxious moments, I recognized where I was—the Potevka safe house.

Who was outside the cabin? Had the mafia or KGB found me?

Adrenalin rushed through my body as my fight-or-flight instincts kicked in. I sat motionless, holding my breath. When the rhythmic banging noise did not subside, I finally realized that the sound was a wooden shutter, which had come loose from one of its hinges, causing it to slam again and again against the window frame because of the fierce blowing wind.

I fell back onto the bed, totally drained from the shock to my system. It took ten or fifteen minutes for my body to return to normal. I was angry with myself because of the needless panic. All too often—especially for me—this clandestine, covert work can lead to excessive mind games and never-ending worry, particularly when one is working alone.

I was now wide awake, not just from the incident of the banging window shutter, but also from the gnawing ache in my empty stomach. Although it was early morning, it was still dark inside the cabin. I decided I would wait until the full light of day before I made my detailed search for the MREs.

Lying in bed with the blankets pulled over my head to keep out the cold, for the first time I heard the eerie, mournful sound. I moved the covers down, propped myself up on one elbow, and listened.

In the distance was the unmistakable howling of wolves. *Wolves? Here in the forest surrounding Potevka? And what does this mean for me?* I suddenly had a new appreciation for the safety and security of my meager accommodations.

After my days and nights on the train, sitting on that hard wooden bench, the warm cocoon of the straw bed seemed like heaven. Not wanting to give it up just yet and confront the bitter cold, I lay there in the dark under the blankets and reflected on the events of the last several months and how foolish political decisions made by our State Department two decades earlier had brought me to this moment in Potevka.

✯ ✯ ✯

In 1954 the U.S. Foreign Service delegation assigned to the Soviet Union moved into a newly remodeled embassy facility—a huge, ten-story, mustard-colored building near downtown Moscow on Tchaikovsky Street. After only a few years of use, the structure was considered inadequate and too small for the expanding size of the U.S. Diplomatic Mission. Not until the mid-sixties did discussions begin between the Soviets and the Americans for each country to be allowed to build new embassy facilities.

Because of the on-going Cold War between the two world super powers and the distrust that each government held towards the other, it took more than ten years of negotiations before a "Memorandum of Understanding" was finally signed, allowing for the construction of new embassies for the USSR and the United States.

The Soviets would build their new compound not far from downtown Washington, D.C.; the

Americans would build in Moscow on a site next to the old embassy on Tchaikovsky Street. Several more years would pass before the actual construction began on either facility.

Although it was during the Reagan presidency that the embassy construction actually took place, it was the previous administration of President Carter that originally negotiated the contract to allow the Soviets to have a major role in building America's new embassy in Moscow. At one point over eight hundred Soviets workers labored on the construction project within the walls of the embassy compound.

Knowing of our history and experience with the Soviet Communists and the KGB, it's hard to imagine why our government policy makers would agree to something so foolhardy and irresponsible. However, what we now know about President Carter and his strong Christian ideals perhaps explains his acquiescence to his White House inner circle to trust the Soviets.

But one has to ask, where were the President's Soviet advisors, especially those within the State Department and the intelligence community who certainly should have known better? Surely, there was *someone* who could have predicted what the Communist government and the KGB were about to do.

After years of construction and the embassy building project nearing completion, the State Department *finally* sent a group of specially trained technicians (sweepers) to Moscow with state-of-the-art equipment that could electronically detect intelligence collection devices that might be planted in the building materials of the new embassy structures. Thus, it was discovered that Soviet intelligence had bugged the new Chancery Building and several other top secret facilities on the embassy compound.

During the pre-casting by the Russians of the concrete walls, floors, and ceilings, thousands of minute listening devices were placed into the modular components. Soviet workers were then allowed to assemble these modular components at the work site.

In August, with over two-thirds of the work completed, the State Department halted the embassy construction and ordered the eight hundred Soviet workers removed from the site. It was later revealed that two hundred and six of the construction workers were actually on the payroll of the KGB.

Because of the security compromise and the political firestorm that followed, two months later President Reagan ordered the multi-million dollar Chancery Building to be dismantled.

The question now became: What damage had been done to U.S. intelligence? How long would it take to evaluate the full extent of the security breach, and how long would it take to fix?

The squandered years and wasted work constructing the new embassy facility had cost the American taxpayers two hundred million dollars—bugs and all. Who was now going to pay for the re-work, when—without question—the Soviet government and its covert apparatchiks within the KGB were the responsible parties?

Although difficult to believe, because of the initial denial and cover-up by our own CIA, NSA, FBI, and State Department—none of these agencies wanted to be tainted or take any of the blame for what had happened—it took sixteen years and twenty congressional studies before our diplomatic corps would finally move into a totally secure, newly remodeled embassy complex in the spring of 2001. The final tab for this Moscow embassy fiasco, to be paid by the American taxpayer, was upwards of four hundred million dollars.

Over the years I've had the opportunity to see first hand numerous problems—some enormous—that resulted from the mistakes and incompetence within several of our government agencies. Perhaps it sounds awfully simplistic, but I have often thought how much better off our country would be if sometimes we left the Washington bureaucrats at home and let a group of common sense, everyday men and women—farmers, bankers, factory workers, small business owners, school teachers, ranchers, etc.—negotiate on behalf of the United States. Certainly they could do no worse, and personally I'm confident—because of their *common sense*—they would do much better.

It was during these years of investigation and negotiation, regarding the repayment by the Soviets for the Chancery Building re-work, that it was discovered what role Koshka and the three other corrupt Communist officials had played in order to commit espionage against the United States and embezzle the tens of millions of dollars from the U.S. construction fund.

Through their political positions within the Supreme Soviet (parliament) these four government officials had received confidential, insider information that the U.S. State Department was going to allow various entities of the Soviet government—construction and construction management—to participate in the building of the new American embassy. Working in concert with the KGB, these crooked officials were able to manipulate the contract process and put themselves in a position of authority over the Soviet portion of the embassy construction work.

Because of the Soviet government's active complicity in these crimes, the years of negotiations with the Russian diplomatic corps to have them hold Koshka and the three other Communist officials accountable were totally futile. Both governments knew the facts of the case and who the liable parties were.

Considering the precedent it would set, as well as the possible political and diplomatic ramifications, there was no way the American government was going to let the Soviets and the guilty officials get away with such brazen criminal espionage, not to mention the theft of millions upon millions of dollars. Perhaps the strongest motivating factor to end this stalemate was the political climate in the country; i.e. not knowing how long the Communists would remain in power or how much longer the Soviet Union would survive.

Therefore, in the early '90s, the Department of State finally reached a decision to forego any further talks with the Soviet government regarding this issue and enlisted the help of U.S. intelligence to conduct a top secret, covert operation to resolve this diplomatic impasse. It was at this time that I was contacted by the State Department regarding my willingness to participate in the mission that would take me to Siberia.

✯ ✯ ✯

As was the case with our new embassy, corruption within the Soviet government and the use of political connections for illegal activities has been part of Russian culture for decades. For centuries, several long-established organizations or families, known as the "Red Thieves," operated in each of the larger cities throughout Russia.

During the three hundred years Russia was ruled by the czars, most of the people lived as poor peasants. Those that rebelled against the czarist oppression were labeled as criminals by the government, yet, were looked upon as folk heroes by the common people.

Many of these groups banded together to fight against the subjugation by the government while carrying on their criminal activities—a type of Russian Robin Hood. Because they posed such a political threat to the new *Bolshevik* government, under the regimes of Lenin and Stalin, these criminal groups were rounded up and put in Soviet prisons or *gulags*.

It was after Stalin's death in 1953, that eight million of these hardened criminals were released back into Soviet society. Within a short time, these criminals, working with corrupt politicians, created the underbelly of a flourishing black-market which, in actuality, helped sustain Russia during the years of the Cold War.

The term or label of "Russian mafia" or "Red mafia" became part of the Russian vernacular in the late 1980s and early 1990s. These criminal organizations rose from the ashes of the disintegrating USSR. The anarchy and instability that reigned throughout the country created ideal conditions for these shadow groups to entrench themselves in every facet of Soviet society.

As time went on, they became not only more powerful but increasingly visible. By the 1990's, Moscow, Russia was considered one of the most dangerous places in the world. There were over six thousand criminal organizations in the former Soviet Union, fighting one another for power and turf. In one year alone, over 1,400 assassinations were carried out by the mob in Moscow.

Historically, the main sources of illicit revenue for these groups were from extortion, kidnapping, and murder. However, in the time since the fall of Communism in Russia, these mafia organizations have become much more sophisticated in the criminal side of building construction, import-export, international narcotics trafficking, prostitution, and murder-for-hire.

Many of the Russian mafia are recognizable by their shaved heads or crew cuts and their common attire of black clothing. Together, out among the public, they openly flaunt their persona as thugs and mobsters as if it were a sign of status or prestige. Reports from Interpol and other international law enforcement organizations document how the Russian mafia conducts most of its illegal business through fear and intimidation based upon their reputation for violence.

Since the end of the Cold War, the Russian mafia has made significant inroads into organized crime in America and sixty other countries worldwide. Along with the threat of international terrorism, the Russian mafia has become one of the highest priorities for the FBI within the borders of our own United States.

I admit, I was concerned about the mafia because of what had happened in Tayginsk and the possibility of them finding me on the train or in Potevka. In fact, despite the known brutality of the KGB, I determined I would much rather be found by them than by the Russian mafia.

However, at this point I was becoming so obsessed with hunger that my worry about either of these adversaries was being replaced by my desperate need for food. It was now more than a week since I'd taken anything of substance into my system other than the one small potato and black tea.

I could tell I was losing weight and getting weaker with each passing day. I was beginning to worry—*How much longer would I be able to hold on?*

Chapter 13

A STRANGER IN POTEVKA

The wolf is at the door.

Norwegian Proverb

Although still somewhat dark outside the cabin, it was now morning. Situated where it was in the USSR, Potevka had only a few hours of daylight this time of year. It was unusually late for Russia's first major snow storm; nevertheless, winter had definitely arrived with a vengeance—not just snow, but a monstrous blizzard. The brutal wind continued to howl and beat against the window, as if determined to blow the storm right inside the *izba*.

Lying there in the warm straw bed, it took almost thirty minutes of deliberation, but I finally convinced myself I needed to get out of my nest after noticing the ice that had formed on the inside of the cabin window over night. However, getting a warm fire started in the stove and finding the food supplies were—without question—my *real* motivation to get out of bed.

I moved my left arm out from under the blankets to look at my watch. It couldn't be—I'd slept for ten straight hours! Suddenly, the call of nature came shouting. I threw the blankets aside, jumped out of bed, then wrestled with my boots and coat in order to get to the outhouse.

As I reached for the door, thoughts of the wolves suddenly flashed through my mind. I moved to the window and watched and listened. It was impossible to see more than thirty feet beyond the cabin because of the falling snow.

Cautiously, I turned the handle. Suddenly, the wind ripped the door out of my hand and slammed it against the inside wall. The icy blast hit me directly, sucking the breath from my lungs. I stumbled backwards into the cabin, landing hard on my backside. I got to my feet and pushed back at the door as the storm blew a cloud of snow across the wooden floor. When I finally got control of the door, I struggled getting outside. Because of my weak, painful arms, it was all I could do to pull the door shut behind me.

I could not see the outhouse; it was snowing horizontally now. I leaned into the wind and pushed through the two-foot deep snow as if I had fifty pound weights attached to each leg. A twenty-five yard struggle and, finally—relief!

After making it back to the safety of the cabin, I told myself that if the storm continued like this, I would have to come up with a new arrangement for the outhouse and me. Perhaps, from now on I would just write my name in the snow outside the *izba* door like my buddies and I used to do back home as kids when sledding on Slaughter Hill high above the frozen Bear River.

With the light of morning, I thoroughly searched the cupboards and storage closet for the MREs. Again, I found nothing. I meticulously inspected the loose planks of the wood floor, hoping that I would find a secret compartment with the rations hidden there. Using my penlight, I even looked around in the beams of the rafters. Nothing! Yet headquarters had assured me there was food here in the cabin.

So, where were these mysterious MREs? Had someone been in the izba before my arrival?

After searching in every conceivable place, it was evident that the only food in the *izba* was the old, wrinkled apples I found the night before. I inspected each apple again in detail. I was *so* hungry! Finding only one worth trying to salvage, I cleaned it on my pant leg, and cut the non-spoiled portion into a few small pieces. My empty stomach growled back at me as I swallowed down each tiny morsel.

Oh, to turn back the years and to be back home this morning, sitting down at the kitchen table with Mom and Dad for one of their big breakfasts of bacon and eggs, hash browns, toast, and bottled fruit. There was always Mom's bottled fruit from those large Mason jars—Utah homegrown raspberries, peaches, and pears.

☆ ☆ ☆

After the measly three pieces of apple, I put on my cold weather gear and grabbed the large ax from the closet. As I made my way through the snow to the woodpile behind the cabin, I pulled the broken shutter from off the outside of the window frame and stood it in the snow against the side of the cabin.

Because of my aching ribs and arms, I was concerned I would be unable to swing the ax, but I really had no choice; it was vital that I get a fire going.

I cleared away the snow, pulled back the tarp, located the driest logs, and carefully started chopping. Although weak and sore, the work actually became a welcome relief as my body began to warm from swinging the heavy ax. I had to stop several times to rest when the pain became too much.

Within thirty or forty minutes, I had cut enough wood to heat the cabin with enough left over to cook something later after I returned from picking up supplies in the village.

I decided that when I finished at the market and my belly was full and my strength was back, I would return to the woodpile and chop enough firewood to last for the remainder of my days in Potevka.

Not long after carrying several armfuls of wood into the *izba,* I soon had a wonderful fire roaring. I pulled a chair close to the stove and watched the beautiful flames dance through the thick glass window. Other than those blissful hours in last night's nest, this was the first time I'd been warm in over a week.

After half an hour or more of warming myself by the fire, I could no longer ignore the pangs of hunger. It was time to make my way to the village for some food.

As I got ready to leave, I said a silent prayer that the *kolkhoz* supply truck had been able to make a delivery to Potevka with food and provisions during the week. Besides the usual cabbage and potatoes, maybe I'd be able to buy some sausages too. It was also critical that I find something at the market that could be used as bandage material for my head wound. There was no way I could risk the possibility of getting infection.

I dressed in my snow gear, put on my backpack, and took the canvas tote from the back closet, which I would use to haul back my provisions. I locked the door behind me and stepped out into the storm.

As I slowly made my way along the ridge road overlooking Potevka, the storm momentarily calmed. From my vantage point on the hillside, I was able to look down on the entire village. Below me nothing moved—everything was covered in deep, white snow. The view reminded me of a beautiful Christmas card of the Bavarian Alps.

There was a peaceful, wondrous quiet, as if the whole earth had stopped to honor the moment—the morning after the first heavy snow of the Russian winter.

Standing majestically in the middle of the village was a small, Russian Orthodox Church. On top of its onion-shaped dome was a once-gilded cross, now rusted and bent but still pointing heavenward.

While looking down on this small sanctuary, my feelings of peace gradually turned to resentment, as I thought of what the Communist government had done to the Soviet people, their religion, and faith.

By declaration of the Communist Party, Russia and the Republics of the Soviet Union were officially atheistic States. In his writings Karl Marx referred to religion as "the opium of the masses." During the oppressive rule of Stalin, the people of Potevka, as in thousands of other towns and villages throughout the USSR, were forced by governmental decree to close down their local church.

In an ongoing attempt to purge religion from Soviet society, Stalin's secret police desecrated, bombed, and burned thousands of churches and monasteries throughout the country. Hundreds of thousands of clergymen and parishioners were exiled to labor camps in Siberia simply because of their beliefs and religious activities.

For sixty years—since the beginning of Stalin's reign—the small church in Potevka had been used only as a barn for cattle and for the storage of farm equipment.

On this morning—knowing that the evils of Communism were finally crashing down all across the Soviet Union—I was struck by the symbolism of the small church, sanctified by the pure, newly-fallen snow, standing proudly in the middle of the village as a reminder to all that seventy years of godless government in the USSR were finally coming to an end.

I made a promise to myself that day. If I ever had the chance to make it back to Potevka, I would pay a visit to her certain-to-be restored and re-dedicated church.

As I continued on my way to the village center, I passed by twenty or thirty cabins, but, strangely, saw no people and very few tracks in the snow as well. When I finally reached the *rynak* (outdoor market), which was surrounded by a high stone wall, I pushed open one of the large wooden doors and stepped inside. To my astonishment, the entire place was empty! *How could this be?*

Near the entrance doors, three young boys were playing, making snow sculptures.

"Where are all the people?" I asked.

"Gone to Moscow for the celebrations," the oldest boy answered.

"What celebrations?" I asked in disbelief.

His father had told him that the local Communist leaders were directed to bus the villagers from the surrounding province all the way to Moscow—several hundred miles away—to celebrate the victory of the government forces for successfully putting down the recent coup attempt against General Secretary Gorbachev. Such forced, government-mandated celebrations were not all that uncommon under the Communist regime.

As a result, in addition to the market being shut down, the small *kolkhoz* store was also closed. And to make matters worse, both the store and market would be closed for the next four days during this unofficial holiday.

This can't be happening!

I had a large supply of *rubles* on me, but what good would they do me now? I'd been without food for six-plus days—and now possibly four more? *There was no way!*

Walking back in the direction of the safe house, wondering what I would do, I was relieved to see two bearded old men resting on their shovels next to a woodpile near one of the cabins. They had just cleared a pathway leading from one of their cabins to a nearby woodshed and outhouse. Both men stood motionless as I approached.

With their white beards and covering of fresh snow, they could have easily been mistaken for crude snow sculptures, except for their frosty white breath and the gray smoke that swirled up from their pipes before it vanished overhead into the storm.

"Dobraye utra," I said with my best Russian accent.

"Dobraye utra," they cautiously replied—almost in unison.

I was uncomfortable having to explain my situation of being a visitor in their village and not having any food.

"I arrived here by train last night to spend a few days in Potevka," I told them. "I had no idea the market and village store would be closed for four days. Is there a chance either of you gentlemen might be willing to sell me a small amount of food to get me through the weekend?"

They looked at me suspiciously—almost as if they were afraid. They turned to one another, each waiting for the other to speak; yet, for whatever reason, neither of them would answer me.

My ability with the Russian language was certainly not native, but surely the two men understood what I was asking of them.

I posed my question again, adding that I would pay them generously for the food, but, unfortunately, I got the same result. Nothing. Perplexed, I stood staring at the two of them.

After several more minutes, *"Spaseeba,"* I said, irritated and shaking my head in disbelief. As I walked away, the thought came to me—*Had someone warned these men about the stranger in their village?*

I was aggravated at the two men. Yet, at the same time, I felt sorry for them and for all the Soviet people living under such a repressive regime as this. So powerful and ingrained was the KGB's influence over every facet of Soviet society, relying on their repugnant system of citizen informants, each person lived with a crippling fear and distrust of everyone—even one's closest neighbors.

Slowly making my way back to the *izba*, the snow and wind continued relentlessly. While I walked, I looked for any cabin where it appeared that someone might be at home. Yet I didn't see a single place with light coming from a window or smoke from a chimney.

While plodding through the snow, I continued to agonize over my food problem. The next town was over fifty miles away and surely, in such a poor outpost as Potevka, no one in the village owned an automobile.

I stopped by the empty railway station and re-checked the train schedule posted on the outside wall. The only opportunity for me to leave Potevka would be in four days, the very train on which I was already scheduled to depart.

Whatever was I going to do?

Chapter 14

RIPE, RANK, AND NAKED IN THE WASHTUB

We never know the worth of water until the well is dry.

English Proverb

Back at the cabin, I started a fire again to heat the place and get myself warm. The more my stomach ached, the more I worried about being four days in Potevka without any food—not to mention that I still had several days yet to travel in order to get back to our embassy in Moscow.

With a fire roaring in the stove, once again I made a search of the cabin, hoping to find the

MREs in a place I'd overlooked. After a futile half-hour, I finally gave up.

Why had HQ specifically told me there were provisions here at the safe house, and, yet, there were none?

I sat at the edge of the bed worrying, contemplating what to do next. My circumstances seemed to keep going from bad to worse. I had to shake the gloom I could feel coming on. Like so many times in recent years, I knew that if I let it, I could waste the entire day worrying and fretting about my situation, my past, and my future—that is, if I had a future.

In an effort to raise my spirits and to forget about my food problem—if only for a while—I decided the next best thing I could do was to fetch water from the village well for a long, overdue bath. Not having bathed for several days—not since before the blood, sweat, and mud incident with Koshka's two mafia goons, not to mention all those wretched days on board the train—I was definitely getting ripe. Sitting on that hard bench seat, I'd dreamed of soaking my aching, sore body in a tub of hot water. But, then again, one benefit from the freezing temperatures of a Russian winter was a body really doesn't stink all that much. And, if I was going to go from cabin to cabin begging for food, I needed to get cleaned up, smelling okay, and make myself as presentable as possible.

I secured two large water buckets and the yoke from the closet, locked up the cabin, and trudged through the snow towards the communal well. The only tracks along the road, other than those barely visible from my earlier excursion, were those of a horse and sleigh.

When I was half way to the center of the village, rather than continue on the same route as before, I chose a different road where several other cabins were located. Of the dozen or so that I passed, I finally came upon one where it looked as though someone might be at home. With my hopes up, I left the yoke and buckets near a picket fence and went inside the yard to the cabin.

Although a light burned inside, there were no tracks outside and not a sound coming from within. No one answered the door. Disappointed, I returned to the yoke and buckets and continued on my way through the storm.

I reached the village well just as a scrawny, weathered old man—his beard as white as the falling snow—had finished loading the last of several small barrels of water onto his horse-drawn sleigh.

"*Zdrastvuitye*," I said.

He stood for a moment looking down at me.

"Got to be the worst, first snow storm of the season in these parts in fifty years," he said in a raspy, worn voice. "Could be a bad one for us."

He stepped down from the wagon into the deep snow.

"I agree with that," I said, showing him my interest in what he had to say. "You must have experienced many a bad winter here in your lifetime. Any idea how long the storm will last?" I asked, eager to engage him in further conversation, hoping I could, perhaps, get him to help me or tell me where I could buy some food.

But the old man made no response to my question. He just looked at me and shook his head. Abruptly, he moved towards his horse and grabbed the halter rope.

"Da svidaniya. Mama zdoat s *garyachiym supem* (Goodbye. Mother is waiting with hot soup)," he said, before giving a whistle and leading his bony horse and sleigh away.

I leaned up against the rock well and watched longingly as they slowly disappeared into the storm. I stood for a moment, thinking how nice it would be to go with the old man back to his home, to meet his wife, to visit with them—even, perhaps, be invited to have a bowl of hot soup.

It was my understanding that the peasants living in the Russian countryside, unlike the people living in the larger cities, were especially friendly and hospitable. Thus far, that theory didn't hold much weight as far as my empty stomach and I were concerned. Nevertheless, I reminded myself that these were desperate times for Russia and its people; it wasn't right for me to be too judgmental.

I pulled water from the well and filled both buckets. I put one on each end of the yoke, carefully balanced it across my shoulders, and started back towards the safe house. Several times I had to stop and set the buckets down when the pain along my sore rib cage became too much.

Finally back at the *izba*, I added extra wood to the fire then poured water into two medium-sized kettles from the cupboard and put them on the stove to boil. Using a combination of boiled water and melted snow, I eventually had enough hot water to fill the round metal washtub waiting for me in the middle of the cabin floor.

I got out of the clothes that I had lived in for the last week and set the awful-smelling Russian lye soap and bristle brush next to the tub. No Head & Shoulders or Irish Spring here.

Very slowly I lowered myself into the hot, steamy water. "Hallelujah Chorus," "Joy to the World," and all three verses of "Tom Dooley"!

Bathing in this small metal tub was actually not new for me. Growing up in Bear River, a wonderful, small town of farmers and ranchers in northern Utah, the house where we first lived on the north end of town did not have indoor plumbing. On Saturday nights our mom would ready a similar tub of water for her tribe of kids—the first tub of hot water for the girls, the second tub for the boys.

Because my brothers were much older than I, I was always the last one in the pecking order to bathe. By the time it was my turn in the tub, the water was usually a murky gray color. Didn't matter to me though, it was the same color as the water in the large irrigation canal that ran near our house. And we *loved* that canal. We swam, floated on makeshift rafts, and played along its banks whenever we got the chance during the long, hot summers.

Regrettably, there are many routine, everyday things in this life I don't appreciate or even think much about. On that snowy day, however, while squatted in that cramped tub of hot water, I vowed I would never again take for granted one of life's simple pleasures—a wonderful hot bath. For almost an hour I soaked, scrubbed, and sang every John Denver and Kingston Trio folk song I could remember.

Although my body was weak from the lack of food, still I remember myself as the picture of speed and athleticism; trying to avoid the cold by springing from the hot water—naked as a jaybird—to feed the fire in the stove and then jumping quickly back to the washtub.

When the temperature of the bath water started to feel like the temperature of the outside storm, it was time to extract myself. I did so with great reluctance. There I stood—scrubbed lobster red—looking more like a large, pale, wrinkled prune, but feeling like a million Russian *rubles*!

For almost an hour in that blissful tub of hot water, I was able to forget about Koshka, the mafia, the KGB, and not having any food.

Knowing that the afternoon daylight would soon be slipping away, I got myself dressed, re-bandaged my head wound, put on my winter outer gear, and again set off towards the village center where the majority of the cabins were located. Surely, I could find someone in Potevka who would be willing to sell me some food.

Chapter 15

A COMPASSIONATE MAN

There in some smoky corner which,
through poverty, passes for a dwelling place,
a peasant wakes from his sleep.
All night he has been dreaming of a pair of boots . . .

Fyodor Dostoevsky
Poor Folk

I knocked on seven or eight cabin doors where, because of a few tracks in the snow, it looked like someone might be inside. Only two people opened their doors. They were both elderly grandparents looking after grandchildren much too young to make the long, several-hundred-mile bus trip to Moscow.

Unfortunately, no matter how much money I was willing to offer, neither would part with any of their food. Because of the collapse of the Communist government, the failing economy, and Russia's uncertain future, food was now more precious than *rubles*.

While searching for other cabins where someone might be at home, I finally reached the other side of the village, approximately two miles from where the safe house was located.

Just as I was ready to turn around and start back, I noticed in the distance, almost obscured by the storm, a structure located off by itself. It was a few hundred yards from the nearest cabin.

As I got closer, I could see it was, indeed, a place where someone lived. However, it was half the size of the other cabins in the village and looked as if, at some earlier time, it had served as a shed or small barn, then later adapted to function as someone's living quarters. There was a light inside and heavy smoke was coming from the chimney.

Please, someone, please answer the door!

I knocked several times. After a long wait, the door slowly swung open with a high-pitched screech.

There in front of me stood a small, thin man, probably much younger in years than he looked, which I guessed to be around fifty. His face was lean and weather-worn. His left leg was noticeably deformed, shorter than his right. He leaned on a crude, homemade crutch.

Sadly, everything about him spoke of poverty. His clothes were old and threadbare. Crude slippers made from rags and held together with twine were on his feet. Just inside the door stood a pair of worn boots, the heels almost gone, portions of the sides rotted away.

Appearing apprehensive that someone was at his door, he stepped onto the front porch and pulled the door shut behind him. When I introduced myself, he hesitated for a moment before giving his name as Arkady.

"Pardon me for troubling you," I said. "I'm staying in Potevka for a few days and, unfortunately, I have no food. I had no idea both the market and communal store would be closed for four days. I've been walking around the village trying to find someone at home, but it appears that most of the cabins are empty."

As I told the man my story, from the expression on his face, I sensed he understood my predicament.

"I'm sorry," he said, "but I can't give you any food. I have very little for myself." He reached behind him and grabbed the door handle.

"Please understand," I said hurriedly, "I don't expect you to just give me food. I will pay you generously for it. I have *rubles* right here in my coat pocket."

"You can see I'm a cripple, and the authorities won't allow me to work. I receive a small pension from the government for my disability, but I tell you . . . I barely get by."

"I'm sorry about your disability, sir, but I will pay you generously for any food you can spare, even if it's only a little."

I showed him the handful of *ruble* bills I'd pulled from my coat pocket.

"It's been several days since I've eaten," I said.

He stood silently, leaning on his crutch, looking not at the money but at the snowflakes collecting on his frayed sweater. After a moment he turned and looked up at me.

"You're obviously not from around here. You don't know that since last month Potevka and all the villages in the surrounding province have been restricted to food rations. The local party leaders have promised to double our rations for the next month if Potevka has a high enough participation at this week's absurd, forced celebration in Moscow. The old *Bolsheviks*, you know, still run everything here in the provinces."

"I apologize, sir," I said. "I didn't know about the food rationing. I now understand why the few people I've talked with have been so reluctant to help. Someone should have told me."

"If someone was to see me give you food or if the word got out that I did, I could have trouble from the local authorities. It could jeopardize my getting any food rations, which is just what some of the villagers here would want to happen."

His brow furrowed, and his jaw tightened as he spoke.

"The people here look down on me because I'm crippled and cannot work. They can't stand the fact that I get a monthly stipend from the government, but I tell you . . . it's not enough! If I didn't have the food I grow in my small garden each summer, I'd never survive—I'd starve to death. We are poor peasant people here. I just can't help you. I'm sorry, but you don't understand how things are for us here in Potevka."

"I do understand about the local authorities, sir, and I'm sorry how you are treated by the villagers, but I have no food. I have gone to several cabins here in Potevka, but not one person has offered to help me . . . not one."

"And . . . you made no plans to bring any food with you?"

"I did bring food with me, but while traveling here on the train, someone in the rail car stole my food sack."

"I'm sorry, but you should have been more careful," he said, turning away. "I can't help you. You . . . you just don't understand."

I was at a loss of what else to say. For an awkward moment, I just stood there looking at him. I said a quick silent prayer, asking the Lord to *please* touch his heart, hoping that he would change his mind. Leaning on his crutch, the man continued to stare out at the storm but said nothing.

In desperation, I pulled back the hood of my coat and removed my *schapka* so the man would see my head. He reeled back, astonished at the sight of the bandages. I told him about the beating I'd received at the hands of the Russian mafia and how weak I'd become from the loss of blood.

Immediately I knew my ploy had backfired by introducing the Russian mafia into the conversation.

"I'm certain you're an honorable man and would help me if you could," I said. I slowly put my *schapka* back on my head. "I apologize for putting you in this position."

In a final attempt to prolong our conversation and, hopefully, gain his sympathy, I asked him about the wolves that I'd heard in the forest.

"Of course there are wolves around here," he said, ". . . just like there are throughout all the forested areas of Russia. It's nothing to worry about. The only time they occasionally kill is when they attack the smaller farm animals that stray from the sheds or barns."

I certainly didn't feel reassured by his comments about the wolves, but I thanked him just the same. I also thanked him for telling me about Potevka's mandatory food rationing. Before leaving, I reached out to shake his hand. Still appearing anxious, surely because of my comments about my altercation with the mafia, he ignored my extended hand and turned away.

"You needn't worry about the wolves," he said, then stepped back into his cabin and pushed the door closed behind him.

So much for an answer to my prayers!

I was angry and upset with myself because of how I'd bungled my lost opportunity. *Mike, how could you have been so stupid?*

I felt certain that the man had understood my predicament and was ready to offer his help until I botched it all by bringing up my confrontation with the mafia. *But, then again, could it be that he, too, had been warned about the stranger in Potevka?*

Hurt and disappointed, I started back towards the village center. *What was I going to do?*

After I was almost up to the road, I heard what I thought was the high-pitched sound of the man's cabin door opening, followed by a muffled whistle. I stopped and turned around.

Through the falling snow, I could barely see Arkady on his front steps waving his crutch back and forth above his head, motioning for me to come back. I hurried down the side road as quickly as I could. When I eventually reached his door, he stepped out onto the porch.

"I apologize for how I treated you and what I said earlier," he said. "Put this inside your coat. But I ask you, please, do not mention it to anyone. If someone were to find out that I gave you this . . . there could be trouble for me."

I stuffed a small paper sack down inside the front of my jacket. He then gestured with his head for me to leave.

I reached in my coat and brought out my wallet of *rubles*.

He shook his head, *"Nyet-Nyet.* It's a gift from me to you."

"Spaseeba, spaseeba, tovarisch (Thank you, thank you, comrade)," I said.

Arkady looked at me, smiled, and extended his free hand. I pulled off my gloves, reached out and shook his hand vigorously with both of my own, causing him to wobble precariously on his one good leg. For a brief moment, we looked at each other smiling—almost laughing.

"Spaseeba, tovarisch." I said again, "I will never forget this kindness."

"It's okay," he said. "And not to worry about the wolves."

Although what he had given me was something small—it was *something*. And please, Lord, please let it be something to eat!

By the time I got back up to the road, the snow had intensified, and the wind had picked up considerably. The storm was, again, a full-scale blizzard. I fastened the top Velcro strap on my coat and pulled the flaps of my *schapka* securely down around my ears.

It was almost two miles back to the safe house. I tried to hurry—almost falling at times—as fast as I could through the blinding snow. The thought of having something to eat gave me more strength than I'd had for days.

In less than an hour I was back inside the cabin. First, I had to sit down; I was so weak from pushing through the deep snow that my legs were trembling. After a few minutes of rest, I stood and shook off the snow.

I opened the top of my coat, and pulled out the sack Arkady had given me. Carefully, I reached in and pulled out three slices of Russian black bread.

Thank you, Dear Lord, and thank you, dear Arkady!

As I held the bread close to my nose and breathed in its wonderful, pungent aroma, tears filled my eyes. I couldn't remember ever being more excited about something to eat. I was so hungry!

After adding wood to the fire, I pulled the rotten apples from the garbage pail where I had thrown them the night before and inspected each one again in detail. The spoiled apples and three slices of black bread would now be breakfast, lunch, and dinner—*survival food*—at least for this day.

I cut the few barely edible parts from the six rotten apples and mashed them together with a fork, making a poor-man's applesauce, which I spread on two slices of bread. I decided to save the third slice of bread for later in the evening before going to bed.

I then boiled water for peppermint tea, which I'd found earlier, hidden from the mice in a metal coffee can on top of the cupboard.

Bread, applesauce, and tea!

After kneeling in a heartfelt prayer of thanks, I tried my best to eat slowly and make the two pieces of bread last as long as I could—they were gone within minutes. Soon, the constant ache in the hollow of my stomach, which I'd carried around for the last seven or eight days, was finally gone—at least for now.

Chapter 16

A SONG OF GOODBYE

God could not be everywhere
so therefore He made mothers.
Jewish Proverb

After eating the two slices of bread, I sat for half an hour near the stove warming myself and resting my tired, shaky legs. Afterwards, I put on my coat, *schapka*, and gloves and braved the storm to chop more wood.

Although still unsteady and weak, I did seem to have more strength this time swinging the ax. In less than an hour, I was able to move enough wood inside the cabin to last me for the remainder of my stay with enough wood left over for the cabin's next occupant.

I cleaned up the mess I'd made from hauling the firewood inside, then lay down on the straw bed and pulled a few of the blankets over me to rest for a while.

As I lay there, I thought about the hardships and suffering of the Soviet people. I thought about the kindness of Arkady and the old woman at the train station and what good, noble people they seemed to be despite all the adversity they had faced in their lives. I hoped to see them both again before I left Potevka.

I thought about the *babushka* and how much she reminded me of my mother. It brought back bittersweet memories of one of my last experiences with my dear mom not long before she died.

☆ ☆ ☆

My mother was a strong, remarkable woman; something I didn't realize or appreciate until I was well into my twenties.

In the small town where I grew up, there were many large families—farm families tend to be that way. And as the last of seven children, I just assumed that most families were as big as ours and that all moms worked from early in the morning until late in the evening as mine did.

Mom was the second oldest in a family of fourteen brothers and sisters. With her younger siblings, she grew up very poor and under very difficult conditions.

Although I never realized it when I was young, our family, too, was poor. Our first home, where we lived on the north end of town, had no indoor plumbing, no central furnace for heat, and no water heater. Mom cooked our meals over a coal-wood burning stove. She did the cleaning, washing, ironing, and mending for our entire family of nine.

In spite of the hardships in her life, she seemed to be a happy person. She loved to laugh, and she especially enjoyed visiting and gossiping with neighbors whenever they dropped by. I can still see her, as if it were yesterday, working in the kitchen—cooking, cleaning, ironing, or whatever—all the while singing to herself. It was Mom who instilled in me my love of music.

When my grandfather—Mom's dad—died at the age of eighty-two, Mom and her brothers and sisters gathered at grandpa's old home across from the town park in Bear River to go through his belongings.

After they divided up all of his possessions, someone in the family asked, "What about the attic?" Somewhat small for my age and probably no more than seventy pounds soaking wet—my older brother Ted's nickname for me was "Rickets"—it was determined that I was the only one present with the size and agility to make it through the small opening up into the attic.

As I explored the cluttered room with a flashlight, there tucked away in a corner, almost obscured by the piles of yellowed newspapers and magazines, boxes, and scattered junk, was an old guitar. After seeing the excitement of my discovery, Mom's brothers and sisters agreed that the guitar should be my inheritance from Grandpa.

I spent the next few days repairing the old guitar with Elmer's Glue, some paint and varnish, replacing a couple of tuning pegs, and putting on a new set of strings.

A week later my brother-in-law, Boyd, drove me in his old, green Chevy pickup to a sheep camp somewhere in the hills west of Tremonton.

There we met with a sheepherder who taught me how to tune the guitar. He also showed me how to position my fingers on the neck of the guitar for the three basic chords in the key of "G." I was thrilled beyond words!

Despite the old guitar's wide neck and my small hands, by the time Boyd and I got back to town, I was able to strum out the three chords while the two of us sang a simplified rendition of "The Battle Hymn of the Republic."

Mom was so proud—my life-long love of music had just begun.

I have wonderful memories of sitting in the kitchen of our old home playing the guitar and harmonizing with Mom as we sang her favorite songs. We were great together on "Red River Valley," but in our version, we always substituted "Bear River Valley" where appropriate.

After Dad passed away, for twelve years Mom continued to live in our family home. In her ninetieth year, she experienced a debilitating stroke, and needed to be confined for the last two years of her life to a rest home in Tremonton. In addition to the stroke, she suffered from a type of

Alzheimer's but seemed happy, unaware of her condition or the world around her.

Because of the stroke, she totally lost her speech, but would jabber away noisily as if we understood everything she had to say. And our mom *always* had a lot to say!

When back home, I tried to visit her at the rest home as often as I could. She loved to go riding in the car, which always required a stop at Van's, the local fast food drive-in. She loved their cheeseburgers, round dogs, tater tots, and caramel shakes. Unfortunately, as her health deteriorated she became bedridden and could not leave the rest home facility.

On the afternoon of Christmas Eve, a few months before she passed away, I drove the eighty miles to the rest home with my boy, Chris, to visit Mom and give her the Christmas gifts we had bought for her. On the way there, the idea of taking Mom back to her home for a short visit kept whispering in my mind.

"Chris," I asked, "what would you think if we were to take Grandma back to her home to be there, perhaps one last time, at Christmas?"

"That's a great idea!" he replied. "Maybe we could even hang some Christmas decorations and have Grandma open the gifts we brought for her."

When we got to the rest home, I explained my proposal to the head nurse. I was surprised that she so readily agreed to it.

"But you must have your mother back here no later than six o'clock," she said emphatically.

"I promise. Mom will be back in time for dinner," I assured her.

With Mom jabbering away at us, we put her in her winter coat, wrapped a blanket around her legs, and wheeled her to the car. As I lifted her into the back seat, a light snow began to fall. Chris seated himself in the back of the car next to his grandmother and held her hand as she rambled on about something or other.

While I drove, periodically checking the rear view mirror, I couldn't help but chuckle to myself. As his grandma babbled away, I saw Chris continually nodding his head: "Yes, Grandma—Uh-huh Grandma—That's right, Grandma."

By the time we had traveled the nine miles to Bear River, the storm was so heavy I debated about turning around and going back to the rest home. Yes, I had made a promise to the head nurse, but I was determined that Mom should spend a few hours in her own home again—especially on this Christmas Eve.

Once parked in front of her house, I left Mom and Chris in the car with the heater running while I found a shovel in the back shed to clean the snow from the sidewalk. With a narrow pathway cleared, I carried her from the car to the front porch.

As Chris and I helped her through the front door into her home, where she had lived for the last fifty years, she suddenly stopped, looked at me with big, excited eyes, and proceeded to pound on my shoulders and chest with her hands. Without a doubt, Mom realized where she was. Chattering loud, unintelligible words, she began to cry, all the while her face beaming with joy. With a lump in my throat, I glanced over at Chris as he turned away from me to hide his own tears.

I walked Mom to the sofa and sat down next to her. She continued to gesture with one hand and then the other, jabbering on about memories and stories we couldn't begin to understand. Chris and I just smiled and nodded in agreement to everything she had to say.

When her rambling finally slowed to a moderate pace, we made sure she was warm and comfortable with her favorite hand-made afghan tucked around her. I sent Chris out to the car to bring in the Christmas presents while I went into the back room to turn up the furnace and run the water in the kitchen sink and bathroom. Only moments later, when I returned to the living room, Mom was curled up on the couch, sound asleep.

While waiting for her to wake from what we expected to be a short nap, I went through the cupboards in the kitchen and pantry looking for anything that might be available to prepare for a meal. I found a variety of canned foods and non-perishables. I decided our early Christmas Eve dinner would be canned tomatoes over elbow macaroni, my favorite meal that Mom would cook for me when I was a boy growing up in that home.

In Mom's back pantry, Chris found a roll of white butcher paper and a box of crayons. "Dad, how about if I make some Christmas decorations for Grandma's table?"

"Good idea," I said. "She'll definitely like that."

While I cooked, Chris busied himself cutting, coloring, and taping holiday decorations. With Mom still asleep and the food ready and warming on the kitchen stove, Chris and I sat on the living room floor next to her, listening to KSL's Christmas music on the large, floor-model Philco radio that had been in our family since I was a boy. Lost in the memories of growing up in that home, the afternoon eventually turned dark as the snow continued to fall.

"Dad," Chris said, "it's going on five o'clock, and it's still snowing. What do you think we should do?"

Remembering my promise to the nurse, reluctantly I told him, "Well, I guess we'd better get Mom back to the rest home."

I cleared the table and poured the macaroni and tomatoes down the sink. After shoveling the sidewalk again, I went out to the car and started the engine. Chris gathered the hand-made decorations and presents and took them to the car. Mom woke only for a moment as we wrapped her up in the blanket and I carried her to the car. She never saw her home again.

At Mom's funeral a few months later, I had the privilege of playing my guitar and singing "Bear River Valley" to her one last time.

Chapter 17

A HOLIDAY DISCOVERED

Where we love is home,
home that our feet may leave,
but not our hearts.

Oliver Wendell Holmes

The memories of Mom and home, along with the sound of the wind blowing through the nearby forest, soon put me to sleep. Two hours passed before I woke with a start.

From somewhere in the forest, again I heard the mournful howling of wolves. Their eerie wailing and the penetrating cold in the *izba* had me now wide awake. I got up and added more wood to the stove and soon had the fire crackling again. It was still snowing heavily outside.

In the evening, with the cabin warm and comfortable and the woodbin full of firewood, I pulled my portfolio from my backpack and began to make a detailed review of my documents. The pangs of hunger started again, but I didn't want to eat the last slice of bread I'd saved until just before going to bed. I needed to occupy my mind with something else besides food.

While studying my calendar, to my utter astonishment, I discovered that tomorrow—Thursday, November 28—would be Thanksgiving Day in America.

Unbelievable!

With all the pressures and problems of the last month—specifically our failed clandestine operation in Siberia—the holiday had totally escaped me. Immediately my thoughts traveled thousands of miles back to my home in northern Utah and memories of Thanksgivings past.

The end-of-year holidays have always been a special time for me. It started when I was very young and has continued throughout my adult years. The glorious, traditional turkey dinner, usually served at both Thanksgiving and Christmas, has always been my very favorite meal. In fact, even today when I go to a restaurant, I always check to see if turkey dinner might be on the menu.

As I contemplated my discovery, heavy feelings of isolation and loneliness came over me. I soon realized that going through my documents might have been a mistake, perhaps it would have been better had I not looked at my calendar at all.

I sat, reflecting on my circumstances. Tomorrow was Thanksgiving in America, one of our most cherished holidays, and here I was in the tiny village of Potevka, somewhere in the hinterlands of Russia, holed up for several days in a humble cabin safe house and with nothing to eat. *Nothing!*

As the evening darkened, so did my mood. I got down the oil lamp from the cupboard and lighted the room. Pulling the table closer to the fire, I started writing several long-overdue letters to be sent home to the States and to Australia.

Because of my operational cover, I would write draft letters in German and then re-write them in English once I got back to our embassy in Moscow.

Besides a long letter to my boy, Chris, I would write a generic letter to my brothers and sisters and their families. I would also drop a line to Bonnie to let her know that her long-lost friend in Russia was doing okay. Thinking about the holiday and everything that was going on back home, I missed them all more than ever.

Tonight my heart especially ached for a young, missionary somewhere in Australia.

Why hadn't I planned things better? Under these circumstances, with Christmas just around the corner, it was doubtful if I could even get a card in the mail to him—let alone a gift. I wished there was someway I could talk to him and explain.

Chapter 18

THE JOYS OF A SON

What is the price of a thousand horses
against a son where there is one son only?

J.M. Synge
Riders to the Sea

I was doing post-graduate studies in Russian at the Defense Language Institute in Washington, D.C. when Chris was born at nearby Andrews Air Force Base. I was thrilled beyond words the day he arrived—I actually had a son!

Immediately, I began planning all the things I'd be able to teach him and all the things we'd do together. However, as a first-time father, my enthusiasm quickly waned when, for his first year—like all new babies—he basically did nothing but eat, sleep, and drool. Then at about twelve months, when he began to walk, the magic happened. It seemed that over night he turned from a helpless infant into a curious little boy, full of happiness and mischief, eager to discover the world around him.

During his youth, when he wasn't in school or with his friends, Chris and I were almost inseparable. We spent thousands of hours on the tennis courts working on his game, and surely we spent just as many hours throwing a football and running pass patterns in our back yard. By the time he was eight years old, Chris could already throw a football dead-on-target from thirty yards away.

Whenever people ask me about my life and what experiences stand out as the very best, without hesitation I answer—the six years when, each fall, I coached Chris' little league football team. They were such a great group of kids who cared about one another, worked extremely hard, and developed into one heck of a football team.

When Chris was young, we purchased a used Volkswagen camper, the kind with a pop-up top that allows for an additional sleeping compartment above the lower level. We affectionately named the vehicle the Mus-Bus because of its mustard-yellow color.

It served as a school bus some mornings, a team bus during football season, a ski bus in the winter, and as a hotel-on-wheels in the summer to take us to our nearby favorite places: up Logan canyon to Ram Station, Bear Lake, and beautiful Jackson Hole, Wyoming.

However, it was during our annual father-son summer excursion to California that the Mus-Bus was relied on the most. With the music of Sting blaring from the stereo speakers, our route of travel usually took us west along I-80 to San Francisco, with overnight stops in Reno and Lake Tahoe. From the Bay area, we would travel down the coast highway to our favorite spots in southern California—Newport Beach and Laguna Beach. Typically, we would also visit San Diego before returning home to Utah through Las Vegas.

As we visited each of our favorite places, it was a tradition to have our own City Tennis Championships, which included bragging rights until the following summer. For years I kept the Traveling Tennis Trophy in my possession until Chris reached fifteen or sixteen years old.

As the power and consistency of his serve and forehand developed, he showed no mercy on his old man whatsoever. By then, of course, I used the excuse that I was suffering from too little sleep; the sounds of the waves from the Pacific kept me awake at night while we slept in the Mus-Bus at a camp site near the ocean.

Our once-in-a-lifetime summer trip took place when I finished a three-month State Department assignment during the time of the Reagan-Gorbachev Summit in Moscow. In June of that year, when my responsibilities in Helsinki and Moscow were over, Chris flew to Europe to join me. Both of us armed with a tennis racquet, back-pack, and small, wheeled suitcase, we spent four weeks together experiencing the magic of Europe and playing on her red clay tennis courts whenever we could.

With our Eurail passes in hand—a ticket that allows for unlimited train travel—we journeyed throughout the seventeen major countries of Western Europe. From Venice and Rome in the South to Copenhagen and Stockholm in the North, we rode Europe's incredible railway system.

Following a day of sightseeing in one of Europe's grand cities, we'd return at night to the train station exhausted. After determining our next day's destination—usually by flipping a coin—we'd board a train for the overnight journey. After bedding down for the night, from his bunk, Chris would repeat the same words he'd said the night before: "Dad, this has been the best day of my life." And I totally agreed. The month we spent together in Europe will always be one of my most cherished memories.

Before returning home to Utah, Chris and I made a stop-over in Washington, D.C. Through a well-placed connection, an invitation had been extended to visit the White House for my winning the men's tennis singles which had been part of the summit activities in Helsinki and Moscow.

The sponsor of our visit to the White House, Colonel Jim Barrett, was the military attaché to the president and had also participated in the diplomatic tennis tournament. Jim and I had become acquainted when we played together as the doubles team representing the American Embassy. Although we made it to the finals, unfortunately, we lost to the team from the Soviet Embassy.

Because of Jim's position at the White House, he had been able to arrange for us to spend a few minutes meeting President Reagan. However, eight hours before we were to arrive at the White House, an American Naval ship, the *USS Vincennes*, mistakenly shot down an Iranian passenger airliner over the Persian Gulf.

Needless to say, the president had an international crisis on his hands and certainly no time for two tennis bums from the Rockies. Although disappointed, the hours we spent that evening at the White House were an experience neither Chris nor I will ever forget.

Having traveled together for nearly five weeks, Chris and I finally returned home to Utah. That fall Chris began his senior year at Davis High where he excelled at both tennis and football. Thanks to his mother, he was also an honor student, which earned him an academic scholarship to the University of Utah. After one year at the "U," Chris chose to take a two-year break from his university studies to serve as a church missionary in Australia.

It was during my State Department mission to Siberia that Chris left for his Church mission. It was strange to think—we were both serving missions but for two entirely different reasons.

I had yet to receive any word from him since his arrival "down under." I was eager to get to our embassy in Moscow; I was certain that his letters were waiting for me there.

I could only imagine all the things he had to tell his old man—things about Australia, the friendly Aussie people, his mission work, and how he was managing without his best friends. And I was especially interested as to how he was coping without his dog, Oscar. Chris and his shaggy, white-haired maltepoo had been best buddies for the last fourteen years.

With it being the Thanksgiving holiday, what I wouldn't give to have access to a telephone tonight here in Potevka, to call him and hear his voice again, even if it was only for just one minute.

✯ ✯ ✯

Not only did I miss my boy, but I was also concerned for him. Chris had an extra heavy burden to carry into the mission field—that of his mother and me finally being divorced. No matter that it was the right thing for all concerned, I'm sure it hurt him deeply to know we would never again be together as a family once he returned home from his two years in Australia.

The failure of our marriage was emotionally devastating. To this day when I hear of a couple going through a divorce, my heart aches. Chris' mother and I stayed in the marriage for so many years trying to make it work, but it never did. And I do accept the majority of the blame for its demise. Looking back, we were just two different people going in two different directions.

While she and I were dating, I was attending Utah State University full-time, hoping to get into law school. I had a full-time job during the week, as well as a part-time job on weekends. She had already finished college and was willing to support me through my final two years of school. At the time, marriage seemed the logical thing to do.

She was bright, beautiful, gifted, and came from a wonderful family. She loved books, academics, the theater, and the arts. My passion was sports—football, tennis, and skiing. She was happy staying at home; I always wanted to be on the go. And at the time, I had stars in my eyes; I thought Utah was just too tame, and I wanted to experience the world.

After graduation I was eager to serve my military obligation, which I had incurred as a member of the Reserve Officer Training Corps (ROTC) at the university. I was hoping to be sent to some far away, exciting place. And as for a career after the military, I didn't want just a normal job. I wanted to be an entrepreneur; to perhaps one day have my own consulting company. I dreamed of traveling and being involved in some type of international work. I wanted the challenge and excitement of working overseas with people and projects that could make a difference in the world. Perhaps that is why, years later, I found intelligence work so appealing.

In spite of our difficult marriage, from our union came an incredible son. Chris blessed our lives and home in so many ways. I believe he grew up knowing that both his parents loved him dearly and would do anything for him. During the many rough times of the marriage, it would have been so easy to go our separate ways, but the love and bond we had for our boy was just too great. So we stayed together and did the best we knew how under the circumstances.

When Chris was in his final year of high school, his mother and I began to talk seriously about the divorce. For years the three of us had an unspoken understanding about what would eventually happen once Chris left home to start college.

Although I knew it would ultimately come, in early spring when the local constable served me with divorce papers, it finally became a reality.

After she moved out, Chris and I remained in our home for a few days more. On the day the movers came and took our belongings, that night Chris and I stayed in our house for one last time. Without beds, we tried to sleep on the carpet, but we actually spent most of the night talking about the good times and reliving the great memories we had shared together in that home.

I remember the next morning taking a final walk through each of the rooms of that empty house with my heart aching. As we walked around outside, Chris and I lingered in the backyard, which we had landscaped fifteen years earlier as a small football field, bordered by maple trees, quakies, and shrubs.

Next fall there would be no worn-out sod to replace; the daily, after-school, neighborhood football game would no longer be played there.

Finally, we walked to the garden where a few months earlier we had buried our dog Oscar under our large peach tree. Oscar had been in our family since Chris was five years old.

As Chris and I drove away from our home for the last time, it was one of the most difficult moments I had ever experienced.

Chapter 19

RISKS OF THE HEART

Endure, and keep yourself for days of happiness.

Virgil

As the wind rattled the safe house window, I took a break from my letter writing and sat on the edge of the straw bed watching the fire in the stove, I thought of home, of Chris, and the sadness that divorce brings. It's hard, sometimes, to understand why life has to be so complicated and difficult.

When I was younger, I always thought that after a person reached a certain age of maturity, life's troubles would finally be behind him. Yet, for whatever reason, the Good Lord apparently has a different plan for some of us.

I walked to the stove and stoked the fire. Standing near the window, I could see the heavy snow still falling through the darkness.

During the last several years of my fading marriage, I determined that once the inevitable divorce was done and behind me, I would never involve myself in a serious relationship, nor would I ever again consider marriage. Based upon my failure as a husband and my imperfections as a person, I was convinced I just was not good marriage material. It seems divorce and a difficult marriage have a way of doing that to a person.

As the years passed, there were days when I would try to convince myself that I wasn't so bad after all, that I did have some value as a person. Perhaps someday I would even get to the point where I would stop blaming myself for everything that had gone wrong in my life and in my marriage.

Then there came a time in my life when I first took notice of her and began to realize what had been there—right in front of me all along. And my conviction that I would never again be involved in another relationship would someday be seriously tested.

☆ ☆ ☆

I first saw her when she walked into our Salt Lake offices to interview for a job opening we had as a receptionist/office manager. She was a small, attractive woman, simply dressed in a charcoal-gray business suit. She gave her name as Bonnie.

While interviewing her, it was evident she was intelligent, articulate, and had excellent qualifications. She was a graduate of Brigham Young University, where both her mother and father were professors. She came from a family of eight brothers and sisters, Bonnie being the oldest.

What I remember most about that first meeting are two things: first, how nervous she was, and, second, how there seemed to be an unexplainable, curious chemistry between us.

Following four days of screening over twenty-five applicants, her name was at the top of our list, so we offered her the position. Immediately, she fit in with the rest of our small team and became dedicated and proficient in her work. We all enjoyed her friendly personality; she seemed to add a special something to the work place.

Over the next few years she and I developed a strong respect for one another and I came to consider her one of my most trusted friends.

As time passed, now and again Bon would talk about her life away from the office—her friends, her dates, and her latest boyfriend. Seldom had I ever been around a person with such a positive, optimistic outlook on life. She was always happy, upbeat, and saw only the good in people. I especially admired her quality of self worth—probably because it's something I've struggled with most of my life. I often thought how lucky some man would be to someday have her as a wife and companion.

We had many conversations and enjoyed challenging one another on various issues. On occasion she would question me about marriage—what made some so successful and others so miserable? As if *I* knew! The only thing I was certain about regarding marriage was that I would definitely never find myself there again. The risk of failure was just too great.

During one particular discussion, she hinted about the possibility of pursuing a relationship with someone several years her senior. At the time, I didn't have a clue as to where her comments were really directed. Months later, in a similar conversation, she asked me candidly if I would ever consider a person like herself as a companion.

I didn't know what to say; the thought had never crossed my mind. I remember laughing at such a foolish suggestion. No doubt my rude response hurt her feelings because she stood up and walked out of the room.

Of course, I was flattered, as any man would be, that an attractive, intelligent, young woman had a mistaken interest in someone like me. Nonetheless, I simply brushed off her comments as a passing fancy. There was no way I would ever consider such a thing. Besides, she already had plenty of other men in her life.

Whenever my assignments took me away from the Rockies to the East Coast or Europe, we remained in contact with one another because of our work connection. On one occasion, I was called on a long-term project by the State Department to Scandinavia. When I left, I remember thinking that she would likely be in a serious relationship or engaged to someone upon my return to the States. Such was not the case. In fact, while assigned to the American Embassy in Helsinki, we communicated at least once a week, and she surprised me with a care package at least once a month. I found myself missing the girl and her one-of-a-kind smile.

After I finally returned back home, we continued our friendship, but that's where it ended. I was determined I would never get seriously involved with someone. Besides, I thought there was too much of an age difference between us.

On occasion we discussed the issue, and Bonnie was very open about her feelings. She was firm in her conviction that the age issue was not a problem, but I was just as determined that it would not be fair to her. Although she was one of the women who graduated from Brigham Young University without finding Mr. Right, there were still so many other men that she could choose from once she got serious about a long term commitment and possible marriage.

In reality there was no doubt I had very strong feelings for Bon. However, there was no way I would admit those feelings to myself, much less to her. If things were never going to work out between us, why should I let her know how I really felt and just complicate our lives even more? So I went on playing the friendship game, never telling her or showing her how I really cared.

At the time, I had a close friend, Brent Frazier, who was a bishop in our Church. He was a marriage and family counselor by profession. One night before leaving for an intelligence assignment overseas, I requested a Bishop's blessing from him. After the blessing, our conversation turned to my future and what it might hold for me. During our talk, I mentioned Bonnie and the special feelings we had for one another. He had already met her and knew of the wonderful qualities she had as a person. We discussed the age issue and my reluctance to get involved again in a serious relationship.

His advice to me was short and to the point: "Brother Mike, you deserve to be happy. And when it comes to the eternities, do you really think age matters?"

He admonished me not to dismiss my feelings without a great deal of reflection and prayer. As a good friend, I knew he didn't want to see me spend the rest of my years alone; he wanted me to be in a happy, loving relationship.

However, because of my lingering suspicions and negative feelings towards marriage, I remained unsure. I thought the world of Bon, but I felt she had too much going for her to be involved in a dead-end relationship with someone like me.

After all was said and done, Bon and I agreed that no matter what the future brought to each of our lives, we would maintain our friendship and try and stay in contact with one another. She was someone special—a true and dear friend—and I only wanted the best for her.

☆ ☆ ☆

It was in late summer, months after my mother had died, that the State Department contacted me and asked if I would be willing to go back to the Soviet Union to be part of the covert mission to Siberia. They guaranteed that I would be in Russia for only six months. Due to the time-sensitive nature of the assignment, they allowed me only twenty-four hours to give them my decision.

Only weeks earlier, Chris had committed to serve as a missionary in Australia, but there were still four months before his actual departure date. The two of us had big plans for those four months, which included trips in the Mus-Bus to the Tetons, Lake Tahoe, and southern California. We also planned to make numerous visits to our favorite local spots: the Mandarin in Bountiful, Hires Big H in Salt Lake, Maddox in Brigham City, and all of our other favorite eating establishments in between. Staring at a two-year absence away from home, and needing to survive the usual daily dose of Aussie Weet-Bix and Vegemite, I wanted Chris to be well fed before he got on that 747 jet to travel to the Land Down Under.

I was faced with a real quandary in making my decision. I had grown up with a strong love and sense of duty for our country thanks to my dad and brothers. My years of serving on active duty, then my time with the 300th MI, and finally with the State Department in Europe had been very rewarding. Nevertheless, I very much wanted to spend Chris' four remaining months with him before he went away to serve his two-year mission.

After receiving the phone call from the State Department, that evening Chris and I ate dinner together at the Mandarin. Afterwards, we spent the hours driving around, discussing the decision that needed to be made.

Following much conversation and long periods of reflection, reluctantly, we both came to the same conclusion—if the State Department needed me in Russia, then I should go.

The next morning, I called Washington and committed to the assignment.

That evening Chris and Bonnie helped me pack. Afterwards, the three of us drove to the Denny's restaurant near the Salt Lake City Airport for a late, farewell dinner.

At midnight, after an emotional goodbye, I caught a Delta red-eye flight to Washington, D.C. via Atlanta. The following morning I was picked up at Dulles Airport and whisked off to a frantic day of briefings at the State Department and at the Pentagon.

Twelve hours after my arrival in D.C. I was back at Dulles International where I boarded a flight to Helsinki, Finland.

Following the hectic day of meetings, exhausted, I settled into my seat on the 747. While reflecting on the day's briefings and carefully reviewing my operational documentation, for the first time I realized the risk and possible dangers of the upcoming mission. I stayed awake the entire night as our nine-hour flight crossed the Atlantic, thinking about what was ahead of me and what I'd left behind. I had the feeling that I was again at a definite crossroads in my life. And I couldn't help but wonder, *Would I ever see Chris, my family, Bonnie, or the Rocky Mountains again?*

Chapter 20

SECRETS, LIES, AND SPIES

An ambassador [government agent] is an honest man sent abroad to lie for the good of his country.

Sir Henry Wotton
Reliquiae Wottonianae

As my overnight flight crossed the Atlantic, I thought about the upcoming mission to Siberia and the burdens and restrictions it would place upon me. Like many of my other overseas assignments, I was required to be incommunicado with the outside world. Regrettably, this included Chris and my family, which at times, was very hard for some of them to understand.

Needless to say, such a mission necessity was also extremely difficult for me. Agents, understandably, are strictly prohibited from discussing their work with anyone, including family, friends—even other agents.

There are occasions when an agent must endure weeks—even months—working on a clandestine operation in which people's lives are at risk or an important aspect of our national security might be in jeopardy. The success or failure of such a mission is highly dependent upon the agent's knowledge, experience, and ability. Yet, through it all, the agent is strictly prohibited from speaking to anyone other than his controller or handler about his assignment. And with most intelligence operations, there is a "seven-year rule," which requires that no information regarding an operation may be openly discussed until seven years after its completion. This is one of the most difficult aspects of doing intelligence work—*never* being able to talk about one's career work, accomplishments, or failures.

To insure there are no intelligence leaks, operatives in high-profile missions are routinely polygraphed to determine if any classified, national security information—intentionally or unintentionally—has been passed on to a third party.

Sadly, intelligence work is the one area of government service where the public only hears about the glaring failures but never about the successes. One such example is the case of the senior FBI officer Robert Hanssen. As a counterintelligence agent for twenty-seven years within the FBI, he was, in fact, a spy—a mole—working for Russia and the KGB. Hanssen, reportedly, did more damage to America's national security than anyone since the Rosenbergs—the couple that was sentenced to death for providing the USSR with America's top secret plans for the atomic bomb.

Because of the FBI's years of ineptness in finding the mole (Hanssen) hidden within the intelligence community, a handful of U.S. agents working in Russian intelligence became the target of the FBI's desperate investigation. For a three-year period, several of us were placed under intense scrutiny with our careers and reputations threatened.

With only months left of access to top secret U.S. classified information, due to his pending retirement, Robert Hanssen was finally exposed by those for whom he was really working, Russia's new Federal Security Service—the new name of the former KGB. The same old wolf in new sheep's clothing.

How someone such as Hanssen—a U.S. intelligence agent—who had enjoyed all the rights, privileges, and blessings of living in America, could betray and sell-out his own country is, to me, incomprehensible.

It is worth pointing out, yet, to no one's surprise, that actual intelligence work is far removed from the "cloak and dagger spies" portrayed by Hollywood. This pop phenomenon, which began with the *James Bond* genre of movies in the early 1960s and continues today, depicts the handsome, swashbuckling secret agent escaping imminent danger at every turn; clandestine rendezvous in exotic, far-away places; high-tech spy gadgets; and being constantly surrounded by beautiful, buxom women. In reality, intelligence work is extremely serious, tedious, and unglamorous; done by balding, pudgy, middle-aged men—and there are seldom any beautiful, buxom women.

Like a typical younger brother who wanted his older siblings to understand that he did have some earthly value, I always wanted my family—especially my four older brothers—to know of the work I was doing, but, of course, I couldn't tell them. Even Chris was not aware of what his dad was *really* doing in Russia. Yet I wanted him to know, especially if something were to happen to me during one of my foreign assignments and I ended up returning home to the Rockies in a pine box.

While on leave back in Utah, I never discussed my assignments or what I was doing in my career, which, regrettably, did not sit well with some of my brothers. With the exception of my brother Dick, all five men in our family, including two brothers-in-law, had served in the military. During his draft-age years, Dick was exempted from service because of a broken back he sustained in a truck rollover trying to avoid an oncoming car while driving down Logan Canyon.

Our dad had served in both World War I and World War II. Avoiding military service was not an option in our family, and we brothers agreed unconditionally. Dad made certain we each understood that military service was not an obligation but an honor. It was a way for us to give back to this great country where we were born and so blessed to live. So when my turn came to serve, I was proud to be able to follow in their footsteps and carry on the family tradition.

From time to time, my brothers would ask what I was doing overseas that was so important I couldn't talk about it. Yet one would think that they should have *some* idea; i.e. I had been commissioned in the Military Intelligence Corps, graduated from the Russian Institute in Washington, D.C., was a graduate from counterintelligence school, and had served numerous missions to Europe, Scandinavia, and Russia. Nonetheless, each year when I returned home, which was usually at Christmas time, I would catch an earful—especially from my brother Ted. Rather than being proud that his younger brother was serving our country, Ted would vehemently harangue me because of my unwillingness to discuss any of my assignments.

"Just what in the heck are you doing that is so top secret that you can't tell us about it?" he would demand.

"Ted, you should be able to figure it out," I'd reply, hoping his inquisitions would stop.

It was as if he had some harebrained idea that I was working for some evil, third-world, drug cartel smuggling drugs out of South America into Russia.

In all likelihood, Ted probably had a good idea what I was doing in Russia. Yet, if I didn't tell him anything about my work, then I was being a prima donna; on the other hand, if I did divulge things about my assignments, I was being negligent—even breaking the law by violating the Uniform Code of Military Justice. It was a no-win situation for me.

But, then again, perhaps it is true what our oldest brother, Dee, has always said about Ted—that he played football too many years at Box Elder High and at Utah State without a helmet.

Chapter 21

FANTASY, FOOTBALL, AND FAITH

I remember my youth and the feeling that I could last forever, outlast the sea, the earth, and all men.

Joseph Conrad

It was ten p.m. when I finished writing the German drafts of four or five letters. I slowly ate the last piece of bread Arkady had given me. Unfortunately, this only seemed to reawaken my hunger. I added more wood to the fire and moved the oak table against the door.

After putting my things away, I knelt down at the side of the bed to pray. I pleaded with the Lord that he would help me find a way to get some food. I had consumed gallons of tea in the last week, but with the exception of the small potato, three slices of bread, and a couple spoonfuls of spoiled applesauce, tomorrow would be my eighth or ninth day of suffering the constant pains of hunger.

I was also beginning to be concerned about my thought process—my decision-making ability. I didn't know if it was because of the lack of food or the amount of blood I had lost, or a combination of both, but I worried that I wasn't thinking rationally. I was getting more discouraged with each passing day and, certainly, getting physically weaker. Most disturbing, I was beginning to have very negative thoughts as to how this arduous journey across Russia would finally end for me.

✯ ✯ ✯

So often, in difficult times like these, I have such little faith and so many misgivings. It's not that I doubt the Lord, but more that I doubt myself. All my life I've struggled with feelings of low self-esteem—believing that I've never measured up to be the person that the Lord would want me to be.

I didn't grow up with religion. That is to say, our family was never active in the local Mormon faith. Certainly, Mom and Dad taught us right from wrong, but as kids we didn't have a foundation of religious teaching in our home. I sometimes think that, all too often, I use this as a crutch. So when times become especially difficult,

I have a built-in-excuse for my doubts and why I lack the inner faith and confidence that the Lord will help me or that He even cares.

As a boy, I remember tagging along once or twice a year with my sister Karen to church. Even at that young age, she recognized I needed all the help I could get. When I reached my teenage years, I attended church now and again but mostly only for social reasons— sports, dances, parties, etc.

So, one might ask, how, then, did I ever end up going on a mission for our Church?

In my youth, my older brothers were my heroes—especially my brother Ted. It had been my dream to follow in his footsteps and play college football at Utah State. To my young, impressionable mind, Ted had definitely made the family name famous with his success on the gridiron. His senior year he was chosen as captain of the football team at Utah State and selected to the All-Conference squad. Maybe my desire to play college football was a way to prove to my older brothers—especially to Ted—that "Rickets" did have some value after all.

As a kid I loved sports, but mostly football, which I played every chance I got on the school grounds during class recess and at the town park on Sundays. Sunday after church was the one day of the week when my friends and I could gather at the park to play sports, ride horses, or just hang out and talk about girls. It was a chance for most of the kids to get away from the never-ending work of growing up on a farm or ranch.

There just couldn't have been a better place for a young boy to grow up than my home town. I have read that a small town is where, if you get the wrong phone number, you can still talk for fifteen minutes if you want. So it was with Bear River. And as far as I was concerned, the people living there were some of the very best people anywhere. They were hard working, cared about their families and each other, and wanted only the best for our little community.

The Bear River area was settled by a small group of pioneer families that came from Scandinavia in 1866. While I was growing up there, the town's population was still small—around three hundred and fifty people. Located in the northern part of the state in Box Elder County, our town was nearly equal distance from the two larger cities of Tremonton and Brigham. A few miles to the east—as if there to protect and watch over us—stood the majestic, nine-thousand foot peaks of the Wasatch Range of the great Rocky Mountains.

We had an elementary school—kindergarten through the eighth grade—a church house, and a cemetery. There was also a small post office, a gas station, and a general store. At Bernard's general store you could buy almost any necessity—from soda pop and groceries to work boots and cowboy hats. A gallon of milk was fifty cents; a pair of Levis would cost you three dollars.

To us teenagers, however, the most important thing was our large town park—and on Sundays it belonged to us. It had acres of green grass surrounded by tall poplar trees. It was big enough to include a playground for kids, a baseball field, a softball field, a soccer area, a rodeo arena, and plenty of grass left over for tackle football games. The park was situated a few hundred feet above the banks of the Bear River, which meandered slowly down below on its long journey to the Great Salt Lake.

While playing a pick-up game of baseball, if one of the older, bigger kids—batting at home plate—was lucky enough to catch a pitch in the sweet spot of his bat, and if the wind was just right, the ball would carry over the fielders' gloves and over the cliffs down towards the river. We'd talk about it for days! What great memories I have of spending Sunday afternoons at that park with my best friends.

As I grew older, my athletic skills improved as well as my speed, but my best talent was my ability to throw a football. I would spend hours with my best friend, Doug Watanabe, running pass patterns or throwing a football through a tire as he rolled it from one side of the park to the other.

When I was a senior at Bear River High School, my greatest youthful aspiration came true—I was designated the starting quarterback on the varsity football team. There were bigger and better athletes on the team than I, but for whatever reason Coach Simmons decided that I could do the job. More than a great football coach and an inspiring teacher, he was a wonderful human being. He helped me understand the value of hard work, sticking to the basics, playing with confidence, and never giving up no matter what the odds. His belief in me at that young age greatly affected me then, and in turn, has continued to influence me throughout the rest of my life.

We had a great football team with exceptional players and coaches. Our All-State tailback, Hugh Davis, had incredible speed, while our fullback, Conger, and our two animal guards, Lamb and Baer, would take out the opposition on those long end-sweeps.

The night of my senior year, when we defeated our cross-county archrival, Box Elder, was a dream come true. It was a dream I'd had ever since I was a boy and saw my first Bear River –Box Elder football game when it seemed the entire county turned out to see which school had bragging rights for the following year. After our victory, as far as I was concerned, my life was now complete. At the end of the season, as region champs, our team made it all the way to the state football championships for only the second time in our school's history.

By then, of course, I was really full of myself; I was certain that I was going to play college football. However, there was one major problem—*I weighed only 129 pounds*. I was skinny as a rope.

Still, despite my small size, at the end of my senior year I was contacted by two junior colleges and encouraged to try out as a walk-on for their teams. Junior college? No way! That was not for me. I was determined I was going to play with the big boys at Utah State University, even if I had to do it without a scholarship.

I took a year off after high school to work full time and save money for college, hoping, in the meantime, that my body would grow and develop.

The following year I enrolled at Utah State where the Aggie football team was nationally ranked in the pre-season polls. I reported for freshman football weighing 132 pounds and was summarily relegated to the practice squad. (Those of us so appointed referred to it as the suicide squad!)

After the season ended, our freshman coach called me into his office and told me there was no way I could continue to take such a beating. He explained, in no uncertain terms, that I had to put on some weight.

Next year's varsity depth-chart had me listed as the number seven quarterback. There were originally eight quarterbacks in all, but the tall, blond, beach-boy QB listed in front of me had returned home to California to be with his girl friend. Personally, I think it was the bitter snows of Utah State's Cache Valley that did him in.

Since my four older brothers were all around 200 pounds, Coach Williams and I agreed—my growth spurt was yet to happen.

"Aren't you LDS, Mike, a Latter-day Saint?" he asked. "Have you ever thought about going on a mission for your Church?"

Now, there's my answer!

Not only would I be able to serve as a missionary like many others my age were doing—maybe even go to a foreign country and learn a foreign language—I would return in two years to Utah State, a strapping 200-pound quarterback!

Admittedly, it was not the best of reasons to go on a mission. Yet I felt I was as capable and qualified as some of my friends who had already been called to serve. The way I figured, it would be an opportunity to experience another culture in another part of the world, serve the Church by serving others, and, at the same time, achieve my goal of putting on weight and muscle.

I spent the summer and fall working on road construction to help finance my next two years, and in November my odyssey as a missionary for our Church began. Off I went to serve in southern Germany and northern Switzerland.

While there, whenever I had the good fortune to do so, I ate their delicious *bratwurst, wiener schnitzel,* and *sauerbraten* with—always—extra servings of *kartoffelsalat* (German potato salad). I needed to put on the pounds whenever the opportunity presented itself. And Germany had the most wonderful pastries in the world. I would even skip meals in order to afford one of their delicious creations every few days. In fact, while serving my mission, I think I actually became addicted to *Bayrische apfelkücken* (Bavarian apple turnovers).

Then came one of the most disappointing periods of my youth. Having been gone for two years, I returned back home to America weighing a whopping 134 pounds. I had gained a measly *two pounds!* With most college players probably weighing a minimum of 230-plus pounds, I was forced to face the fact that my dreams of following in my brother Ted's footsteps and playing college football were over.

Admittedly, at the outset of my mission, my main interest was not proselytizing but putting on bulk as a future college quarterback. However, as the weeks and months passed and my frequent bouts with homesickness subsided and I dedicated myself to the work, I saw the great good and positive change that the Gospel could bring into people's lives.

Although my mission was a challenge and not without problems and disappointments, what I gained from my experience was not brawn and pounds, but, rather, a great love and respect for the German and Swiss people and a deep appreciation for the joy and satisfaction that comes while in the service of others.

While I didn't realize it at the time, my decision to volunteer those years of service to our Church as a missionary in a foreign country would be of significant value to me later in my life.

Chapter 22

AN LDS SPOOK IN THE WORLD OF SPIES

In time of [cold] war, when truth is so precious, it must be attended by a bodyguard of lies.

Winston Churchill

After my Church mission, I returned home and continued my studies at Utah State University. It was while enrolled in one of my political science classes that I first became aware of the opportunities in the field of intelligence and its importance to our country's national security. As I gained a basic understanding of all that it encompassed, I became intrigued and began to consider intelligence as a possible career choice. Following the example of my father's and brothers' service in the military, I enrolled in the university ROTC program.

Upon graduation, I made application to Military Intelligence as the corps in which I wanted to serve during my years of active duty. It was later that I found out, despite my ordinary academic record, it was my Church mission experience of living abroad and my ability to speak a foreign language that were the primary factors in being selected for an officer's commission in the intelligence corps.

As new intelligence officers complete their mandatory schooling and required on-the-job training, those few who are eventually selected for actual covert assignments are sometimes faced with a peculiar dilemma—dutifully fulfilling the operational mission while remaining true to their religious convictions. During my early years of intelligence work, I, too, found it difficult to reconcile my beliefs with certain mission requirements and with being a totally effective agent.

My first experience with the serious nature of this work took place just three weeks before I was to graduate from Russian language school. As a young counterintelligence officer, I was finishing the year-long resident course in Washington, D.C., when I was unexpectedly summoned for a meeting at the Pentagon. I'd seen the mammoth, strange looking building many times, but only from a distance. Having never been inside, to a first-time visitor it was definitely intimidating. Upon my arrival, I was escorted to a special security area in one of the building's lower levels. When I entered the room, I was introduced to a group of eight senior officers from various intelligence agencies who were reviewing my personnel file and other background information.

After twenty minutes or so of general questions and conversation, the senior officer asked me point blank, "Lieutenant Ramsdell, would you have a problem if you were asked to be involved with the termination of an individual for the sake of our country's national security?"

Needless to say, having such a profound question asked of me was the furthest thing from my mind. Stunned, I didn't know what to think or how to respond.

What does he mean . . . "be involved"? Is he asking me if I would be willing to be a hit man, a hired gun? Assassination was the dark side of intelligence that no one ever talked about or even admitted that it ever took place. *How could these men ask such a thing of me, knowing I had not even started my career yet?*

"Sir," I said, "could I ask you . . . please repeat your question?" I wanted to make certain I'd understood him correctly. Appearing somewhat irritated, the colonel posed the question a second time. I sat erect, looked around at those in the room, placed my hands on my knees, and cleared my throat as though I was about to give some profound answer, but nothing came out.

The panel of officers obviously realized I needed time to think things over. Following a twenty-minute break—presumably time for me to come up with my answer—the group reconvened. I asked the colonel who had posed the question,

"Sir, would I be permitted to know who the individual was, what he had done, and the reason he needed to be terminated?"

With every eye in the room on the colonel, his answer to me was an emphatic . . . "NO!"

The room became awkwardly silent. Again, not certain of what I should say, I stumbled with my words. "Gentlemen . . . I'm sorry . . . but I don't feel I would be able to comply with such a request because of my beliefs."

Not wanting to sabotage my career before it even got started, I made an effort to qualify my answer.

"However, sir . . . I feel that my views about being involved with someone's termination could possibly change if . . . if I were given access to additional information about what the person had done to our national security and . . ."

The group of officers apparently didn't like this response either—especially the colonel. I was immediately excused from the meeting.

Before being escorted out of the room, the colonel walked up to me.

"Remember Lieutenant, this meeting never took place," he said. "Do you understand?"

"Yes, sir . . . I understand." I replied.

I've often wondered what they had in mind for me had I answered in the "affirmative" to whatever it was they were looking for me to do. As a brand new intelligence officer, that was my introduction to the harsh realities of the world of intelligence—secrets, lies, and spies.

☆ ☆ ☆

As my career progressed, so did my enthusiasm for the work. Yet, as my assignments became more involved and my responsibilities increased, I continued to struggle with what was expected of me during some of my missions and how it conflicted with my religious beliefs. During several of the clandestine operations to which I was assigned, naturally, there were times when I was required to work undercover and take on a new identity and represent information that was totally misleading and factually untrue.

Believing, however, that I was accomplishing the better good, I always put the success of the mission above any of my apprehensions. As a young officer, I never dared speak to my superiors about this dilemma, concerned what it might do to my career—but I definitely had issues.

A partial resolution to this dilemma came as I was given more opportunities to travel and serve abroad, specifically in Western Europe and Scandinavia. It was from these foreign assignments that I first became aware of the large number of former missionaries serving within the U.S. intelligence community.

In the forties, fifties, and sixties, most of the recruiting by the CIA, FBI, and NSA was done on the East Coast among the Ivy League schools.

Today, however, one of the top places for our government agencies to recruit is on the campuses of the colleges and universities in the Rockies.

It was as if the federal government, only in the last few decades, had finally become aware of such a valuable resource in the Rocky Mountain West. Utah, Colorado, Arizona, and other neighboring states have a large population of young adults, men and women who have had exposure to living abroad as missionaries for an extended period of time—eighteen months to two years. And as such, a great number have learned to speak at least one of the fifty major languages of the world with exceptional fluency.

Another important factor for their recruitment is their healthy life style, usually free from the problems associated with alcohol and drug abuse. A further aspect of their appeal to recruiters is that most of these young men and women tend to be patriotic and loyal to the ideals upon which our nation was founded.

It was during my very first assignment as a mission team leader in Scandinavia, that I realized I was not alone in my struggle to reconcile certain operational requirements with my religious convictions. I was sent to a pre-operation briefing in Frankfurt, Germany as one of five agents representing the five geographic regions for intelligence collection in Europe, Scandinavia, and the Eastern Bloc.

As we assembled the first morning in a secure conference room, waiting for the briefing to begin, the five of us introduced ourselves to one another. Of the five agents in that room, four of us had served years earlier in various countries as church missionaries.

Later that night, the five of us were having dinner at a German *Gasthaus* near the Frankfurt Railway Station, when the subject came up as to how we each came to terms regarding the conflict between our religious beliefs and our work as intelligence agents.

The oldest of the group, a senior officer with over twenty years of service, was the only one with whom I had previously worked. He was a devout Catholic and a wonderful man. He explained that in spite of our government's imperfections and shortcomings, he felt great pride to work in a job that helped protect our national security interests, which, in turn, helped preserve America's freedom and our democratic way of life. Even though his own family and friends would never know of his specific contributions in keeping our country free, he found immense satisfaction in his service.

Another officer related his feelings regarding his belief that the Constitution of the United States is divinely inspired. Because of this, he seldom questioned his work as being at odds with his Church membership. Two of the other agents even referred to passages of scripture that relate stories of several religious heroes being involved in clandestine spy work when their country or their people's survival depended on it.

By the time the evening was over, I felt that a heavy burden had been lifted from my shoulders.

It was comforting to know that other agents with strong beliefs had similar concerns as mine, and, yet, they continued to serve honorably.

I can't say that I never again had reservations about some of our government's decisions or any of my assignments, but from that time forward, I no longer questioned my service as an intelligence officer as being in conflict with my membership in the Church.

☆ ☆ ☆

After finishing the draft letters and spending so much of the evening reflecting on my life and my career, the temperature inside the safe house had dropped considerably. The outside wind was howling through the trees, causing a cold draft inside the cabin. I walked to the stove and added more wood to the fire. I went to the window to make one last check of the storm. By now there was well over three feet of snow on the ground.

Although I'd finished the last piece of bread given to me by Arkady and had nothing for tomorrow, I determined that a positive attitude was my new best approach. I decided I would spend the entire next day in the village visiting every single cabin if necessary. I told myself that by a show of faith on my part, and with the Lord's help, before darkness settled over Potevka the following evening, there would be food in the cabin for me to eat.

I took off my boots, crawled into bed, and pulled the blankets over me. With a heart longing for home, I settled into the straw mattress and lost myself in wonderful memories of my family and their activities during this Thanksgiving weekend.

I thought about the holiday meal preparations, decorating the home, the smell of hot cider, visiting relatives, the end-of-season college football games (the Utes hoping for a win against LaVell's BYU Cougars), my brothers cussing while trying to hang the strings of outdoor lights, and the frenzied first few days of Christmas shopping at the stores and malls.

I wanted to enjoy every thought, every memory, every one—except those related to food, which, of course, was next to impossible since the Thanksgiving holiday is synonymous with food: the fat, roasted turkey stuffed with sage dressing, buttered mashed potatoes with home-made gravy, hot rolls with raspberry jam, sweet buttered corn, wild rice, yams, cranberries, and pumpkin pie piled high with real whipped cream—I could taste every delightful bite.

The candle on the table finally burned out, but not before I was in a wonderful deep sleep, dreaming I was back home with my family, gathered around our dining table, enjoying the Thanksgiving feast.

As the blizzard continued, strong winds out of the North moved and drifted the snow throughout the night.

Chapter 23

PANDORA'S BAFFLING BOX

No passion so effectively robs the mind of its powers of acting and reasoning—as fear.
Edmund Burke

The next morning, just as the first light of day came into the cabin, I was awakened by the sound of an approaching vehicle. Startled, I sat up in bed, keeping perfectly still.

How could this be? Since my arrival in Potevka, I'd come across only four or five broken-down farm vehicles, but I had not seen or heard a single working automobile or truck.

The vehicle stopped on the ridge road not far from the cabin. I heard what sounded like a truck door open, then the faint noise of a person struggling through the snow towards the cabin. Immediately, I thought of Koshka and his mafia thugs and quickly got out of bed.

Suddenly, without warning, something slammed against the cabin door. Fearing the worst, I grabbed my boots and hid behind the tall storage closet at the back of the cabin.

The vehicle, which now sounded more like a jeep than a truck, started to drive off. I rushed to the window. Through the falling snow, I was barely able to see the taillights of a dark colored vehicle heading along the ridge road in a direction away from Potevka.

I ran back behind the storage closet, crouched down, and waited for the blast. My heart hammered in my chest.

Who had been here? And more importantly . . . what exactly was at the cabin door?

With trembling hands, anticipating the explosion, I struggled pulling on my boots and getting them laced. Hurriedly, I put on my *schapka*, coat, and gloves, then stood momentarily frozen, barely breathing. As I waited behind the closet, everything became so quiet and still, I was sure I could hear the snow falling outside the cabin.

After an insufferable amount of time, probably ten or fifteen minutes, I decided I must do something. I left the protection of the closet and walked across the room to the front door. Ever so slowly, I moved the table away from the door and carefully pulled it open a few inches. There in the snow next to the stone steps was a package approximately the size of a shoebox.

This certainly was not a mail delivery. As in most small Russian settlements, the villagers living here in Potevka picked up their post at the *kolkhoz* store every four days when the train passed through.

What was in the box? Who had brought it? And was it some kind of explosive device?

With several forced deep breaths, I reminded myself to stay calm and try to think clearly. Pulling the door open a few more inches, I looked down to where the box lay and then up towards the road where the vehicle had stopped.

Seeing the large boot tracks in the snow, it appeared that the person who brought the box had thrown it towards the cabin from a distance of fifteen or twenty feet away. That seemed strange.

If the package contained a bomb of some sort, wouldn't throwing it that far have caused it to detonate on impact?

I began to pace nervously back and forth from the open door to the back of the cabin, hearing again in my mind the words about Koshka's rage when he learned of our plan to smuggle him out of the country.

Was this an early "Christmas gift" from him?

From the back of the cabin, I grabbed a broom. With the door almost closed, I carefully stuck the broom handle through the slight opening. With my head protected behind the heavy oak door, I gently pushed and poked at the box with the broom handle. Nothing happened. After a few more minutes, I laid the broom aside and started to breath normally again.

Who brought this package here and why? Maybe it wasn't Koshka. Perhaps it was the KGB trying to get back at us.

It was a well-known fact that Russia still possessed large stockpiles of nuclear and biological weapons. One of our agency's recent covert operations had exposed several collaborating Soviet scientists and KGB agents trying to sell top secret, nuclear information to representatives of a Middle-Eastern country. It had been front-page news around the world and a significant embarrassment for the Soviet government. In such social and economic chaos, keeping Soviet nuclear-biological secrets and weaponry from third-world extremists had become a major focus of U.S. intelligence.

So, was the ominous box from the KGB? Were they trying to kill a U.S. agent in an attempt to get even?

Following a long period of fear and indecision, I finally pulled the cabin door all the way open. With the heavy snow still falling, I walked around the area where the box lay then up to the ridge road where I inspected the tracks of the vehicle. From the size of the tire tread and the apparent ease with which the vehicle had maneuvered through the deep snow, it must have been equipped with four-wheel drive—perhaps a military vehicle.

I returned to where the package lay and again poked it and pushed it around with the broom handle. After several more minutes standing over the box, I reached down and carefully picked it up and took it inside the cabin. Still hesitant, I purposely left the door open behind me.

I set the box on the table and began to study it over. Like everything purchased at that time in the USSR, whether fish, fruit, or furs, the package was wrapped in heavy, tan butcher paper. On my initial inspection, the box seemed to have no markings. It was secured with heavy twine all around.

Following more doubt and uncertainty, my worry-self began to take over. Under normal operational procedures, I would immediately notify our control center about such a package. But here, with no way to communicate with HQ, that was impossible. Besides, no one was to know I was here in Potevka.

Cautiously, I put the box to my ear but heard nothing.

Was this package meant specifically for me? Was it something good—or the bigger question—was it something to cause pain . . . even death? Was this, perhaps, the reason I had come back to Russia?

Eventually I decided that whatever was in the package, there was plenty of time to think more about it before I did something foolish and lost some of my fingers or my eyesight. I placed both hands securely around the box, walked through the open door, and carefully pushed through the snow to the outhouse where I placed the box on one of the large planks of the wooden floor.

When I finished my other business there, I pushed open the outhouse door.

Fifty yards away near the edge of the forest I saw them—five gray Russian wolves. Startled, they stood motionless, each yellow eye piercing the storm, looking directly at me. Surely, the rest of their pack was somewhere nearby.

Without the ax or any other weapon to protect myself, I was terrified. At least, for the moment, there was the safety of the outhouse. I slowly stepped back inside and closed the door.

Through a crack in the door, I stood watching the wolves, occasionally my eyes glancing down at the menacing box on the floor. It seemed I was now faced with two grisly choices: Would I rather be blown up by a box of explosives or torn apart by a pack of wolves? After a twenty minute standoff, the predators finally lost interest and disappeared back into the trees. Yet they knew someone was now occupying the vacant cabin near their territory in the forest.

Although I was freezing in the sub-zero weather, I waited another five minutes before pushing the door open. As I hustled back to the cabin, I kept a close watch over my shoulder. I decided then and there that whenever I made this trip again, I would carry the large ax with me, its blade newly sharpened.

Safely back inside the cabin, my mind drifted from the wolves back to the package. And then, for whatever reason, the thought came to me of the legendary story from Greek mythology—Pandora's Box. With all the problems and bad luck I'd been experiencing lately, I wondered . . . *Did this box have my name on it?*

Chapter 24

THE DEPTHS OF LOW AND A MURDER OF CROWS

You pray in your distress and in your need; would that you might pray also in the fullness of your joy and in the days of your abundance.

Kahlil Gibran
The Prophet

Back inside the cabin, I started a morning fire in the stove and began to heat water for tea, all the while pre-occupied with the mysterious box. My obsession for food was now replaced by my obsession with the package. It was obvious that—besides the pack of wolves—someone, somehow, knew that the agency safe house in Potevka was now occupied and that I was the house guest.

The storm had abated, at least compared to the fury of last evening, but the cold wind continued to blow out of the North as cruel as ever. Last night's winds had caused the drifting snow to pile up on one side of the cabin all the way to the edge of the roof.

I warmed my body with the hot, peppermint tea, which again re-awakened the hunger pains. I had no other choice, I needed to make another attempt to get food from somewhere in the village. I decided that this time I would try to locate the old *babushka* whom I had met at the train station the night I'd arrived. I should have discussed with her the incident of having my food sack stolen while on the train when I arrived in Potevka. Surely, she would have helped me.

I put on my snow gear, placed the hatchet in my backpack, locked up the cabin, and slowly plodded my way towards the village, all the while agonizing over the package.

When I reached the village, I knocked on the doors of the few cabins in which I could see a light burning. I was able to speak with only one couple, again elderly grandparents and much too old to have made the long, difficult trip to Moscow. But no matter how much I pleaded, they were not willing to part with any of their food.

"Is there a chance either of you know where the old woman lives who takes the mail from train when it stops here in Potevka?" I asked.

They shook their heads. "I'm sorry," the old man said, "we don't."

With only sixty to seventy families living in Potevka, to an outsider it might seem impossible that everyone did not know one another personally and know exactly where everyone lived. However, those who have lived in Russia know all too well the paranoia of the Soviet people because of the lingering fear of the KGB and its system of informants. In the huge, government housing projects of the larger cities, it was not uncommon for people not to know their neighbors—neighbors who had been living a few feet away in the same stairwell for years—even decades. Such fear and paranoia was what remained from Stalin's infamous purges when over twenty-two million Soviet citizens were taken from their homes and exiled to Siberian labor camps or summarily killed for being considered "enemies of the state."

While standing on their front step, still trying to persuade the old couple, I noticed a large apple tree in their side yard.

"Would it be alright with you if I were to look for any apples that might be under the snow?" I asked.

The old man nodded his head.

"You're welcome to look . . . but I'm certain that we picked all the apples a few months ago."

I thanked the old couple and bid them goodbye. I walked over to the tree and set my backpack down. There were a dozen or so apples still on the tree, but shriveled and frozen, now the size of a walnut.

With my gloved hands, I dug in the deep snow until I was able to locate a few apple remnants. As I pulled them from the frozen ground, each rotten piece came apart in my hands. It was clear that this was not a good idea. As I turned to walk away, I saw the window curtain drop where the old man had been standing, watching me.

I stood near the apple tree, rubbing my frozen hands together trying to get the circulation back, hoping the old couple might reconsider my urgent need for something to eat. After a few more minutes, I picked up my backpack and walked away. I needed to get my cold, stiff body moving again.

Although terribly weak, I struggled through the heavy snow along the ridge road to the other side of the village towards Arkady's cabin. I was concerned about going there and bothering him again, but I was desperate. As I approached his cabin, I was thrilled to see smoke coming from the chimney.

Regrettably, once I got there, Arkady would not answer my repeated knocking at his door. Giving him the benefit of a doubt, he probably couldn't hear me because of the ferocity of the wind beating against his cabin door. After a time, resting from the elements under his porch overhang, I turned and walked out into the storm.

By this time, both the power of the North wind and the amount of snow it brought had increased significantly. Visibility was almost down to zero; I could barely see four or five feet in front of me. As the blizzard increased, it became so bitterly cold I knew I had no choice but to get back to the protection of the safe house. It was crucial that I be able to follow my tracks in the snow before the storm got so bad that I wouldn't be able to find my way.

Plodding through the deep snow and drifts was so fatiguing that I had to stop several times to rest. After fighting against the storm for what seemed like hours, my body became so weak I couldn't go on. My legs simply gave out. I sat down and fell back in a large snowdrift near the side of the road. I pulled the hood of my coat completely down over my face. Totally spent, I stretched out on my back in the deep, soft snow.

As I lay there in the darkness I had created, my labored breathing eventually slowed; everything became quiet and still. I thought to myself . . . *Why not just lie here and rest until the worst of the storm passes?* Yet I knew if I didn't get up and force myself to move on, hypothermia would set in, and I would freeze to death.

Lying there, totally spent, with the blizzard raging around me, thoughts of dying began whispering in my mind. But rather than anguish or fear, strangely, I felt totally at peace. If it was my time to die, at the very least I would be able to see Mom and Dad and my sister, Kathleen, again.

After resting in the snow for I don't know how long, my body heat dissipated to the point that I began shivering uncontrollably. Then off in the distance I heard them—the howling wolves. In an instant I came to my senses. I might give up my life by freezing to death, but I certainly was not going to be survival food for a pack of hungry predators.

"Mike," I said to myself, "no matter how tired you are or how bad this blizzard is, you *have* to get up and get moving."

I rolled over and propped myself up in a kneeling position in the snow. While there I asked the Lord for His help, but for the first time in several days, my desperate prayer did not mention a thing about food—only for protection and the strength to make it back to the izba.

I struggled to my feet. I covered the exposed area of my face with my scarf, adjusting it just enough so that I could see directly in front of me as I walked. Again, I pulled the hood of my coat over my *schapka*. From my backpack, I pulled out the only protection I had if I were to come upon the wolves. With the hatchet firmly secured in my gloved right hand, I pushed on through the storm. It took over an hour and a half to make it back to the cabin.

Although I could not see them, I felt a great sense of relief as I approached the *izba* when I heard the crows in the nearby trees cawing their obnoxious banter. It meant that in a matter of minutes I would finally be out of the blizzard, protected by the shelter of my temporary home.

I had great difficulty trying to get the key into the lock and the door open; my fingers were useless stubs. My hands were so stiff and cold, it was all I could do to pull off my gloves. I removed the scarf from around my neck and face and managed to partially open my coat and the tops of my two wool shirts. With my arms folded across my chest, I placed my aching hands under each armpit. As the warmth of my body began to thaw my frozen fingers and thumbs, the unexpected pain felt like a thousand needles being forced deep into each of my hands. After ten minutes or so, I was finally able to get my fingers to work and maneuver the key into the lock. By the time I got inside the cabin, every inch of my body was numb.

The fire in the stove had burned itself out hours ago. Walking across the room, I looked in the mirror and saw that ice crystals completely covered my beard and mustache; I had no feeling in my face whatsoever. Somehow, I managed to light the candle sitting on the table.

Still wearing my coat and *schapka*, I walked past the lifeless stove and crawled onto the bed and dragged the pile of blankets over me; my numb feet in my frozen boots extended over the end of the straw mattress. I lay on the bed staring across the room, the flickering candle casting bizarre shapes on the cabin ceiling, as a mountain of dark feelings came over me.

From time to time during my career, I thought about the inherent risks of this work, about the possibility of dying, and under what circumstances it might happen. But never once did I consider that my life could possibly end like this. Rather than dying as a patriot at the hands of the KGB or Russian mafia while in the service of my country, I would only be remembered for having died of starvation or freezing to death in some far-away place due to my negligence of not being properly prepared for the Russian winter.

After all the service and sacrifice I have made for our country, how could this be happening to me? I had suffered a severe beating, my aching head had a hole in it, I couldn't hear out of my left ear, some of my ribs were probably fractured. And why would someone on the train steal the only food I had to eat? And why had my own headquarters abandoned me out here without any support whatsoever? How could these people in Potevka be so callous and uncaring? I might be a stranger in their village, but I'm still a human being! And, most heartbreaking of all—after I was able to survive the gunshots and confrontation with the mafia back in Siberia—why would even the Lord now abandon me in Potevka, leaving me here to die?

I know I'm far from perfect and have made more than my share of mistakes in life . . . but it seems that I continue to struggle, year in and year out, without any indication whatsoever that the Lord knows who I am or that He even cares.

Tears rolled off the side of my face onto the straw pillow, as I lay on the bed watching the candle slowly burn down and down—and then, finally, die.

I'm not asking for the heavens to open . . . but why, just once, couldn't You—someway, somehow—let me know that You are there? Some small token of reassurance would mean a great deal to me right now, especially in such dire circumstances as these.

And, yes, Lord, I do realize that there are many people in difficult situations throughout the world that need Your help a lot more than I. But, regardless, at this moment—at this crucial time—this is me! It is my life on the line! I would like the chance to see my boy again, to see my family, my home, and the Rocky Mountains at least one more time. I'm the one who every day has desperately been pleading for Your help, but, again, it's obvious—You simply don't care!

My aching body, the constant hunger, the relentless storm, the cold and darkness, and the feelings of abandonment, they were all part of the depressing gloom that was beginning to consume me. Despite the storm and my weak condition, if it weren't for the wolves, I would have taken my self-pity and gone up the hill to the road above the *izba* and continued my diatribe against the Lord. Unfortunately, I knew the only thing that would accomplish would be—once again—to scatter the cantankerous crows into the night.

Following what seemed like an endless period of time wrestling in the darkness with my demons, the anger and hurt eventually subsided. And then came the guilt—guilt because of my thoughts, but mostly because of my words.

After lying on the straw bed for the better part of an hour, trying to make sense of it all, I threw back the covers and walked to the stove. I restarted the fire. Fifteen minutes later, long enough for the fire to take the chill out of the cabin, I took off my coat and *schapka* and sat at the edge of the bed with my head in my hands, staring at the floor. I knew I needed to do something to shake the awful despair that had come over me.

In an attempt to occupy my mind and focus on something positive, I sat down at the table, pulled my portfolio from my backpack, and forced myself to work on the draft letters. My spirits momentarily lifted to know that my family would finally hear from me as soon as I got back to our embassy in Moscow and mailed their letters home.

As I wrote, more troubling thoughts crept in. *Was there a chance I might never see Chris, my family, or Bonnie again? But then . . . would it really matter to anyone if I didn't make it back home?*

The dark feelings were still there, oppressive as ever.

I stopped, put my pen down on the table, and— *What had I written in the letters?* So many negative thoughts ran through my head. I began to worry that my family might detect from my words just how bad things were for me and how discouraged I was. They didn't need to hear any of that.

I gathered the letters together and walked over to the stove. One by one, I slowly placed them into the fire. I stood and watched the red, orange, and blue flames curl around each page and turn it to ashes. As the last letter disappeared up in smoke, I stepped back from the stove mesmerized, as tears again ran down my face.

After several minutes staring at the fire, more feelings of guilt and shame came over me.

Mike, now what have you done? How could you be so stupid and selfish, especially in regards to your own son?

For the second time in his life, my boy Chris had recently left home and was now halfway around the world, struggling as a new missionary. He was living in a foreign land, dealing with an unfamiliar culture. He, too, must be experiencing times of discouragement and homesickness. What he needed was a letter from his old man. He needed to hear words of encouragement and support, of how proud his dad was of him and the work he was doing.

I brooded around the cabin, full of remorse and self-pity because of what I had done with the letters and my earlier outburst towards the Lord. I stopped my pacing and stood in front of the old, pitted mirror hanging on the cabin wall. What I saw was the ghost of a man I didn't want to be.

How could my life have reached such an awful low point? What had happened . . . to my honor and pride, my sense of duty to my family, to my country, and to myself?

In that moment, I remember being more discouraged and depressed than I had ever been in my life.

I tried to reason with myself, to make some sense of what was happening. The last several days could have occurred to any agent with an assignment like mine. And I knew when I chose this line of work there could possibly be days like this. I reminded myself that I had willingly accepted this current mission and how proud I felt to be part of what U.S. intelligence was trying to accomplish at this critical time during the collapse of the Soviet Union. Yet, despite my best efforts to convince myself otherwise, what was happening to me, both physically and emotionally, was more than I ever bargained for.

☆ ☆ ☆

The gray daylight soon gave way to winter's darkness. I sat at the table still thinking about the letters I'd burned, ashamed for what I had done. I picked up the three photographs I'd carried with me since leaving home—a photo of Chris, a small snapshot of Bonnie, and a group photo of my family. I placed the photographs on the table and tried to focus on them, on home, and the good things in my life. I took out my notebook and pen and set them on the table, intending to start redrafting the letters.

Before I began, I fixed more hot tea, telling myself that as long as I had fluids I could make it three more days until Sunday when the train would take me away from Potevka and to the American Embassy in Moscow.

Thinking about being back on the train and making that first stop at a large railway station and my chance to buy some food, I became distracted from my writing. Instead of the letters, I wrote out the Russian words and phrases I would need for my future conversation with the first old *babushka* I saw who would sell me her awful smoked salt-fish and cabbage rolls—at least it was food!

Then unexpectedly from out of nowhere—survival training from twenty years ago—*Would it be possible to set some sort of snare or trap to catch one of the crows that nested in the nearby trees?* My mind raced with the possibilities. *And, better yet, if I could catch a crow . . . then why not a rabbit?* I knew I had seen one or two of the furry creatures hopping around in the bushes the previous day while on my way to the village. *Which would be easiest to catch—a crow or a rabbit?* I decided my chances were better trying to trap one of the crows. There were dozens upon dozens of the irritable, noisy things at the edge of the forest less than fifty yards from the *izba.* I thought of how easy it would be to boil the meat off the bird and then re-boil the bones to make broth for another meal. I could almost taste the steaming meat sitting on a plate in front of me.

But what about the wolves? How would I keep them from my trapped prey? I would think of something.

Energized by the possibilities, I took my penlight to the back of the cabin and searched through the storage closet, trying to find anything that I could use as a trap. I set aside one of the water buckets and a long length of twine that I would experiment with when daylight returned. I had now come up with a plan—a plan that had a real chance of succeeding. I told myself that by mid-morning tomorrow there would be a crow under the water bucket—if not two, maybe even three.

But what would I use for bait to entice the crows to my trap? Why hadn't I thought about this earlier? I should have saved a crust from the three slices of bread Arkady gave me. In spite of this possible flaw, I was determined that I would figure out a way to make it all work.

I'm ashamed to admit it, but while so desperate for something to eat—especially with the thought of catching, killing, and eating a crow—another idea began to stir in my mind, *What were my chances of breaking into one of the empty cabins and taking just enough food to get me through the next few days?*

Most of the villagers, after all, were several hundred miles away in Moscow, and surely, I would be honorable and leave them more than enough *rubles* to make up for the few food rations I would take. *After all*, I told myself, *it wasn't really stealing—it was survival.* The idea kept turning over and over in my mind, becoming more enticing the more I considered it. It definitely seemed a lot more palatable than eating crow.

The devil had now offered me his solution in my struggle to survive.

It is amazing how all-consuming food becomes when one has gone several days without any and what measures a person will take to satisfy that most basic of all human instincts.

Following an extended period of time, debating the pros and cons of breaking into one of the cabins, I finally came to my senses. *Of course it would be stealing! How could I involve myself in doing such a thing? Especially to think of all the problems and trouble it would cause if I were to get caught.*

Oh the cruelty of hunger—how it can blur one's perspective about what is right and wrong.

And to think, only a few days earlier I was *furious* that someone on the train would be so callous and corrupt as to steal my food sack.

So, I wondered, *how would crow actually taste?*

Chapter 25

A FORTUNE COOKIE

O Lord my God! When I in awesome wonder
Consider all the works Thy hands have made,
I see the stars, I hear the mighty thunder,
Thy power throughout the universe displayed.
Then sings my soul my Savior God to Thee,
How great Thou art! How great Thou art!

Stuart K. Hine
How Great Thou Art

After dismissing the idea of breaking into one of the vacant cabins, I sat at the table wrestling with the idea of how crow might taste when suddenly—as if to complicate things even more—thoughts of the package I had stashed in the outhouse came flooding back stronger and more powerful than ever. But this time, something was different.

Not really knowing why, I pushed my letter-writing aside and rose from the table. I unlocked the door and went out into the night—even leaving my coat, *schapka,* and the ax behind. Foolish as it might sound, for some inexplicable reason all my fears and concerns about the package were gone. Something told me, *Whatever is in the box . . . is not a bad thing.*

With little concern for the wolves, I pushed my way through the snow to the outhouse, opened the door, picked up the package, and carried it back to the cabin.

Once inside I set it on the table and brushed away the snow. I carefully studied the box, turning it from side to side, end to end. Again I put it to my ear but heard nothing.

With no further excuses, I took a deep breath and ever so carefully began to undo the twine.

As I pulled away the outer layer of Russian butcher paper in which the package was double-wrapped, my eyes immediately fixed on the address label that was glued to the side of the box. There, written on the label was my name and the APO address of the American Embassy in Helsinki, Finland. I was dumbfounded. *It couldn't be!* There was no mistaking whose handwriting this was—I had seen it a thousand times before. The handwriting was that of my sister, Karen.

Three years older than I, Karen was the next youngest in our family. In our youth, she and I were like typical brother and sister—most of the time at odds with one another. Although we grew up in the country, she wasn't interested in ridin' horses, huntin' for birds, or fishin' down on the Bear River, and she especially wasn't good at sports of any kind; therefore, I really had little use for her. Yet, for whatever reason—and usually against my wishes—Karen took it upon herself to look after me, her little brother. Perhaps she did it to help our mom, who was along in years and, by then, justifiably worn out.

Mom had already raised a large family under poor and difficult conditions. My dad, a forty-five year old patriot, twenty-plus years beyond draft age, left Mom and us kids to serve in World War II.

Actually, at the age of my parents and as poor as they were, I'm certain I came into our already-large family as an unwelcome surprise. According to my older siblings, when Mom found out she was pregnant with me—her seventh child—five months passed before she ever spoke to my dad again.

As I matured into my late teenage years and became aware that there was more to life than football and hanging out with my buddies, I came to realize what a wonderful sister Karen was. It was during this time that we became best friends.

Could it be that this was a care package from Karen? If so, it was typical of her kindness. Like my sister Sally, Karen seldom forgot a birthday, a holiday, or special event.

But, still, how on earth did the package get from Torrance, California, to the American Embassy in Helsinki, Finland, and then find its way to me in the tiny village of Potevka, Russia? And, strangest of all, how did it manage to arrive at my cabin door on Thanksgiving Day?

My heart raced as I slowly removed the lid from the box. It was crammed full of things, all unrecognizable because each item was individually wrapped in newspaper from the *Los Angeles Times*.

I held my breath as I carefully removed the largest item first. As the newspaper wrapping fell to the floor, there in my hands was a box of Kraft Macaroni and Cheese. I was STUNNED—I couldn't believe it! I now possessed the main course for my Thanksgiving dinner! Next, I unwrapped a small jar of artichoke hearts, one of my very favorite, rare indulgences. Yes! Then, out of the box came tomorrow's breakfast—a mini box of Kellogg's Frosted Flakes. Next came a small plastic bag filled with crumbs and dark broken pieces of something, most of it now powder from the months or more of travel. On the side of the plastic bag I was able to make out the worn, discolored words—"Oreo Cookies." Holding the bag of crumbs in my hands, I thought to myself—*Oh . . . if this cabin's accommodations only came with a cow!*

My hands were trembling, my heart pounding, and my stomach growling. Miraculously—somehow, someway—I had food. I was a million miles away from home, but I was *definitely* going to be able celebrate Thanksgiving! And to think, only a few hours earlier, I was worried that this package might blow up in my face!

Then, to my delight, I next pulled from the box, what was for me, *The Holy Grail*—a Hershey's with Almonds Chocolate Candy Bar. *Rapture!* Still to this day, my one true addiction.

Next was a small bag of gummi bears and a pack of Black Jack Chewing Gum—my very favorite—the kind we used to buy for a nickel at Bernard's General Store when I was a boy. Growing up in our little town with Karen, only she could know what all these things would mean to me.

The last items in the box were two small candle figurines—Thanksgiving Pilgrims. At the bottom of the box was a beautiful Thanksgiving card signed with words of love.

With the butcher paper and newspapers scattered across the floor, I placed the items on the table and reminded myself to breathe again. It was truly a miracle! There before me on the table was food—*American food.* This was going to be a Thanksgiving unlike any other, and crow would definitely *not* be on the menu!

I couldn't believe that someone had brought this treasure to the safe house and in such a storm as this. *But how . . . and why . . . and by whom?*

I sat on the bed trying to collect my thoughts, totally amazed by what had happened. At that moment, I would have given anything to be able to telephone Karen and try to explain. She would never believe all that I had to tell her.

Holding the box of macaroni and cheese next to my chest, I stood and walked to the window and looked out at the falling snow, my heart and mind seven thousand miles away back home in America.

No longer could I hold back the tears, for these were tears of joy for a loving Heavenly Father, for belonging to a wonderful family, and for a dear sister, who had remembered me on this Thanksgiving Day. I pulled a chair away from the table, dropped to my knees, and poured out my heart in a prayer of gratitude to the Lord.

By now it was early evening. Darkness covered the village as the snow continued to fall. I added more wood to the fire and readied the table for my Thanksgiving meal. I used a thin blanket from the closet as my tablecloth. The two pilgrim candles were my centerpiece. Although desperately hungry, I forced myself to set aside a portion of the contents of the box for the following day.

Using boiled snow-water, I took longer than necessary to prepare the macaroni and cheese—it was my Thanksgiving dinner, and I wanted it to be as perfect as possible.

Finally, everything was ready. The delightful aroma of cheese sauce and pasta filled the room. I placed the food on the table and lit the pilgrim candles. As I knelt down to ask a blessing on the food, once more the wonder of what had happened filled my heart. Again, I was overcome with emotion as I expressed my gratitude to the Lord for this miracle and for reminding me of one of life's important lessons:

It is not the Lord's way or His plan to take away our hardships and difficulties. It is these challenges that give us the opportunity to grow in faith, character, and understanding. And if we won't give up, He will be at our side to help us see them through.

While on my knees, I asked Him, again, to please forgive me for my doubts, my lack of faith, and for the regrettable words I had expressed to Him in anger.

I sat down at the table. Words cannot express how wonderful the hot macaroni and cheese tasted! Ravenous as I was, I was determined to make the meal and the evening last as long as possible by eating only one noodle at a time.

Such an idea brought a smile to my face as I thought back to my youth and Mrs. Billy Bean, my first grade teacher. During lunch period in our small grade school cafeteria back in Bear River, she would admonish—actually demand—that we kids appreciate the food we had to eat, to think about the starving kids in China, and chew each mouthful at least twenty times. *Yes, Mrs. Bean, tonight—I promise—I will definitely comply with all three of your requests.*

With the noodles disappearing one by one, and me savoring each and every bite, I glanced over at the discarded newspapers on the floor. As I looked down at them, I soon realized they were not just random newspapers but a collection of the sports sections from several Sunday papers. Thank you, dear Karen! Not only Thanksgiving dinner but, also, the gift of hours catching up on football and other sports back home in America for a once-skinny high school quarterback.

When I reached down to pick up the section of newspaper nearest me, something fell out of it. There on the cabin floor was a fortune cookie broken apart. I moved my chair, knelt down, and picked up the pieces, including a small strip of paper—a hand-written fortune. I placed the broken cookie on the table, then held the tiny piece of paper close to the candlelight. It read:

"Little Brother, Although you are away from us this Thanksgiving, always remember how much we love you and how proud we are!"

I will never forget that moment.

After several minutes trying to contain my emotions, I couldn't help but notice that for some reason the night darkness outside the cabin seemed to be fading—almost as if it were morning. As it grew brighter, I pushed the chair away from the table. I stood and walked to the window.

I was amazed to see that for the first time in days the storm had totally subsided. No snow—no wind. I grabbed the blanket from the chair where I was sitting and draped it around my shoulders. Opening the cabin door, I stood on the steps, awestruck by what I saw above me in the night sky.

A large, winter moon was shining down through the high, broken clouds, which now illuminated the entire snow-covered Potevka valley. Within minutes the night sky became so placid and clear that it seemed I could see every galaxy in the entire universe as a billion stars blinked on and off in the dark, blue abyss.

With the absence of the howling wind, it became so incredibly quiet, not even the annoying crows in the nearby trees dared make a sound to break the powerful silence. Time seemed suspended. Though thousands of miles away from my home and family, a warm, indescribable feeling came over me—a feeling of peace and love and that *I was not alone*.

I stood looking out over the valley, into the heavens, humbled and amazed by the goodness of the Lord and the wonder of His universe. For the first time in my life, I had an overwhelming sensation—an undeniable awareness that in spite of all my shortcomings, mistakes, and little faith, the Lord really did care about me and loved me.

Awed by what I was experiencing, the music and words of the beloved, old, Swedish hymn began to whisper:

Then sings my soul my Savior God to Thee,
How great Thou art! How great Thou art!"

Then, in that tranquil, serene moment something happened—something that even now, years later, I cannot explain. I heard no voices, I saw no personages, nor did I see a bright light. It was as if my consciousness was touched and I was made to understand:

One of the greatest gifts that God gives to each of us is the love we share with our family, friends, and fellowmen. It is this divine gift of love that enriches us, gives meaning and purpose to life, and makes it all worth living. Everything else in life is secondary. Everything. And when our time here on earth is over, our lives will not be measured by the riches we accumulate, the honors we receive, the degrees we acquire, or the professional success we achieve, but by our capacity to love and be loved.

The message was simple and clear; not one of reprimand or guilt, but one of love. It was something that I needed, especially at this time in my life. In the last few years, I had hardened my heart because of my failed marriage. I was constantly feeling sorry that my life wasn't what it should be, foolishly thinking that I was the only person with problems. I was so caught up in the things of the world, trying to compensate through my work and career for my failures, that I had forgotten many of life's most important things.

Everyone has challenges and problems; it was time I stopped complaining and blaming. We are all on this journey of life together, each given certain gifts to make this world a better place and to help make one another's burdens a little lighter along the way.

And as for my future and my concern about being alone—sure my son was now a young man and on his own, but still, he would always need a dad. And my brothers and sisters each had their own busy lives and families, but I could still be a brother to them. And I had wonderful friends who cared about me and supported me; it was time I started giving back to those relationships. It was time that I started to focus on the good and appreciate just how blessed my life was.

The isolation and the longing for home I had suffered for the last several months were totally gone. I'd never before had such a profound emotional experience, one that I did not want to end.

It might sound trite in today's world, but on that frozen winter night, standing alone outside the *izba* in that small Russian village—undeserving as I might have been—I truly believe that for one brief moment the Lord touched my soul. And for that once-in-a-lifetime experience, I will forever be grateful.

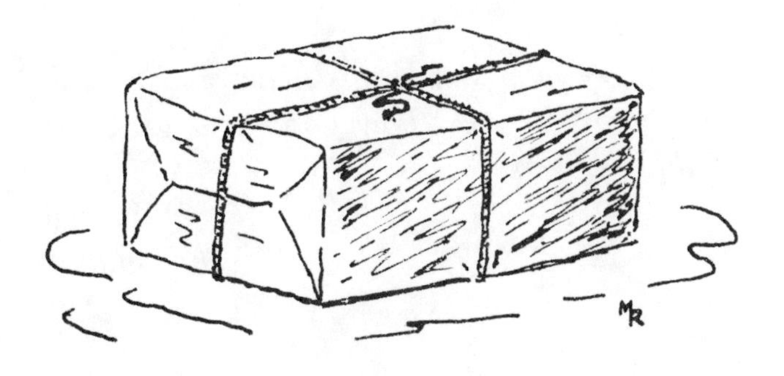

Chapter 26

GUMMI BEARS AND CHRISTMAS CAROLS

Let every man search his heart and his life and consider . . . how good and gracious God has been.

Editorial
The Outlook

The storm's momentary lull soon ended. The winds began to pick up and blow dark clouds back over the Potevka valley and, with it, the snow. The frigid temperature soon became too much to ignore. Reluctantly, I left the cabin steps and went back inside.

With the blanket still draped around my shoulders, I added more wood to the fire and then sat down at the table. I tried to focus on what had just happened. I wanted to remember in detail everything I had seen and, especially, what I had felt. I got out pen and paper and started writing.

An hour passed before I returned to my dinner. After reheating the mac and cheese, I finished the few remaining noodles. Then I remembered that I even had Thanksgiving dessert yet to eat.

I counted out fifteen gummi bears, exactly one fourth of the packet and made a rainbow of my colorful friends around the rim of my dinner plate. For each gummi bear devoured, I offered up my short rendition of a favorite Christmas song.

Back home in the evening hours, following our big Thanksgiving feast—after the adults had taken their naps, the kids were back inside the house from their football game in the snow-covered pasture, and most everyone was ready for a cup of hot chocolate or cider and another piece of pumpkin pie—a long-standing family tradition would take place. We would all gather together in the living room to sing Christmas carols. After singing for an hour or more, we always had to finish with "Silent Night," which never failed to make Mom cry.

My Potevka Thanksgiving lasted into the late evening. Even my two roommates, Ma and Pa *meeshka,* went to sleep fat and happy, having devoured every crumb I threw near their living quarters—a hole in the corner of the cabin wall. They appeared especially delighted with the pieces of Oreo cookies. As if to show their gratitude, they would sit on their little haunches and consume each bite right in front of me without taking their treasure back to the safety of their hiding place.

The snow continued to fall all through the night.

In the morning, following a long, restful night's sleep—my first in months—I eagerly dressed in my snow gear for a walk to the far side of the village. Motivated by the goodness of my sister Karen, I returned to the cabin where Arkady lived.

Smoke was coming from his chimney, but this time I didn't attempt to knock. Expecting he would not answer the door, I left him a short note telling him of my good fortune and thanking him again for his kindness. Along with the note, I left this fine man his first Hershey's with Almonds Chocolate Candy Bar.

✯ ✯ ✯

In the next two days, I had ample time to reflect on what had taken place and what it meant for my future. My Potevka experience certainly changed the way I looked at the world and my place in it. During the long hours of contemplation, waiting out the storm, I made several important decisions that affected the rest of my life, but none more important than the promises to myself that—*everyday I would appreciate the miracle of life that God gives to each of us; I would show greater love to my family and friends; and never again would I take for granted the wonderful, simple, everyday things of life.*

As I contemplated my future, thoughts of Bonnie kept getting in the way. How long was I going to deny the feelings I had for her? I hadn't seen her for so long, and by now she could very well be engaged or involved in a serious relationship.

Whatever the case, I promised myself, then and there, that I would take to heart the advice of Bishop Frazier. If Bonnie was still unattached when I returned back home to America, and if she was still interested in our relationship, I would finally be honest with her about my true feelings. Perhaps we could find a way to make it work after all.

☆ ☆ ☆

Two days later I rose early in the morning, dressed, and built a final fire in the stove. After some peppermint tea and the last six gummi bears, I cleaned and organized the cabin. When it became light enough, I went outside to the rear of the cabin and chopped more wood for the cabin's next occupant. Back inside, I repacked each of my bags.

Just before noon I locked up the *izba* for the last time and hid the key under the large rock next to the cabin. I pushed my way through the snow storm to the small station where I would catch the scheduled train that would finally take me to Moscow and to the American Embassy.

At the railway station, I was thrilled to see the old *babushka* I'd met the night of my arrival. She seemed as genuinely pleased to see me as I was to see her.

I told her about what had happened during my stay in Potevka and about my efforts to find her. She was truly sorry that my visit had been so traumatic. She explained to me exactly where she lived and insisted that I stay with her if I ever made it back to Potevka.

I never did have that opportunity to return, and I have always regretted that I didn't think to leave two envelopes full of rubles for her and Arkady. They were both kind and noble people whom I will never forget.

I survived my days in Potevka and one of the worst winter blizzards that area of Russia had experienced in decades. It was an emotional moment as I boarded the train, as if something were pulling at me to stay. I told myself that I would return, but I knew in my heart it would never happen.

Looking back, as the train slowly pulled from the station, the old *babushka* was standing on the platform waving her scarf high above her head.

Potevka had taught me so much about people and about myself. I would always remember my days spent there and the life-awakening experience I'd had. But now it was time for me to leave. In a matter of days I would be back at our embassy in Moscow—finally safe—among Americans.

☆ ☆ ☆

The train to Moscow was almost identical in every way to the one that had brought me to Potevka—over-crowded, foul smelling, and miserably slow. The one redeeming thing, however, was that the boiler worked. Unfortunately, this increased the putrid smells inside the rail car, but at least we had heat. I kept my schapka stuffed inside my duffel bag and wore a stocking cap pulled over my head to hide my bandages.

When I boarded the rail car there were no seats. For my first four hours on board, I alternated between long periods of standing, holding on to the overhead luggage bar, and sitting on my duffel bag in the aisle way. A seat finally became vacant when a worker sitting near me got off the train after reaching his destination. I sat on a bench next to two young teenage boys whose parents and little sister occupied the row in front of us. Following a half day of sitting next to them, the boys finally warmed up towards me, as did their parents, when I began to teach the boys some basic German words and phrases. They seemed to enjoy a game I made up of how many things the boys could remember—in German—both inside and outside the rail car as we traveled; anything to kill the endless hours on the train.

During one of our first long stops that evening, the father was kind enough to buy me a loaf of bread when he left the train with his children to take a break from the monotony of the journey. In the afternoon of my second day on board, the father bought me not only a new loaf of bread but also six apples and four sausages. I was so thankful for the food, for which I paid him generously. I continued to consume the awful Russian black tea that was available at the end of rail car.

For the next three days on the train, I didn't worry that much about the mafia or KGB. After what I had survived, I felt the Lord had a reason for me to make it back to Moscow without further incident. I tried to sleep as much as possible on the noisy, rocking train. Yet I mostly kept thinking of the moment when I would finally arrive in Moscow and hitch a ride from the Yaroslavski Railway Station to our embassy, when off in the distance I would be able to see a red, white, and blue flag, the flag of the United States of America, flying proudly over the embassy compound. Finally, I would almost be home.

Chapter 27

A DOLLAR FROM DOWN UNDER

A joy that is shared is a joy made double.
English Proverb

I ended up spending more than two weeks at the American Embassy in Moscow recovering from my injuries. While being treated by the medical staff, they discovered my head wound to be more serious than expected. Because of the amount of blood lost, I was put on a special medication to help speed up its regeneration. Also, x-rays showed four of my ribs were fractured. I was placed on extended medical leave in order to receive the proper treatment I needed and assigned a temporary duty apartment on the embassy compound. The additional days of rest would give my sore body more time to recover.

Besides getting medical care, my first week at the embassy was spent with agency officials in long, grueling debriefings. In an effort to create a mission damage report—blame had to be placed on someone—every aspect of what went wrong in Siberia was dissected over and over.

During the afternoon of the fourth day, I was taken into a conference room where I was surprised to see my Helsinki supervisor, his boss from European headquarters, and two officials from the Special Operations Directorate in Washington, D.C. Once again, a detailed chronological review of the events of the aborted mission took place.

The following day, in a similar meeting with the same group of people, the ranking official from D.C. revealed that mission headquarters had made a grave error by sending me to Potevka, which—unbeknownst to me—had placed my life in peril.

Three months prior to my arrival there, our agency had designated the Potevka safe house as non-operational—shut down and off limits. The agency had reason to believe that the safe house had been compromised by the KGB.

As a result of this mistake, a controller and his supervisor at headquarters had been relieved of their duties and an internal investigation was underway. The investigation stemmed from the decision by certain individuals at HQ to leave me alone in Tayginsk after the failed mission, unprotected and without any backup or support, while sending the two senior agents back to Moscow to the safety of our American Embassy.

Several ranking officials—part of the "Good Old Boy Washington Establishment" that had given me problems from our mission's beginning in Helsinki—were now in serious trouble.

At the end of the week of meetings, I was notified that because of the events that took place in Siberia and the mafia threat against me, rather than sending me back to the States, Washington agreed to let me complete my remaining two months in a low-profile, low-risk assignment a few hundred miles from Moscow.

After Siberia, the dreadful days on the train, my struggles to survive in Potevka—and in spite of the awful week of debriefings—being at the embassy was like heaven. Besides receiving medical treatment for my injuries, I was able to mail letters home, take multiple hot showers daily, and stay in the embassy cafeteria for as long as I wanted.

Most importantly, at the embassy post office I was able to pick up my mail, which included five letters from a young missionary now serving in the land of koalas and kangaroos. He was doing just great. I read each of his letters over and over, at least a dozen times or more. Among the other mail, there was even a letter from my brother, Ted.

Although I'd never admit as to the cost of the postage, I boxed together the three staples of Chris' diet, which I was able to buy at the embassy store: two large cans of Hunts' Spaghetti Sauce, a couple boxes of spaghetti noodles, and a bottle of A-1

Sauce. The Christmas card had to be a handmade one.

☆ ☆ ☆

During my second week at the embassy, after more food, showers, and rest, I started feeling much better. I was even gaining back some of the weight I'd lost during the previous month.

Despite the political unrest in the Soviet capital, on one particular afternoon, free of meetings and medical treatments, I got permission to walk downtown to see some of the historical sights of Moscow. As I was advised would happen, within minutes of leaving the embassy compound, a KGB agent—a shadow—began to follow me. This had nothing to do with what had happened to me in Tayginsk but was normal procedure for any unknown foreigner exiting the American Embassy.

After walking a half hour or so, I came to the *Arbat,* a busy, congested area in the heart of the city full of small shops and outdoor kiosks. Because of its central location and heavy foot traffic—but due primarily to the dire circumstances in the Soviet capital—the sidewalks were lined with thousands of poor, ragged people selling anything and everything imaginable in order to get money to buy food. Along with the ever-present drunkards and beggars, there were artists and musicians performing their talents in hopes of being given a few *rubles* from those passing by.

While pausing for a moment to listen to a trio of classical musicians, without warning, on the opposite side of the large crowd I spotted them—

two men dressed in black, approximately one hundred feet away, walking directly towards me. My breathing stopped; my legs refused to move. From a distance, in their dark suits and dark overcoats, there was no doubt they were Russian mafia. Forty or fifty feet away, our eyes made momentary contact.

This can't be happening after all that I've gone through . . . and right here in downtown Moscow!

For the last two weeks, Siberia and Tayginsk, Koshka and his mafia men—they all seemed like a distant dream. But now, here I was, a mile from our embassy, alone, without a weapon or communication device. My legs turned to Jell-O.

I looked behind me to check the location of my KGB shadow. He had stopped when I had, pretending to be looking in a shop window. He had not seen the two men coming towards me, nor could he anticipate what was about to happen. He had the authority to intervene and help me, but would he?

My heart pounded in my chest.

As the two men got closer, it became even more evident—because of their business-like attire—how they stood out from the hundreds of shabbily-dressed Muscovites along the busy *Arbat.* To my astonishment, however, both of these men wore smiles as large as the big, furry *schapkas* on their heads. And, *INCONCEIVABLE*, as they walked past me—close enough for me to reach out and touch—I couldn't believe my eyes—both had Mormon missionary name tags pinned to their overcoats!

I stood dumbfounded, totally unable to utter a word, as they walked right by me. They were ten or fifteen feet past me before I was able to get my mouth to work. "ELDERS!" I yelled out through the crowd.

They stopped, turned around, grinned.

As we walked towards each other, I was so excited I couldn't help myself. Without saying a word, I brushed aside their extended hand shakes and gave them both a big bear hug.

It was a great thrill—*actually a great relief*—to meet them. They were part of the very first group of missionaries that had been sent by the Church to Moscow. They introduced themselves as Elder Pitts from Broken Arrow, Arizona and Elder Redd from Farmington, Utah.

Chris was not going to believe this! In one of his letters that I picked up only a week earlier when I'd arrived at the embassy, Chris told me that one of his high school classmates had been sent to serve his two-year Church mission in Moscow, Russia.

"Dad," he wrote, "If your travels ever take you to Moscow, please locate Elder Redd and take him and his companion to dinner." Chris had included a dollar in his letter as a bribe.

I carried the dollar in my wallet with my supply of *rubles* as a reminder of my obligation to his friend.

But what Chris didn't understand, at this point in time a permanent place in Moscow had not been found where Church meetings could be held on a regular basis, let alone the existence of a mission headquarters. Therefore, I had no way of making contact with his high school friend. Yet, at this very moment, here stood Elder Redd right in front of me.

When I introduced myself to the elders and told them my name, Elder Redd immediately asked, "You wouldn't happen to know any Ramsdells in Farmington, Utah, would you?"

"Elder Redd," I replied with a smile, "I'm from Farmington and Chris Ramsdell is my son."

Suddenly, Elder Pitts was holding Elder Redd's backpack and briefcase, while two grown men engaged in another long back-slapping bear hug.

Elder Redd had been an exceptional student, and the more we talked, the more certain I was that I could remember him when, as a parent, I had attended various student-scholar award assemblies at our local junior high and high school.

Elder Redd was tall, dark, and handsome but much too thin if he was going to survive his two years in food-scarce Russia. His companion, Elder Pitts, on the other hand, was pushing five-foot-five and seemed as wide as he was tall. Elder Pitts would *definitely* not have to worry about surviving his two years. It was a joy to be in their company and to feel their positive, upbeat spirit, especially after all the darkness I had experienced during the last few months.

They seemed as excited to meet me as I was to meet them—an American in Moscow and a Westerner to boot! I wanted to hear everything about their experiences and how their work was progressing. I wanted to know about their lives, their families, and what news they'd heard from back home in the States.

After our initial few minutes of spirited conversation, I proposed taking them to dinner later that evening. After all, I had Chris' dollar in my wallet! Unfortunately they had to decline. Following seventy years of Communist isolation, the Russian people were starved for news and information from outside the Soviet Union. With their new-found freedoms under Gorbachev, including religious freedom, many in this city of twelve million were interested in learning about other faiths and churches beyond the borders of Russia. The dozen missionaries assigned to Moscow couldn't keep up with the demand. Elder Redd explained they had teaching appointments from early morning until late each evening.

"Then you do have meetings tonight?" I asked, hoping I'd heard wrong.

"Yes, Brother Ramsdell, we have three appointments set for this evening." Elder Redd replied.

Although disappointed, obviously their work had priority, but I was thrilled for them just the same. Due to the Russian's interest in religion, these two young men were having such a memorable experience, teaching the people while helping the Church establish a foothold here in the Soviet capital.

"However," Elder Redd interjected—my ears alert for what he was about to say—"all three of tomorrow's evening appointments have canceled on us."

My heart suddenly beat a little faster.

"If it would work out, I'd be happy to take you both to dinner tomorrow night," I said, trying not to sound too eager.

"We do have several appointments in the afternoon," they said, "but after six o'clock we could be free for dinner if you'd like."

"That would be great," I said.

We agreed to meet at six p.m. at Gorky Park near the main entrance, a place convenient for them and not too far from the American Embassy for me.

After bidding them goodbye, I continued my walk along the *Arbat*, however, this time with a little extra spring in my step. For the last week at the embassy, it had been so good to be around Americans and hear English spoken again. However, tomorrow night's dinner guests not only spoke English, and Utahn, but they spoke Mormon too. Food, conversation and companionship, it was going to be a great time for the three of us! Besides hearing of their experiences, I had a few to share with them myself—especially one about the goodness of the Lord and modern-day miracles.

I arrived back at the embassy just as the early winter darkness was settling over the city. I debated about placing a phone call to Chris to tell him of the great news. In his first letter to me, he had included his phone number in Australia, but according to missionary guidelines, it was to be used only in case of an emergency. Tonight I was definitely tempted to bend the mission rules. Instead, I spent the evening back in my room at the embassy writing a long, long letter.

Chapter 28

THE GREAT AMERICAN CUISINE

You always pass failure on the way to success.

M. Rooney

The next evening could not arrive soon enough. Dressed for dinner in a sport coat and tie, my long winter coat, *schapka*, and gloves, at four-thirty in the afternoon I caught a rickety city bus in front of the old embassy building on Tchaikovsky Street. With my unwanted shadow sitting several seats behind me at the back of the bus, I traveled down past the *Arbat*, past the Soviet Foreign Ministry and across the Krymskiy Bridge, which spans the

Moscow River. I got off at the stop near the entrance to Gorky Park.

Although I wasn't to meet the elders until six o'clock, but knowing I had a KGB agent following me, I wanted to get to the park early and observe what his intentions might be. I certainly didn't want any unforeseen problems, especially not this evening.

Gorky Park is one of the most popular attractions within the city of Moscow. Recent storms had covered the city with a foot of beautiful, new snow. The park air was cold, yet refreshingly clean; a welcome relief from the normal pollution and stench of this decaying, old city. The trees in the park stood naked against the winter snow, bare of their summer foliage.

Using antiquated shovels and makeshift brooms of bundled birch branches, hefty female workers with orange safety vests pulled over their coats, busily pushed snow from the walkways throughout the park as daylight began to fade.

I made my way through the park entrance and meandered among the crowd of old bent *babushkas* and stout middle-aged mothers, all clothed in their worn, drab coats, sweaters, and scarves. They sat on dilapidated park benches, keeping a close watch over the children. Red-faced and sweating, dressed in their bulky winter snowsuits, the children ran and played in the snow.

These families had come from the huge, Soviet government apartment buildings near the park. They were there to enjoy a rare afternoon of sun during the long, dark months of another Moscow winter.

Forty-five minutes later, my two dinner guests entered the park. I looked back to the opposite side of the entrance to see my KGB shadow begin to stir and finally show some signs of life. Bundled in winter clothing, he too, had been fighting the effects of the warm, late afternoon sun. For the last half-hour, he had been watching me from his concealed perch behind a monument near the park entrance.

After the elders arrived, I maneuvered my way through the crowd and was soon standing directly behind them.

"*Dobry vyechyir tovarischee* (Good evening comrades)" I said.

Two handsome faces, under two huge *schapkas,* greeted me with wide smiles and the obligatory, strong, pumping handshake. Both had a look of excitement. Although it was Moscow, and not American food, the three of us were going to a *real* dinner in a *real* restaurant.

At the time, there were few places in this city of twelve million where one could get a safe, edible meal. There were only three restaurants recommended for safe food consumption by the U.S. Embassy. Although owned and run by three different Moscow crime families, these restaurants catered specifically to Soviet government officials, members of the Russian mafia, and to foreigners with American dollars.

"The best of the three restaurants is only a twenty-minute walk away," I told the elders.

The decision was made; off we went. As we walked, Elder Pitts playfully slid along the frozen sidewalk.

So as not to alarm the elders, now and again I casually looked back over my shoulder—the three of us would not be going to dinner alone.

Of the two, Elder Pitts was definitely the talker.

"Brother Mike, do you happen to know any of the latest college football scores from back home?" he started. "Have you heard anything about the Church buying property for a temple here in Russia? What about the rumor that LaVell is going to leave BYU to coach in the NFL? And did you hear . . . ? And what about . . . ?"

I hadn't seen or heard this much excitement since crossing paths months earlier with a large group of young missionaries at the JFK Airport in New York on their way to serve in Europe.

The enthusiasm of Elder Redd and Elder Pitts was certainly understandable. Russia was experiencing a renewed interest in religion and foreign missionary work was just beginning there. Communism and the infamous Iron Curtain had kept the borders of the Soviet Union sealed from the outside world for the better part of the entire twentieth century. This situation, however, was now about to change.

With my years of involvement in Soviet studies and my work in Soviet intelligence, I was often asked, "Mr. Ramsdell, do you think the Soviet Union will someday fall? Will this Communist government ever allow its people to live like the rest of us in the free world?" My answer was always the same, "Never. . . . At least not in my lifetime." And ninety-nine percent of all Soviet scholars felt the same; these Communist leaders would never relinquish the grip they and the KGB had around the neck of every Soviet citizen. And yet, here I was tonight in Moscow, in the very heart of Great Mother Russia, about to go to dinner with two American missionaries who had been allowed into the USSR to bring the Gospel message of Hope to the Soviet people. *Remarkable!*

"Tonight, for only a handful of *dyengi* (money), we'll be able to eat like Russian Czars!" Elder Pitts said.

Yet, I knew that once we got to the restaurant we would likely find, as usual, only one entrée available from the menu—probably the obligatory Chicken Kiev served with *borsht* or cabbage soup and cucumber salad. But with that offering, we'd be very happy just the same.

The usual main course for Russians—endless bottles of vodka—would remain unopened and left on our table. In this nation of 300 million people, few, if any, had ever heard about the Word of Wisdom—our religion's health code—which admonishes against the use of alcohol, drugs, and tobacco.

A few blocks later, Elder Pitts reminded us just how far from home we really were.

"Hey, guys," he said, "wouldn't it be awesome when we get around this next corner to find a Golden Corral Buffet waiting for us there?"

I laughed while Elder Redd just shook his head and gave his companion an annoyed look.

After twenty minutes, we were standing in front of a large, concrete, windowless building. The three of us bounded up the flight of steps to the entrance. We were immediately confronted by a very unfriendly doorman who best resembled an overstuffed pit bull with a gold earring, wearing a black turtleneck several sizes too small.

"*Dobry vyechyir*," I said excitedly as we approached.

As we got closer, I noticed that rather than looking directly at me, he looked over my shoulder, across the street to the KGB agent who had been following me for the entire evening since leaving the embassy. Glancing down the stairs in the direction of the agent, the doorman gave a subtle nod and then turned back to us with a loud, "*Nyet*! You are not allowed to eat here!"

Even today, in the former Soviet Union, American missionaries are occasionally mistaken for CIA or other U.S. intelligence operatives, believed to be there to keep watch on the activities of the Russian government and its people.

I had to smile, because tonight, my shadow had his hands full. Normally he and his KGB comrades were very adept at keeping track of just one person, but a half hour earlier, I had been joined by what he had to believe were two other American intelligence agents. He had to be asking himself why the three of us were together, and what were we up to? Tonight, my shadow—no doubt—had more than he could handle.

I continued to work the doorman with my best school Russian and western wit, but to no avail. It was getting us nowhere. I turned to the elders to reassure them—not to worry.

"When such difficulties arise and nothing else seems to work—which is often the case in Russia—the clincher of last resort is to pull out one's diplomatic passport."

It had never failed me before, that is, not until tonight. The doorman shrugged off my diplomatic status as if it were nothing.

In exasperation, I pleaded with the mafia moose, "My guests are American Christian missionaries, and not what you think!"

He just shook his neck-less head and again decreed loudly, enunciating each word: *"Nyet, Nyet, Nyet."* He then turned his back and refused to speak to us any further.

There they stood at my side—young, handsome, engaging, dressed in dark suits with white shirts and ties—recognizable in most parts of the world but not yet in Russia. My frustration and disappointment became more evident by the volume of my words to this mafia slug. Yes, I felt bad for myself, but much worse for the elders I'd invited to dinner. I was mad but mostly embarrassed.

As I continued my losing efforts with the pit bull, Elder Redd reached out and grabbed my shoulder.

"Brother Ramsdell, it's okay, everything will be all right. We'll find another place."

Following this incident, I had my doubts about our chances at the other two restaurants, but we agreed to give them a try. I'd wanted this to be such a great evening—especially for the elders.

With my KGB shadow in tow, we went across the city by metro.

When we reached the second restaurant, it was as if we met the previous doorman's brother; he would not let us enter. By now I was an unhappy and frustrated dinner host.

We agreed there was no sense in trying the third restaurant. At the very least, we could go down to the *Arbat* market, find a park bench, and create our own dinner with a few apples, some fruit juice, and the food staple of the Soviet nation, Russian black bread.

"And guys," Elder Pitts said, "if we're lucky, maybe we can find an old *babushka* at the *Arbat* still selling her home-made cabbage rolls off a cardboard box."

Disappointed, but determined to make the best of a bad situation, off we went, but this time kicking at the chunks of ice along the sidewalks a little more aggressively than before. It would take us a half hour to get to the *Arbat.*

"Da apples best not be too vormy!" Elder Pitts said in his best pit bull, bouncer voice.

We all had a good laugh, and by that time—after all that had happened—we needed a good laugh.

Ten minutes into our walk to the *Arbat* our conversation faded. Moments later, Elder Pitts, who was leading the way through the snow, suddenly stopped in his tracks, spun around, and confronted Elder Redd and myself with big, excited eyes.

Then, as if to communicate with every Muscovite living in the surrounding apartment buildings, he yelled out, “McDONALD’S!”

For fourteen long years, McDonald’s of Canada had negotiated with the Soviet government to be allowed to open the first McDonald’s in Russia (because of the ongoing Cold War, the Soviets would not consent for the Americans to be involved). It had been fourteen years of Soviet bureaucratic “*Nyets*.” But finally, someway, somehow—probably during one of those long, cold, Russian winter nights, in the inner sanctum of the *Kremlin*—some *politburo* bureaucrat finally said, “*Da*.” Following years of construction, bribes, delays, and more bribes, McDonald’s had finally opened its doors in Moscow.

“It’s near Pushkin Square.” Pitts exclaimed.

“American food for three hungry Americans,” I said, absolutely thrilled to learn of the news. I could already smell the grease from the burgers and fries!

With no further discussion, off we went. This time our feet hardly touched down; we just skated along the top of the frozen sidewalks, forcing our unwelcome guest to double-time in order to keep up.

It seemed like we would never get there, but even with the wintry conditions, we probably made it in record time. As we wound our way through the streets of downtown Moscow and turned the corner on Tverskoy Boulevard, there in the distance loomed the Promised Land, Moscow's newest landmark—those magnificent Golden Arches of МакДоналдс. My heart surely skipped several beats.

However, we couldn't believe what else we saw—a crowd so large that it almost obscured the entire McDonald's building. On that cold winter night, the line of people waiting to get inside extended from the building entrance, across the street, and then serpentined back and forth several hundred yards throughout the park at Pushkin Square.

"There are hundreds and hundreds of people here," I said in disbelief.

"Why is it I never have my camera when I need it?" Elder Pitts complained.

"I haven't seen this many Russians in one place since attending the *Bolshoi Ballet*, a few years ago," I told them, astonished by what we were witnessing.

"People back home will never believe this," Elder Redd added.

Elder Pitts and I nodded our agreement.

We stood motionless and watched in amazement. Not one of us spoke a word for at least fifteen minutes, as the reality of our situation began to sink in. With a crowd this size, it would be hours before we would be inside, devouring *Bolshoi Maks* or anything McElse.

Once again, it looked as though we were headed back to the *Arbat* for a meal of apples and Russian black bread. At this late hour, our *babushka* with her cabbage rolls had surely gone home by now.

As we started to leave, I apologized to the elders. It seemed our evening had gone from bad to worse. Then, suddenly, an idea came to me.

"In as much as we're here," I said, "I'm intrigued to know approximately how many Russians are waiting here in line."

"I agree, Brother Ramsdell, it would be an interesting fact to know when re-telling this experience back home," Elder Redd responded.

Off we went, headed toward the entrance, which was hidden somewhere underneath the Golden Arches.

Our plan was to walk from the front door of the McDonald's building and count, by threes, fours, or fives, the number of people waiting in line. Once we were at the front entrance—and that was a mistake because then we really *could* smell the grease—the three of us did an about-face; then began mumbling numbers and making additions as we passed along the mass of bodies that snaked its way through Pushkin park.

As we muttered and walked, it seemed that every Russian eye waiting in line was watching us. *What were these three weird foreigners doing—still looking for Anastasia?*

When we reached the end of the line, we huddled. With little debate, all three of us, surprisingly, came up with the same rough number. Difficult to imagine, but on that frozen winter evening in Moscow, Russia, we estimated that 2,000 Soviets were waiting in line to experience the great American cuisine of Ronald McDonald. *Who back home would ever believe this?*

Fifteen minutes earlier, when we'd stood near the McDonald's entrance, the smell of greasy burgers and fries had made our bellies growl. We were ravenous, but 2,000 hungry men, women, and children were now standing between us and the Promised Land.

"Can't we pull rank somehow? After all . . . isn't this an American thing?" Pitts asked sarcastically. "Doesn't this entitle us to some consideration . . . *pazhalusta* (please)?"

As we stood in the cold, dark evening, looking wistfully back across the park towards the entrance, it was as if, in one defining moment, all 2,000 waiting Russians looked back at us to declare—*Don't even begin to think about butting in line boys!*

It had been over two hours since I had met the elders at Gorky Park. The night had been eventful, to say the least, but this was certainly not what we had planned. By now we were ravenous. Having already caught a whiff of the wonderful burgers and fries at the McDonald's front entrance, the thought of apples, fruit juice, and black bread at the *Arbat* had lost its appeal. Perhaps it was time to call it an evening and end this futile idea that we were going to be able to enjoy dinner together somewhere in the city of Moscow.

Yet, little did we know—our evening was just beginning.

Chapter 29

SASHA'S GOLDEN ARCHES

Youth, even in its sorrows, has a brilliance of its own.

Victor Hugo
Les Misérables

The three of us stood motionless looking back across the park at the mass of people moving imperceptibly like ants towards Ronald's food.

In the moment that we were ready to leave, suddenly, I felt something tugging at my pant leg. I glanced down and saw the gaunt, dirty face of a beautiful, young Russian boy. He couldn't have been more than six or seven years old. His ragged clothes and coat hung on him like hand-me-downs from a poor grandfather.

"*Prēvet (Hi)*. Are you foreigners?" he asked.

"Yes, we're Americans," I answered in Russian.

A smile lighted his face. "And . . . you really speak Russian?"

"Yes, all three of us speak Russian," Elder Pitts offered, as he stepped towards the boy.

"And you're here to eat at my McDonald's, right?"

"Well . . . uh . . . yes," I said, pointing to all the people standing in line in front of us, "but . . . we do have a problem."

"No worries, mister," he replied in a confident, high-pitched voice. "My name is Sasha. I work here at McDonald's, and I'll take care of you."

He pulled off his worn right glove and gave each of us a hand shake. Then grabbing my hand, he started pulling me down the line of people in the direction of the distant McDonald's building.

Not knowing exactly where we were headed, Elder Redd and Elder Pitts followed close behind.

I couldn't help but wonder where he was taking us and what was going to happen. As we walked, I watched this skinny, frail boy at my side. His tousled, blond hair and engaging smile reminded me of a time gone by and another small, blonde boy, now a missionary in the Land Down Under, and the wonderful years I had being his dad.

After passing a hundred or more people waiting in the line, Sasha stopped and introduced us to his best friend, Pavel. Pavel was the same size and wore similar tattered clothes as Sasha.

"Pavel, too, works with us here at McDonald's," Sasha said.

"*Prēvet.* Where ya from?" Pavel asked, stretching forth his small hand to shake ours.

"They're from America." Sasha answered excitedly. "This is Mr. Mike, Mr. Redd, and Mr. Pitts. And they even speak Russian, too," he said, looking impishly into Pavel's face.

"They're Americans!" Pavel yelled proudly to the Russians waiting in line around him.

Sasha grabbed my hand and pulled me away from where Pavel was standing.

"Now, let's go get you some food," he said.

We continued down the line of people towards the McDonald's building, with Sasha giving high-fives now-and-again to other friends who were standing in line. From Sasha's stride and how proudly he held his head, it was as if the elders and I were his own personal trophies.

As we walked, Sasha explained that he and his friends started work each morning at ten when McDonald's opened and didn't go home until closing time at ten each night.

He related to us how several of his buddies were strategically located throughout the crowd. While some of his friends held their place in line, others kept a lookout for foreigners who had come to eat at *their* McDonald's.

"Being good to foreigners is really important for us," he said; something which the elders and I would only fully understand later.

When he mentioned going home at night, I couldn't help but wonder if Sasha really did have a home. Never once in our conversation did he mention his parents, a family, or attending school.

Moscow, like several larger cities in Russia, had thousands upon thousands of orphans who were living on the streets. This was due, primarily, to the extreme poverty or chronic alcoholism of the children's parents. There were Soviet government orphanages where these children could live, but the conditions at these institutions were deplorable at best. Against great odds, Sasha and his friends somehow found the courage to try and survive on the streets.

As I looked down at this handsome, young boy, I couldn't help but wonder what his life might be if he was given a real chance, a chance to escape all the poverty, corruption, and danger he faced, day-in and day-out, simply trying to stay alive.

While thinking of Sasha and what life had already dealt him at such a young age, I was ashamed to think of my own situation and how I had gone through the last few years feeling so sorry for myself.

When the four of us finally reached the McDonald's entrance, Sasha leaped up to the top step where one of his ragged friends was holding a place in line. Sasha looked down at me with a big grin and held out the palm of his hand.

"Just one American dollar, Mister Mike, and I'll put you and your two friends right here, right now." He stomped on the step nearest the front door with his worn-out shoe. "This spot is yours!" he said.

So this is how they do it—selling their place in line to impatient, hungry foreigners for American dollars. *Incredible!* Who could possibly resist this kind of salesmanship?

Capitalism in Russia!

Sasha explained that at the end of the night, the boys were forced to pay an exorbitant amount of their earnings to the local mafia thugs. As is the case throughout Russia, the normal thirty percent extracted from most businesses by the mafia is referred to as "protection money," but in reality, it is simply blatant, criminal extortion. The boys vehemently hated the mafia and their involvement, yet, there was nothing they could do. It was either pay the mafia what they wanted or suffer a severe beating. The only other choice for the boys was to walk away from the flourishing, business they had created, which would only put them back on the street, starving and struggling to survive.

At the end of each night, thugs from the local mafia would show up one hour before closing time to extract their share from the boys' daily earnings. Unfortunately, because they were so young and easily intimidated, rather than the usual thirty percent, the mafia would take almost all of the money, leaving each boy only one or two dollars for his day's work.

However, it is important to point out, at that time in Communist Russia, most Soviet workers were paid approximately the same salary by the government—the equivalent of ten to fifteen U.S. dollars per month. Sasha and his friends were averaging one or two dollars a day each. In actuality, these kids were cashing in big and proud of it. Proud, of course, because of the money, but also because of the notoriety they got by associating with foreigners, something that until Gorbachev's recent policy of *glasnost*, Soviet citizens were strictly forbidden to do.

Capitalism at its very best, right here in Moscow, Russia—and not a whole lot of business overhead here in the park for these future Soviet MBAs. And to think, this gang of ruffian entrepreneurs had probably not yet spent a single day in school.

With the neon golden arches flashing above our heads, there we stood—our new friend Sasha, Elder Redd, Elder Pitts, and myself—at the front door of the newest and largest McDonald's in the world (seven-hundred-person capacity). Finally we were about to have dinner, not just any dinner but fabulous American burgers, fries, and shakes. We three foreigners would be joined at our table by a young Russian boy, who not only saved the evening for us but had also touched our hearts by reminding us—as Americans—just how blessed we were.

I turned towards Sasha and reached in my wallet for the American dollar that had made its way from Brisbane, Australia all the way to Moscow, Russia for this memorable evening.

As the McDonald's security personnel opened the doors for us to go inside, Sasha stuffed Chris' dollar bill, along with several more that we gave him, into a pocket of his dirty, worn trousers.

Suddenly, above the noise of the crowd, my ear caught the words of a marvelous, new Russian phrase, which, until that moment, I'd never heard before, "*Dobro pazhaluvat f Mak Donalds. Shto vwe khatyetya zakazat?* (Welcome to McDonald's. May I take your order?)"

Sasha's face beamed when seeing my reaction to what I had just heard. He grabbed my arm, "Thanks for the dollars, Mister Mike." he said. "And Mr. Mike, if you might have time tomorrow, I'd be happy to show you around Moscow."

I looked down at him. "Sasha," I said, "I'd be delighted for you to show me Moscow tomorrow."

"What about Sunday?" Elder Redd asked. "What are you and your friends doing on the Sabbath?"

A puzzled expression came over Sasha's face. He looked over at Elder Redd, then at me, then back to Elder Redd.

"What's a Sabbath?" he asked.

While thinking of Sasha and his young friends, I looked through the maze of people waiting to order at the McDonald's counter.

Although we had been inside for only a few minutes, somehow, sitting alone at a corner table was Elder Pitts, his tray covered with food. He was already working on the first of three *Bolshoi Maks*.

Shaking our heads in disbelief, Sasha, Elder Redd, and I looked at each other, smiling, then back towards Elder Pitts. We couldn't wait to join him!

Following a marvelous hour of fantastic food—we truly made fools of ourselves—and great conversation, regrettably it was time for us to leave. When the elders excused themselves to go use the WC, Sasha and I walked outside and stood on the front steps.

From our vantage point, standing on the steps of the McDonald's entrance, we waited while looking out over the crowd. Sasha stood next to me with his arms folded across his chest, proudly enjoying the moment.

And then my eyes suddenly spotted him, a dark figure, approximately sixty feet away at the edge of the crowd. With the events of the last hour, I had completely forgotten about my KGB shadow, but he had not forgotten us. Obviously, he had been in the darkness all along and observed everything that had happened.

As a government agent, there was no doubt he could easily cause trouble, not only for me and my two American dinner guests but also for young Sasha—and the last thing I wanted was for Sasha or the elders or the Church to have any problems on my account.

Trying to stay calm and think of what I should do, I unexpectedly found myself walking back inside to the McDonald's counter where I ordered a Big Mac, large fry, and a shake.

When I rejoined Sasha waiting at the front entrance, I pointed out a certain man in the crowd.

"But why, Mr. Mike?" Sasha asked.

"It's okay. There's no need to speak to him; just hand him the sack and say 'thank you,' nothing more. Can you do that?"

"Of course I can, not a problem," he answered.

Without hesitation, Sasha took the McDonald's sack, walked down the steps and through the crowd to where the man was standing. I watched as Sasha handed him the sack, acknowledged the man with a nod of his head, and made his way back up the sidewalk to where I was waiting.

Ever so slowly, the KGB agent maneuvered himself out from the line so as to have a clear view of where I was standing. As our eyes made contact—not knowing what was about to happen—my mouth became dry; my heart beat heavily in my chest. Then in a moment, which seemed to last forever, he looked directly at me. With one hand he held the sack above his head, with his other hand he gave me a "thumbs-up."

Totally unexpected, I stood motionless, unable to respond. After a few deep breaths, I gathered myself, and with a grateful smile, I respectfully nodded back at him and mouthed the word, *"Spaseeba."*

From its ominous beginning, what an evening this had been! My dinner invitation with Elder Redd and Elder Pitts had been fulfilled; I'd made a new, young friend; I was able to show my thanks to my KGB shadow for his non-interference; and my obligation to my missionary in Australia was now complete. And for me—unlike millions of others each day around the world—grabbing a quick bite to eat at a McDonald's would never again be quite the same.

Chapter 30

CHRISTMAS IN THE ALPS AND SECOND CHANCES

Will you stay with me, will you be my love
among the fields of barley
We'll forget the sun in his jealous sky, as we lie in fields of gold
I never made promises lightly and there have been some I have broken
But I swear in the days still left, we'll walk in fields of gold

Sting
Ten Summoner's Tales

Near the end of my second week at the embassy, I was notified that HQ was unable to finalize the details of my follow-on assignment. Inasmuch as the Christmas holidays were fast approaching, they suggested it would be best that I take administrative leave for the last two weeks of December. I was told to report back for duty at the embassy in Moscow at the first of the year.

I couldn't believe my luck—finally! With my medical release in hand and two weeks off, I now had the chance to fly back home for the holidays. America, the Rocky Mountains, Bear River—here I come!

As I bounded through the snow across the quad to the embassy travel office, my feet hardly touched down. Unfortunately, after spending several hours there, trying to make arrangements for a flight back to the United States, the travel staff had exhausted every possibility. With over sixty foreign embassies and a large number of multi-national companies represented in Moscow, Foreign Service personnel and international businessmen, along with their families, had ninety-nine percent of the seats totally booked on every flight back to the States during the upcoming holiday. Even connecting flights through other major European cities were full. The airlines made sure that the few remaining last-minute seats still available were priced so high that only the very wealthy could afford them, something well beyond my financial means.

Later that evening, after several prayers and hours of deliberation, I decided to take a bold chance.

The next day at the travel office, I made arrangements for a round-trip ticket from Salt Lake City to Frankfurt, Germany and back. After several months of not being able to communicate with one another, I sent a fax to Bonnie explaining that in the evening, Rocky Mountain time, a courier would make a delivery to her apartment where she lived with her sister, Tanya. The delivery—a Christmas card from Russia. Inside the card she would find the round trip ticket to Europe and a note:

Dear Bon,

I apologize I haven't been able to communicate, but perhaps you understand. I hope I'll have the chance to explain.

This is terribly short notice—and I'll totally understand if you decline—but I'd like you to consider coming to Europe for two weeks over the holidays to spend Christmas in the Bavarian Alps. You've probably already got other plans—and, Bon, that's just fine—but I thought I'd at least ask.

Merry Christmas

Mike

PS: If you decide you can come and you need a tour guide and translator, I would be happy to make myself available.

The rest of the day, I checked hourly at the embassy communication center for her reply. In the evening, I double-checked several times, but still no answer.

That night I lay on the bed in my room thinking how egotistical and foolish I'd been to expect that she would drop everything and come to Europe for two weeks, especially when she hadn't heard a single word from me for so long. Besides, for all I knew, she could be engaged by now anyway.

Thinking of her engaged to be married made me sad, yet happy for her at the same time. If anyone deserved to be happy it was Bon; she was one of the best people I had ever known. Before falling asleep, I decided that tomorrow I would be a gentleman and send her a second fax and apologize for my arrogance.

During the night, I was awakened from my sleep two or three times by a dream about Bon, but I couldn't make any sense of what it meant. Perhaps it was a deserved annoyance for what a fool I had been.

Early the next morning, I was roused by a telephone call from the commo center; a fax had come in from America with my name on it. I quickly showered and dressed.

As I jogged from my quarters to the commo center, I thought about Bon's goodness; it was just like her to overlook my tactless vanity and have the courtesy to fax me back to let me know that her life was now headed in a new direction, that she was very happy and wished the same for me.

I picked up the fax and carried it to the embassy cafeteria. After staring at the envelope through two cups of hot chocolate, I finally opened it:

Dear Mike,

I eagerly accept your generous offer to travel to Europe this Christmas. And yes, I will definitely need a tour guide. I can't wait to see the Bavarian Alps, but most of all . . . I can't wait to see you!

Love, Bonnie

✯ ✯ ✯

Four days later, as the blue government van left the embassy compound, we encountered the snarled Moscow traffic—a result of several inches of new snow that had covered the city during the night. It took more than an hour and a half to drive the twenty-six miles to the Sheremetyevo Airport on the outskirts of the city.

Looking out of the windows of the airport shuttle, I could hardly contain my excitement; I was leaving the gloom and despair of Russia, even if it was for only two weeks. It was the Christmas holidays and in less than six hours I would see Bon again.

Because of the holiday, the airport was jammed with passengers, as was my flight. There was not an empty seat on the aircraft. I passed up the lunch meal and anxiously thumbed through several magazines, unable to concentrate enough to read any of the articles.

Speeding towards Germany at an altitude of 30,000 feet, I gazed down at the snow-covered landscape below and thought of Bon. I tried to picture in my mind where her flight, coming from JFK in New York, might be at that very moment. *Was she still somewhere over the Atlantic or had her plane reached landfall over Western Europe?*

Forty-five minutes before our scheduled landing, the captain's voice came over the intercom. Rather than providing information about our impending landing, he explained that he had some bad news; the airport at Frankfurt was completely fogged-in.

Please . . . this just can't be happening!

With all that I had endured over the last few months because of brutal weather conditions—it would be a long time before Old Man Winter and I would ever be friends again.

Once over Frankfurt's airspace, the control tower put our flight in a holding pattern high above the city along with dozens of other aircraft also waiting to land. I worried about Bon. If our plane couldn't land, then neither could hers. My flight was scheduled to arrive one half hour before hers. We had planned for me to be at her arrival gate when she landed.

After two anxious hours of circling the airport, our well-laid plans were in definite jeopardy. The captain announced that a decision was being made at Flight Control Center Europe whether or not to re-route all the airplanes hanging in the sky above Frankfurt to other major airports in Germany.

Surely, all the planes, including mine and Bon's, would not be sent to the same location. We might be facing a scenario of my flight landing in Munich in the South and her flight going on to Berlin in the North—two cities three hundred and fifty miles apart. *And then what . . . ?*

Perhaps our prayers, high in the sky above Germany, were in close enough proximity to the heavens: another thirty minutes passed when the captain announced that the fog had lifted enough for us to land within the hour. *Hallelujah!*

Once I disembarked the aircraft, I picked up my bags and watched the overhead electronic information board for Bon's flight. When her flight number finally appeared on the monitor, no arrival gate was given, only a flashing message that indicated "ON APPROACH."

After waiting another half-hour, the board indicated that her flight had landed, but still did not indicate an arrival gate. I went to Delta Customer Service and stood in line with hundreds of other travelers who'd also had their travel plans turned upside down by the fog and winter weather.

While standing in line, I was startled when I heard my name paged over the airport intercom: "Mr. Michael Ramsdell, please go to airport security immediately."

Immediately? What had happened? Had Bon's plane landed safely? Was she okay?

I made my way as fast as I could across the terminal to security, my fearful heart pounding in rhythm with each urgent stride.

Just as I approached the security counter, I heard an excited, beautiful voice, one that I had not heard for almost half a year. "Hey, Mike Ramsdell, over here."

I turned around. There in the middle of a mass of holiday travelers was Bon, frantically waving her arms, almost completely hidden because of her petite, five-foot frame. We bumped and jostled our way through the crowd towards each other.

Finally, we were standing face to face. As if on cue, we dropped our bags and Bon leaped into my open arms. With tears of joy, not a word was spoken. Nothing needed to be said.

In that moment of long embrace, I knew that inviting Bon to Europe was the right thing to do and that this holiday was going to be something more than special.

☆ ☆ ☆

It was so good to be with Bon again, catching up on all the news and things that had happened in each other's lives.

During our first few days together, we spent a portion of our mornings and afternoons at the American Military Hospital in Frankfurt. I needed to have additional exams, x-rays, and follow-up treatment for my head injury.

We spent our evenings, bundled in our cold-weather gear, meandering through the beautiful, old city, seeing the decorated shops and stores, and visiting the famous outdoor *Christkindl Markt* (Christmas markets) of Frankfurt. Being together at this special time of year with all the beauty, sights, sounds, and smells of the season was nothing less than magical.

Once my medical appointments in Frankfurt were over, we traveled by train several hundred miles south to Garmisch–Partenkirchen, a winter ski resort near the German–Austrian border which had served as the venue for the Winter Olympic Games decades earlier. The beauty of the area at this time of year was breathtaking.

Under the terms of an agreement between Germany and America, Garmisch was designated as the primary recreation center in Europe for the U.S. Armed Forces. American military and government officials had access to several charming, old German resort hotels. There were wonderful restaurants, movie houses, places for down-hill and cross-country skiing, ice skating, indoor swimming, and tennis.

On the days when we were not on the ski slopes, we visited the nearby cities of Salzburg, Berchtesgarden, and Innsbruck. In the evenings after dinner, we would walk along the village streets of shops and stores, all wonderfully decorated with Old World charm for the holiday season.

One afternoon Bon and I took the train to Murnau and from there up the mountain to Oberammergau where, as a young lieutenant, I had begun my career as an instructor at the U.S. Intelligence School–Europe. As we visited the area, I shared with Bon some of the joys and sorrows I had experienced there many years before and how my life had been changed by my friendship with a young air force officer, Yuri Novotny.

On Christmas Day, Garmisch-Partenkirchen awoke to the sound of church bells echoing from one side of the mountain tops to the other. An overnight storm had left the alpine valley covered with a beautiful layer of fresh snow.

At nine a.m., I met Bon in the busy dining parlor for a continental breakfast of hot chocolate, *brötchen*, cheese, yogurt, and fruit. For a special Christmas morning treat, Frau Klein, the resort's innkeeper, had made fresh-baked *apfelküchen*—I was in heaven!

Following breakfast we bundled up and took a long, invigorating walk through town out towards the *Zugspitze*—the tallest mountain peak of the German Alps.

After our late-morning excursion, we returned to the resort where we exchanged gifts in the parlor next to the huge Christmas tree. My gifts for Bon included a hand painted *matrushka* dolls (Russian nesting dolls), a small Russian painting, and an amber brooch. Bon's practical gifts for me—a pair of fur-lined leather gloves, ear muffs, and a pair of ram slippers.

For the rest of the afternoon, we sat in the parlor with other guests near the fireplace enjoying the spirit of the holiday and listening to beautiful Christmas music. In the late afternoon, several of the guests gathered around the large stone fireplace to sing German Christmas carols.

Days earlier I had made reservations for us to have Christmas dinner at the General Patton Hotel. I signed us up when I found out that the Patton would be serving a traditional Christmas feast of turkey, goose, and baked ham with all the trimmings. Throughout the afternoon, all I could think about was that moment when we would be sitting down at our evening dinner.

Certainly this Christmas feast would not be as emotionally profound as my humble Thanksgiving meal in Potevka only a month ago, but it would definitely be more physically satisfying. This time around there would be no rationing of *any* food items. And rather than Gummi bears for desert, there would be pumpkin, minced, and pecan pies, piled high with real whipped cream.

Upon our arrival in the early evening at the General Patton, we heard the sobering news that Mikhail Gorbachev had resigned as President of the USSR and that in another week, on December 31, the Soviet Union would officially cease to exist.

The CNN report from Russia described this once powerful, invincible nation in turmoil: there were strikes and demonstrations, the economy was near collapse, tens of millions of people were without adequate food, and crime was rampant in the major cities.

Russia's new president, Boris Yeltsin, was struggling to establish control over the new government. Throughout the member states of the former Soviet Union, political parties were fighting one another to gain power and control over what was left by the fall of the Communist regimes. The world watched and waited as Russia struggled for its survival.

Our conversation during dinner was, at times, difficult. In another week our time together would be over and I would be on my way back to the anarchy of Russia to face whatever was waiting for me there. In spite of the disturbing news, we tried to make the best of a worrisome situation. After all, it was Christmas, we were together, and for that we were both extremely grateful.

Not only was it the Holidays, and I was spending it with my best friend, but we had been able to dutifully stuff ourselves—especially me—with a glorious Christmas feast. Yet there was to be one more highlight to this memorable day.

Following dinner I walked Bon the several blocks back to her room at the resort.

"This Christmas Day has been wonderful, Mike," she said when we got to her room. "But go on now and make your phone call before it gets any later. I'll be just fine."

"Thanks for understanding," I said.

She gave me a hug and kissed me on the cheek.

"You'd better get going, and tell him hello for me. I'll see you in the morning," she said, as she tied my *schapka* earflaps down around my chin.

With a light snow falling, I walked the several blocks to the downtown *Postamt* (post office), which was open around the clock on Christmas Day—one of the few places in Garmisch where one could make an overseas phone call. After giving the clerk a deposit of fifty German *marks* and the phone number, I waited near the bank of phone booths until my name was called. With the kind, efficient help of an international operator—I had no idea regarding the difference in time zones—the overseas connection finally rang through. A Polynesian-like voice answered.

"Hello, Elder Hai Hai."

"Elder, is this the apartment of Chris Ramsdell?"

"Yes it is," he said. "Just a moment, he's right here."

"Elder Ramsdell," I heard him say, "it's for you . . . and it sounds really far away."

And then, "Hello, this is Elder Ramsdell."

"Hey, Elder, how's your tennis game?"

"DAD! Oh my gosh, it's you!"

"How are you Son?"

"Fine, Dad. I'm doing just fine. Where are you? Are you doing okay? Are you still in Russia?"

"Well . . . I was able to make it out for a few days. They gave me some time off for Christmas because . . ."

"Dad, it's so great to hear your voice. Will you have to go back? We hear about a lot of ugly things going on over there."

"It's great to hear your voice, too, and, yes, I'm doing fine, especially right now talking to you. And how are you doing? Are you staying healthy?"

"I haven't heard a thing from you, Dad. I've been worried. You need to write me, and let me know where you are and that you're okay."

"I promise I'll do better," I said. "So . . . how is it there?"

"The Aussie people are incredibly friendly and the Gold Coast area here is absolutely beautiful. The work is going really well and the members here are awesome. You and I have got to come back here someday."

"I'd like that, Chris."

"One day each week we have a thing called service day. My companion and I volunteer at the local Meals-on-Wheels. We spend the entire day delivering food and meals to shut-ins. It really makes me feel like I'm making a contribution to the less fortunate here."

"It sounds like you're staying busy. By the way, what time is it there?"

"It's eight o'clock in the morning, the day after Christmas."

"Well, I almost got to you on time . . . just ten hours late."

"You called at a perfect time. In another half hour my companion and I would have been gone."

"I know I'm bending your mission rules. I promised myself I'd call only for a minute, but I needed to hear your voice again and wish you a Merry Christmas."

"Don't worry about it, Dad."

"In a few weeks you should be getting several over-due letters and a small box I sent from Moscow. I'm sorry about the delay. Someday when we're together I'll have a chance to explain. And when you open the box, remember . . . it's the thought that counts."

"You didn't need to, Dad, but thanks. I've tried not to think about home this time of year, but it hasn't been easy. Dad, please try and write me whenever you can."

"I promise I will. Merry Christmas, Son. I'm really proud of you and what you're doing over there."

"Merry Christmas, Dad. I love you, and . . . I'm so grateful that you're my dad."

I tried to respond—to say something—but couldn't. My heart was suddenly in my throat. Then the connection went dead.

The cold night air stung my face and eyes as I tried to hold back the tears while slowly walking back through the now quiet, slumbering town towards the resort, thinking how blessed my life was and what a marvelous Christmas Day it had been.

✯ ✯ ✯

Following a wonderful week together in the Alps, Bon and I traveled thirteen hundred miles by train north to Scandinavia. When we reached Stockholm, Sweden, we caught a Silja Line passenger ship for Helsinki, Finland where we would spend our remaining week together.

Helsinki had been our agency's base of operations during the planning and training for our covert Siberian mission. I still had my apartment there in the downtown area, which I had rented under a mandatory six-month lease.

Like America, most countries in Europe celebrate the year-end holidays for the entire month of December and into the New Year, and Helsinki was no exception. Not far from the Arctic Circle, this part of Scandinavia had only three or four hours of daylight during this time of year. Thus, both day and night, the city was beautifully dressed in colorful, brilliant Christmas lights.

Due to Helsinki's brutal temperatures, Bon and I didn't spend as much time outdoors as we had in Germany. Nonetheless, the time we spent together was grand. Staying indoors near the fireplace gave us hours to talk, relax, read, listen to beautiful music, and just enjoy one another's company.

In celebration of the holidays, we were invited to a lavish New Year's Eve ball at the American Embassy. There was dining and dancing throughout the evening. Those in attendance were decked out in their finest formal wear. Birgitta, my apartment landlord and dear friend, loaned Bon her fur stole for the evening.

The two of us—at least we thought—made a dashing, handsome couple. We thought we fit right in with the beautiful gowns and tuxedos of the diplomatic personnel and the striking blue and red formal uniforms of the embassy marine guards, gliding across the ballroom floor with their elegantly-dressed dates.

Bon and I had a marvelous evening. Even with my still-tender ribs, we seldom sat out a dance. Before the night was over, she even had me waltzing—and quite well according to her.

Just before midnight, we ventured out into the frigid, arctic air onto one of the embassy balconies. Alongside the other revelers, we welcomed in the New Year with noisemakers, sparklers, and handfuls of string confetti. We were one of the very last couples to leave the party—well after 2 a.m.

Throughout the evening, neither of us made mention of what we were facing in the morning. Tomorrow, I would spend New Year's Day packing my things to go back into Russia. Bon would have two more days before her return flight to America. It had been an absolutely perfect evening—one that we didn't want to end.

☆ ☆ ☆

Mid-morning the next day, I heard her footsteps coming down the hallway from the guest room. I was up and already packing when she came into the living room. After giving me a hug, she curled up opposite me in the large sofa chair, pulling her knees to her chest and wrapping both arms around them.

With her chin resting on her knees, she sat and watched me pack. Neither of us spoke. Following several minutes of silence, she re-positioned herself in the chair and made a soft sound as she cleared her throat.

"Mike," she began, "I have something to say that I've never told you before."

I looked up at her from where I was sitting on the floor and waited.

"What I have to say is very precious to me, and perhaps . . . only me," she said, hesitating as if unsure of her words. "This might sound very strange, especially at a time like this, but . . . I want you to know it just the same. And I feel guilty that in all our conversations over the years about our relationship . . . I've never told you this before."

I looked at her, giving her my full attention and closed the lid of my suitcase.

She took a deep breath.

"I know this may sound weird, like something out of a Harlequin romance novel, but years ago . . . remember, Mike, that day when I came to your office to interview for that job? Well, crazy and strange as it might sound, while I was there talking with you that day, I had this foolish premonition . . . that someday we would marry, and I would be your wife."

She began to wipe tears from her eyes.

"I've gone over it a thousand times . . . and I still don't know the how or why. I didn't know a thing about you; I had never even met you. I just remember trying to answer your questions during the interview, while at the same time an inner voice was telling me, 'Bonnie, this is the man who will someday be your husband.' After I was offered the job as office manager, every day I would go to work wondering how this could ever possibly work out between us and if I should even be there or not."

She shifted uneasily in her chair.

"For years I've wanted to tell you what happened that day . . . but I never dared. That's why, for these past years, it has been so frustrating when I would drop hint after hint about the possibility of us being more than just friends, and you just didn't get it. You were just . . . you know . . . clueless."

I looked at her and smiled while she cried and giggled at the same time.

"After it was decided—actually you decided, Mike—that we'd never be more than just good friends . . . it broke my heart. But I never let you know that. And I never gave up hope that somehow it would all work out and we'd end up together."

She stared down at the floor, her cheeks streaked with tears.

"I've had many wonderful male friends over the years and I dated a lot of them. But when a relationship started to get serious, even when I truly wanted it to work, it just didn't happen. It just never ever felt right."

She looked over at me.

"Do you understand any of this . . . ?" she asked, shaking her head from side to side. "Mike, these last two weeks with you have been the very happiest of my life. I know that you have to leave tomorrow and go back to Russia, but I don't want these two weeks to end."

She exhaled with a deep sigh.

"When you left the States for Russia, I constantly worried about you . . . and prayed for you every morning and every night. I repeatedly asked the Lord, no matter what happened between us . . . to watch over you and keep you safe."

Dabbing her eyes and nose with a tissue, she moved to the edge of her chair and looked down at me.

"Mike Ramsdell . . . whether you like it or not . . . I love you and I will always love you. Now I've said it . . . I've finally told you. And that's all I have to say."

I got up and walked to her side. I reached down and cradled her face in my hands and softly brushed the tears away. Taking both her hands in mine, I pulled her up to me. She buried her head against my chest and began to cry. My heart ached with love. I held her so tightly I worried that she might break. Gently, I lifted her chin and looked into her beautiful brown eyes.

"I do love you, Bon. I'm sorry for being so dense and stupid . . . and I'm sorry for all the years I didn't want to see what was right there in front of me."

I wiped away my own tears.

"Bon, I'd like the chance to make it up to you. I'm sorry I've been such an insensitive jacka_ _."

She reached up with her small hand and covered my mouth. I grabbed her hand and held it against my cheek.

"I hope you'll give me the opportunity to make it up to you. Here we are in Helsinki, half way around the world, at the beginning of a new year and . . . I'm asking you, today, for a second chance."

Bon never used the return portion of her airline ticket.

☆ ☆ ☆

We spent the rest of a memorable New Year's Day getting me packed and Bon unpacked. We were able to meet with Birgitta and add Bon's name to the apartment lease to make her stay official. In the evening, we both placed phone calls to our families back home in America to let them know of our decision.

I also made several calls in the local Helsinki area; I wanted to make sure that I left Bon in the capable hands of my friends within the American Embassy community and the local Finnish Branch of our Church. With such good people—Finns and Americans—I felt confident Bon would be well looked after until I returned from Russia.

Early the next morning, the lingering tears, hugs and goodbyes finally ended with the sound of the taxi's horn waiting at the curb below. An hour and a half later, I sat at my seat on board the Finn Air flight taking me back to Russia, all the while thinking of Bon back in Helsinki and my boy in Australia. Although I was returning to the darkness and chaos of Russia, on this particular morning everything seemed right with the world.

☆ ☆ ☆

As promised by headquarters, I was assigned to a low-profile surveillance operation a few hundred miles north of Moscow. My responsibility was to report on the activities of the new Russian government, specifically the changeover from the old KGB to the new Federal Security Service.

There were few moments of excitement or challenge in my new assignment. The dark days of the Russian winter seemed to flow one into another without end. Not being able to communicate with Bon, Chris, or my family, made for the longest January–February I'd ever experienced.

I counted down the weeks, days, and hours until my assignment in Russia was finally over. The morning I left Moscow, as our jet screamed down the runway and was airborne, I could hardly contain my excitement—the aircraft just couldn't fly fast enough.

Similar to what had happened months earlier in Frankfurt, when I disembarked the airplane I had a difficult time locating my five-foot friend among all the people and passengers. Then, there in the middle of the crowd, hidden at the end of a huge bouquet of colored balloons, was a beautiful someone waiting just for me. *O frabjous day! Callooh! Callay!*

To say we were thrilled to see one another again was an understatement. I was out of Russia, and we were together, eager to begin making plans for our future.

Bon was excited to tell me about her two months in Helsinki, what she had learned about the wonderful Finnish people and their culture, and she was especially proud of her new-found skill with the Finnish language. She was also eager to introduce me to the several new friends she had made during my time away.

One week after my return from Russia, Bon and I were married in a modest civil ceremony in the charming old Finnish courthouse next to the city park. Although there were only three other people present, the local city magistrate and two elderly witnesses, for Bon and me it was a joyous occasion just the same. Our only regret was that our family and friends back home were not there to share the experience with us.

Before going to one of Helsinki's most famous Chinese restaurants, where we had dinner reservations to celebrate our wedding, Bon and I had another appointment. At a photo studio, located not far from the courthouse on the other side of the park, we had arranged to have a portrait taken to commemorate our marriage day.

As we walked through the deserted, beautiful, winter-clad park, we were enveloped by a magical, surreal beauty—a fitting moment for such a special occasion. Overhead was a steel-blue, starlit sky; sparkling hoarfrost covered the snow; millions of ice crystals covered every branch of every tree.

Halfway across the park, we stopped long enough for Bon to open a box that I pulled from my tote bag, something to help warm her ears—a wedding gift I had brought back from Moscow: a Russian, white fox, fur hat.

The wedding photo perfectly captured the newly married couple, posing together on their wedding day, crowned with their Russian *schapkas—the* Cossack and his Russian Czarina.

Months later Bon and I traveled by ship to Sweden where our marriage was solemnized in the Stockholm Temple. One year later, at Christmas time, we would return to the United States to celebrate our marriage with our family and friends.

From time to time I've heard it said that it's possible to have a piece of heaven while here on earth through the joy and blessings of a happy marriage. I am one of those individuals who can attest this to be true. After all my doubts and concerns about marriage, marrying Bon turned out to be the best thing that I ever did.

Chapter 31

EPILOGUE

In spite of everything I still believe people are really good at heart.

Anne Frank
The Diary of a Young Girl

Bon and I were barely getting settled in Scandinavia, when I was asked to return to Russia for a long-term assignment. Happily, this time I would not have to go alone; Bon would be able to live there with me. Russia—what a way to start our married life together!

Fully aware of the potential risks and hardships we would encounter, still, we both felt that going back to Russia was the right thing to do. It would not only provide me an opportunity to further my career, but we would be able to live among the

Russian people and experience their life and culture first hand. It would also give us the chance to be of service through our Church affiliation in an area of the world where help was so desperately needed. Bon and I spent the next six years living in Russia; four in Moscow and two in the old Russian city formerly known as Gorky—now Nizhni Novgorod—located on the Volga River several hundred miles deeper in Russia.

✯ ✯ ✯

When Chris completed his missionary service in Australia, he returned back to Utah and enrolled again at the university. Because I was in the middle of an on-going project, I was unable to leave Moscow and fly home to see him. Not having been together for two and a half years, we immediately started making plans for him to spend the summer with us in Russia when he finished his spring semester classes.

Through the long months of winter and into spring, I counted down the days until his arrival. The night Chris got off the plane at Sheremetyevo Airport on the outskirts of Moscow, Bon and I were waiting at the arrival gate. What a thrill it was to see him! After two and a half years, he seemed taller, a little heavier, and, of course, more handsome. Following the bear hugs and embraces, we loaded his luggage and two over-sized boxes into a taxi-van and headed into the city.

At our apartment, we celebrated our reunion with a delicious late-night meal, which Bon had prepared for us. After dinner, Bon and I excitedly opened the two large boxes of food and necessities we had asked Chris to bring with him from America. From the boxes we pulled treasures all but impossible to acquire at that time anywhere in Russia: cake mixes and cereals, soups and sauces, ketchup and soy sauce, spaghetti and noodles, cookies and candy, soap, socks, and paperback books.

For Bon and me, it was like opening presents on Christmas morning. And, of course, for me personally, I couldn't help but think back to a similar experience two and a half years earlier while in the village of Potevka, opening a much smaller box that was filled with magic and wonder.

In one of the two large boxes was my one absolute, non-negotiable request for Chris to bring from America, a twenty-four-count box of Hershey's with Almonds Candy Bars.

While Bon slept, Chris and I never went to bed that entire first night. We stayed up eating junk food and catching up on all that had happened in each of our lives during the last two and a half years. And, oh, the stories we had to tell!

It was so good to be with my boy again. And what a summer we had, not only experiencing Russia but, also, two unexpected trips out of the country—one to Scandinavia, the other to Western Europe—where the three of us were able to visit several of our favorite cities. Chris spent almost four months with us before returning to the States in the fall and to his studies at the university.

It was during one of his pre-med classes at the university that he met his wonderful wife, Jen.

They now have two dazzling, young daughters. Although they're both still young, besides being bright and beautiful, I can already tell my granddaughters are both going to be *awesome* at tennis!

After Chris finished his undergraduate studies at the U, he went on to dental school at the University of Maryland. It was while he was in Maryland that I called him to discuss the possibility of selling our old Mus-Bus. During the previous month, I'd had several offers from people who wanted to buy it. Chris' response to my inquiry, "Absolutely, unequivocally . . . NO WAY! Dad, we're going to bury you in that thing. Besides, you've got two little granddaughters who have already heard magical stories about the Mus-Bus and going camping in the Rocky Mountains with their dad and grandpa when they finally move from the East Coast back to Utah."

A few weeks after that phone conversation, the Mus-Bus got a major overhaul, new tires, and a new paint job. On weekends—depending on the season—it can still be seen roaming around the tennis courts, kayaking spots, and ski slopes of northern Utah.

My sister Karen still lives in southern California. She recently lost her husband and soul mate, Frank, to an unexpected illness, and now spends much of her time visiting her grandchildren in San Diego and Salt Lake City as often as she can.

Elder Redd is now Doctor Redd, a graduate of Ohio State University Medical School. He is married with three children and is an orthopedic surgeon in El Paso, Texas.

Elder Pitts, I was told, is a manager of a Burger King in Scottsdale, Arizona.

And as for what happened to our young friend Sasha? Well, that's another story for another time.

During my six years living with Bonnie in the former Soviet Union—although I did think about it from time to time—I was never confronted by the KGB or Russian mafia about Koshka or the events that had taken place in Tayginsk. One can only assume that years earlier during my time in Siberia, the KGB and their mafia thugs had definitely botched things and let that German oil field manager get away. For all they knew, the *Kraut* had made his way back to Bavaria, to the *Hofbräuhaus* where he spent his evenings listening to German oompah bands, eating *wiener schnitzel* with "extra" helpings of *kartoffelsalat,* and, of course, *apfelküchen* for desert.

As for Koshka and the three other corrupt, Communist politicians who, with the KGB, had committed espionage and embezzled the millions from the embassy construction fund, the State Department was never able to prosecute any of these men. When I last inquired about their whereabouts, I was told that one of the four men had died. Nothing was known about the other two. Koshka, however, was still actively involved in the operations of the Russian mafia and dividing his time between his estate on the outskirts of St. Petersburg and his villa on the Mediterranean in southern Italy. INTERPOL and U.S. intelligence are patiently waiting for Koshka or his men to make their next ill-advised, foolish move.

★ ★ ★

Several years have now passed since the fall of the USSR, when the people of Russia and the Soviet Republics rid themselves of the cancer of Communism. During its existence, the Soviet regime had built a counterfeit superpower, a military–industrial complex that instilled fear and distrust, not only among its own citizens, but also among the nations of the world.

There was a time when the Soviet military numbered 180 divisions totaling five million troops; factories produced eight tanks, eight artillery pieces, five fighter planes, and one inter-continental ballistic missile *every single day*.

Yet, because the Communist leaders refused to allow their own citizens the dignity of simple basic rights and freedoms, the world's other superpower is now a thing of the past. And, in the end, the most significant factor in bringing down the USSR was the Soviet people themselves.

The greatness of Russia has always been its people. During the seventy years of the USSR, any meaningful accomplishments or achievements were a result of the populace, not the Communist Party. It was the Soviet people that preserved the moral values of truth and goodness, not the mistaken ideological dogma of Marxism. And, today, that is still the hope of Russia's future—its people.

The fall of the Soviet Union changed the lives of millions, including the hundreds of millions around the globe that were affected by the fifty-year Cold War. Although things in Russia have improved, the majority of the population continues to suffer. Unfortunately, it will take the passing of several generations to escape the memories and the terrible effects of Soviet tyranny. While the Soviet bear may be hibernating, the ghost of Communism will continue to haunt Russia and the rest of the world for decades to come.

✯ ✯ ✯

In the years that Bonnie and I lived in Russia, I tried, through our own intelligence agencies and even through operational contacts with our so-called "new allies" in Russian intelligence—the former KGB—to find out how Karen's package had arrived in Potevka at my cabin door that memorable Thanksgiving day. No one knew a thing.

In the immediate years following Potevka, I gave a great deal of thought to Karen's package and spent many hours trying to unravel its mystery. I still don't believe that someone within our own agency delivered it; they wouldn't have any reason not to tell me so. On the other hand, if the KGB was somehow involved, how did they get the package when it was sent from the USA to our embassy in Helsinki for delivery by diplomatic pouch to our American Embassy in Moscow?

If someone working within the KGB knew where I was, had access to the package, and chose to get it to me at the safe house in Potevka, *Why?* This theory, regrettably, assumes that someone within our own intelligence service, possibly a double agent, informed the KGB about my stopover in Potevka.

I'd like to think that, in spite of all the chaos during the collapse of the USSR, along with the hostility and mistrust the Soviet government had towards America, somewhere within the vast organization of the KGB, someone's heart was softened. Maybe this individual knew exactly who I was, where I was—stranded in Potevka—and understood the concept of Thanksgiving in America. And, perhaps, he also knew what it would mean for me to receive such a needed gift on the very day of one of our most cherished national holidays. If such speculation were true, how thrilled I would be to someday meet this former Russian adversary and thank him personally for what he did. In my view, this improbable act of kindness, by a so-called enemy, is simply another testament to the basic goodness of man and the intervention and love of a concerned Heavenly Father.

I've heard it said that the Lord works his miracles through angels living around us in the form of our family and friends—sometimes even complete strangers. Now, many years later, when the holidays come around, or whenever I hear the beautiful music of "How Great Thou Art," I can't help but think back on Potevka and my life-changing experience in that far away Russian village.

Still to this day, I do not know for certain how the package got to me or who delivered it. That will likely always remain a mystery. Most important is the fact that Potevka, the storm, Karen's package, and a loving Heavenly Father changed my life forever.

And, yes, I do believe in angels. As a young boy, growing up in that wonderful, small town of Bear River, I had the blessing of being a little brother to one. Then, many years later another came into my life . . . to heal my heart, teach me to love again, and bring peace and joy to this marvelous journey we are now traveling together called Life.

The End

A Train To Potevka

The Cossack and his Czarina

Highlights Of Russian History

- 6th century: East European Slavs migrate into Russia.
- 8th century: Vikings arrive to trade amber and furs. Warring Slavs choose Viking, Rurik, to govern them.
- 863: Greek missionaries, Cyril and Methodius, develop the Cyrillic alphabet.
- 988: Descendants of Rurik convert to Christianity.
- 1147: The founding of Moscow.
- 1237: Mongols invade; Russia splits into dukedoms.
- 1462: Russian principalities defeat the Mongols.
- 1547: Ivan the Terrible crowned czar of all Russia.
- Late 1500's: Poles and Swedes try to conquer Russia.
- 1598: The end of the Rurik dynasty.
- 1613: Romanov 300-year dynasty of Russia begins.
- 1637: Russians explorers reach the Pacific Ocean.
- Early 1700's: Peter the Great strives to modernize and westernize Russia.
- 1703: The founding of St. Petersburg.
- 1712: The Russian capital is moved to St. Petersburg for a 200-year period.
- 1700's: Russia is ruled by women for most of the century.
- 1762: Catherine the Great, a German princess, comes to the Russian throne.
- 1809: Sweden cedes Finland to Russia.

- 1812: Napoleon's army invades Russia; Moscow is burned. The Napoleonic Wars bring new ideas, debate, and dissent to Russia.
- 1861: Serfs are emancipated in Russia.
- 1867: Russia sells Alaska to the United States.
- 1891: Trans-Siberian Railway's 25-year construction begins.
- 1904-05: Russia is crippled by defeat in the Russo–Japanese War.
- 1905: Protests in St. Petersburg against the Czar.
- 1914-18: Russia loses 3.5 million soldiers in WWI.
- 1917: Bolshevik Revolution forces czar to abdicate.
- 1918-20: Lenin seizes power in Russia.
- 1919: The founding of Communist International.
- 1924: Stalin seizes control of the Communist Party through purges and collectivization.
- 1933: United States officially recognizes the USSR.
- 1936-38: Stalin exiles 15 million citizens to Siberia; 10 million die from starvation and disease.
- 1939: Stalin signs nonaggression pact with Germany.
- 1941: Hitler invades Russia; the 900-day siege of Leningrad begins.
- 1945: By the end of WWII, 22 million Russians had died.
- 1956: Soviet Union invades Hungary.
- 1957: Russia's first Sputnik is launched, beginning the space race between the USA and the USSR.

- 1962: Khrushchev puts nuclear missiles in Cuba.
- 1964-82: Brezhnev rules Soviet Union during the height of the Cold War with the United States.
- 1968: Soviet Union invades Czechoslovakia.
- 1979: Soviet Union invades Afghanistan.
- 1980: USSR hosts the Olympic Games in Moscow. In protest of the Soviet invasion of Afghanistan, the U.S., along with several other nations, refuses to participate.
- 1985: Gorbachev appointed head of the USSR.
- 1985-88: Gorbachev introduces freedoms and openness through his policies of *glasnost* and *perestroika.*
- 1986: Chernobyl nuclear plant meltdown.
- 1986-90: Kremlin's control over the Soviet Republics significantly diminishes.
- 1989: The Berlin Wall, separating East and West Germany, is torn down.
- 1991: August political coup against Gorbachev fails.
- 1991: USSR dissolved; Gorbachev resigns.
- 1992: Boris Yeltsin becomes Russia's first freely-elected president.
- 1994: Deadly conflicts with the rebellious republic of Chechnaya begin.
- 1997: Vladimir Putin replaces Boris Yeltsin as the president of Russia.

Glossary

AGENT—an individual employed by an agency to carry out clandestine intelligence operations.

APPARATCHIKS—a Russian official blindly devoted to his superiors or their cause.

APPROACH—the method used to entice an individual for recruitment for clandestine work.

ASSESSMENT—the evaluation of a potential clandestine source or agent.

ASSET—any resource available to an intelligence service for operational use.

BLOWN—one's true identity is known by the enemy.

BOLSHEVIK REVOLUTION—the "Russian" or "October Revolution" in 1917 led by Lenin and other radicals to overthrow the czar and his imperial government.

BOLSHEVIKS—the radicals led by Lenin during the Russian Revolution who wanted to overthrow the government rather than accept gradual change.

BUG—a concealed listening device used for clandestine audio surveillance.

CASE OFFICER—the person responsible for directing and controlling a specific agent or net in a clandestine agency.

CCCP—Cyrillic (Russian) letters meaning USSR: the Union of Soviet Socialist Republics

CELL—the lowest, most expendable group in an espionage network.

CHECKA—the Office of State Security for the Bolsheviks from 1917-1922.

CIA—Central Intelligence Agency. America's premier foreign intelligence agency, responsible for obtaining and analyzing information about foreign governments, corporations, and individuals; instrumental in promoting U.S. Foreign Policy abroad. Most CIA activities are undisclosed.

CIPHER—a method of cryptography that involves the replacement of each letter in a message with another letter or number.

CLANDESTINE—done in secrecy.

CLANDESTINE OPERATIONS—intelligence collection, counterintelligence, or covert operations conducted against a hostile target; i.e. a government, their military, intelligence, and security agencies.

COLD WAR—the fifty-five year period after World War II of nonviolent hostility between the Soviet Union and the United States.

COLLECTION—the procuring, assembling, and organizing of information for further intelligence processing.

COLLECTIVE FARM—a Soviet cooperative group of farmers who labor on government-owned land and are required to give back to the state what they produce.

COMMISSAR—Communist government department head in the USSR.

COMMITTEE FOR STATE SECURITY—the Soviet KGB.

COMMUNISM—an economic and social system where all production is owned by citizen workers and controlled by the state for the common good.

COMPROMISE—the exposure of information or material to unauthorized persons.

CONTACT—a person who is not an agent but is used for intelligence collection.

COUNTERESPIONAGE—operations intended to prevent clandestine collection efforts by agents of foreign governments or covert agencies.

CONTROLLER—an individual who directs an intelligence operation.

COSSACKS—Russian frontiersmen organized as cavalry in czarist army.

COUNTERINTELLIGENCE—activities to protect against foreign espionage, sabotage, and intelligence collection.

COVER—the identity used by an agent or case officer to conceal his espionage activities.

COVERT—activities carried out in a concealed or clandestine manner to make it difficult to trace the activities back to the sponsoring intelligence service.

COVERT ACTION—methods used by intelligence agencies to influence countries or targets through paramilitary actions, bribery, kidnapping, counterfeiting, and propaganda.

CRYPTOGRAPHY—the creation of codes and ciphers, secret writing.

CZARS—emperors of Imperial Russia from the seventeenth century until the Bolshevik Revolution—an absolute monarchy.

DAMAGE REPORT—the assessment of damage to an agency or operation caused by the compromise of an agent or operation.

DEAD DROP—a physical location used to exchange (deposit and pick up) information and/or materials.

DEBRIEFING—the acquiring of mission-related information from an individual or group after the accomplishment of an assigned mission.

DIA—U.S. Defense Intelligence Agency

DOUBLE AGENT—an agent who is recruited to work against his original intelligence service.

ELDER—male priesthood holder in the LDS Church.

ESPIONAGE—the tradecraft or practice of spying.

FBI—Federal Bureau of Investigation. The U.S. government agency responsible for counter-intelligence and enforcement of federal laws.

FSB—Russia's Federal Security Service, successor to the KGB.

G-2—military staff officer for intelligence.

GLASNOST—a Russian word meaning "openness." Under Gorbachev the loosening of government control and greater freedom of expression.

GORBACHEV, MIKHAIL—General Secretary-President of the Soviet Union from 1985 to 1991.

GRU—Soviet military intelligence.

GULAG—a network of labor camps under the penal system of the USSR.

HANDLER—a case officer directly responsible for the operation of an agent or a net of agents.

IMPERIAL RUSSIA—the totality of the old Russian empire.

INTELLIGENCE—the result of the collection and processing of information regarding actual and potential situations and conditions relating to domestic and foreign activities.

IZBA—a Soviet/Russian private village house, cabin, or hut made of wood.

KARL MARX—a German scholar of the nineteenth century; the founder of Marxism and author of the "Fundamental Theory of Communism."

KGB—the Committee for State Security within the USSR; the Soviet agency responsible for all security and intelligence functions both foreign and domestic; similar to all fifteen U.S. intelligence agencies combined, including the CIA and FBI; the major enforcer for the practice of Communist ideology; in its prime said to have numbered over 500,000 employees.

KHRUSHCHEV, NIKKITA—Soviet Premier in the late 1950s through early 1960s. He sought peaceful coexistence with the West.

KOLKHOZ—Soviet collective farm.

LATTER-DAY SAINT or "LDS"—a member of the Church of Jesus Christ of Latter-day Saints, also known as a Mormon.

LDS MISSIONARY—a Church member, male or female, usually in their early twenties, who volunteers to serve as a non-paid missionary for eighteen to twenty-four months; may be assigned to serve anywhere in the world.

LENIN, VLADIMIR—spearheaded the overthrow of the czar in 1917 during the Bolshevik Revolution; founder and leader of the Soviet Union until his death in 1924.

MICRODOT—the photographic reduction of writing or other material to facilitate its transfer from one location to another without detection.

LUBYANKA—headquarters for the KGB in the USSR; it included its infamous prison.

MOLE—a high-level agent or person within an enemy's government or military, able to provide intelligence information.

MORMON—a member of the Church of Jesus Christ of Latter-day Saints.

NATO—North Atlantic Treaty Organization; founded by allies of World War II after the Soviet blockade of Berlin in 1948.

NEED-TO-KNOW—a determination made by the holder of classified information and/or material whether or not a prospective recipient has a need for access to or possession of the material.

NET OR NETWORK—a group of agents or individuals who have common espionage targets and who are managed by the same handler.

NKVD—Stalin's secret police.

NSA—National Security Agency within the U.S. government.

OLIGARCHY—a government entity in which a small group has control for corrupt and selfish purposes.

OPEN SOURCE—intelligence derived from sources available to the general public.

OUT IN THE COLD—an agent in enemy territory.

PENETRATION—planting agents or monitoring devices (bugs) within a target organization or facility to gain access to its secrets or to influence its activities.

PERESTROIKA—economic restructuring under Gorbachev.

POLYGRAPH—an electronic device to determine if a person is lying. A "lie detector" measures breathing, blood pressure, pulse rate, and palm perspiration. Not admissible in a court of law.

PROLETARIAT—the lowest social, economic class; the working people, the masses.

PUTIN, VLADIMIR—early career with the KGB, minor player in Yeltsin's administration, unexpectedly appointed as acting president of Russia after Yeltsin's resignation, elected president in 2000 on law and order platform, won a second term in March 2004.

PUZZLE PALACE—slang name for the Pentagon.

RECOGNITION SIGNAL—a tradecraft term for a sign or password used to indicate a clandestine rendezvous.

RED THEIVES—criminal families or groups that banded together to fight against the czarist government, often revered as folk heroes.

ROMANOVS—the family that ruled Russia from the seventeenth century until the Bolshevik Revolution in 1917.

RUSSIAN MAFIA—well-established crime families or groups in the larger cities of Russia. Many of these criminal groups rose from the ashes after the collapse of the USSR.

SAFE HOUSE—a safe, sterile location often used to meet or debrief agents or individuals. Also used as a place to hide when necessary.

SANITIZE—to remove specific material or revise a document in order to prevent the identification of intelligence sources and collection methods.

SECURITY CLEARANCE—access given to military, government, or contractor personnel to classified information for the performance of their work.

SERFDOM—a system of servitude in which the serfs were bound to the land. They could not be thrown off the land nor leave it voluntarily.

SHADOW—spy jargon for a tail or someone who follows, usually covertly.

SPETSNATZ—Russian special warfare forces; similar to U.S. Navy SEALs.

SPOOK—a person involved in intelligence activity or collection; a spy.

SPY—espionage agent.

STALIN, JOSEPH—ruthless ruler of the Soviet Union after the death of Lenin until his own death in 1953. During his brutal purges, tens of millions of Soviet citizens were killed or exiled to Siberia.

STEPPE—the millions of square miles of vast barren plains located in eastern Russia.

STERILIZE—to remove everything from a clandestine operation that could identify it as originating with the sponsoring organization.

SURVEILLANCE—close watch kept over someone or something.

SWEEPERS—the term for an electronic technician who examines or "sweeps" an office or facility to determine if electronic listening devices (bugs) have been planted.

TAIGA—a coniferous forest so vast that it stretches over Eurasia and North America, covering one-fifth of the earth's landmass.

TARGET—a person, agency, facility, area, or country against which intelligence operations are targeted.

TRADECRAFT—techniques and skills used by practitioners of espionage.

TRANS-SIBERIAN EXPRESS—the 6,000-mile railway extending from Vladivostok in the Far East to St. Petersburg in the West; the longest continuous rail line in the world; built at the turn of the 20th century.

URALS—a mountain range in western Russia, extending from the Arctic tundra to an area north of the Caspian Sea, which forms the traditional border between Europe and Asia.

USSR—the Union of Soviet Socialist Republics, fifteen republics in all.

YELTSIN, BORIS—in 1991, became the first freely elected President of post Cold War Russia; strong proponent of privatization and economic reform.

Acknowledgements

I am grateful to those who encouraged me to write *A Train To Potevka.* I owe a special thanks to my sister, Sally Munns, who, when Potevka was a short story of ten pages, kept urging me—actually bugging me—to turn it into a book. But then, what are older sisters for?

To my dear friends Terry and Judy Brewer, thank you for your unwavering support. To my friend, Dean Hughes, thank you for helping me get started. To Lt. Colonel Chuck Horton, thank you for your vision for this book. Chuck, we will never forget you.

A special thanks to those who offered their advice regarding the manuscript: Howard Bahr, Ph.D.; Steve & Lana Barlow; Gaylen Buckley, Ph.D.; Susan Chadaz; Steve Crain; Joyce Elison; Col. Ken Feaster; Val Karren; Vadim Klishko, Ph.D.; Col. Al Love; Joe Platt; Brian Smits; Col. Bob and Dar Stack; Wynn Stanger, Ph.D.; Jess Taylor, Ph.D.; and Dick and Irina Williams.

And finally, my greatest thanks to my Bonnie who lived a significant part of this story with me. I will forever be grateful for the love, support, and inspiration that you bring into my life.

Mike Ramsdell

ABOUT THE AUTHOR

Photo: U.S. Intelligence School – Europe*

Mike Ramsdell was born and raised in Bear River, Utah. He attended Utah State University, the University of Utah Law School, and the Russian Language Institute in Washington, D.C. He was commissioned as an officer in the Military Intelligence Corps. His career specialty in Russian/Soviet counter-intelligence has taken him on missions throughout Europe, Russia, Scandinavia, and to Asia. Lt. Colonel Ramsdell has served with the U.S. and NATO militaries, various U.S. intelligence agencies, and the U.S. Department of State. He had the opportunity to work in support of the first Reagan–Gorbachev Moscow Summit. His last foreign assignment was for a six-year period in Moscow and Gorky, Russia. He currently lives in Layton, Utah with his wife, Bonnie, and their two cats, Ralph and Koshka. Active in racquetball, tennis, and skiing, he also serves in the Sunday school of his local Church. *A Train to Potevka* is Mike's first book.

*Early career photo in Russian Military uniform – Oberammergau.